Early one morning, standing in the rain,
Round the bend come a long freight train

"*Railroad Bill*"
Traditional

Also by Alfred M. Struthers:

THE THIRD FLOOR MYSTERY SERIES
The Case of Secrets
The Curse of Halim
The Demon Tide
The Stone Ghost
The Grim Fugue
The Watchman's Keep

CHAPTER BOOKS
(illustrated by Cathy Provoda)
Did You Hear That?

PICTURE BOOKS
(illustrated by Cathy Provoda)
Pepperoni Macaroni

Available at:
Thirdfloorbooksllc.com

The PhantomVale

A Third Floor Mystery

By Alfred M. Struthers

thirdfloorbooksllc.com

First edition paperback copyright 2022 by Alfred M. Struthers

Second paperback edition copyright ©2023
Published by Third Floor Books, LLC
Thirdfloorbooksllc.com

ISBN: 979-8-9870736-2-9

10 9 8 7 6 5 4 3 2

Book design by Third Floor Books

For Mom and Dad,
who gave me the strength to believe,
and the courage to dream.

Prologue

August 2, 1943

The field was barely visible through the thick stand of maple trees. Thinking the property was another quarter mile up the road, Nathaniel Hammond nearly drove by. It was the barn, weather-beaten and worn, perched at the edge of the field, that caught his eye. He braked and pulled off onto the shoulder. Eyeing the building through the trees, he recalled the description he'd been given by the gray-haired clerk at the Mansfield Post Office. If what the old-timer said was accurate, this had to be the place. He grabbed his flashlight from the toolbox on the floor and the thick leather satchel from the front seat, and got out.

The old road was deserted in both directions when he stepped onto the sunbaked pavement. The air was still and the only sound was the distant chatter of songbirds deep in the forest. A surge of anticipation washed over him as he waded through the tall, roadside grass and climbed over the stone wall. At the edge of the field, he paused. On the near horizon, the Green Mountains loomed like sleeping giants, but Hammond's eyes were focused on the ramshackle barn.

He pulled a mid-1800s equipment catalog from the satchel. It was small and thin, its pages stiff with age. At the top, printed in ornate lettering, were the words *Dorsett Brothers Tractor Supply Company, Abbotsville, Vermont.* Just below that was a detailed drawing of an immense steam tractor, parked in front of a large, timberframed barn. He held the catalog up at arm's length and compared the drawing to the structure across the field. They were identical.

According to the postal clerk, Abbotsville had occupied roughly eight square miles. When the town incorporated in 1890, the name had been changed to Mansfield. Now only a handful of area elders recalled Abbotsville at all. By the time of the name change, of course, the Dorsett Brothers were long gone, killed years before when a steam tractor they were working on suddenly exploded. Most believed that this overgrown field and sagging barn were all that remained of their family legacy. But Hammond thought otherwise. He was convinced that another piece of Dorsett family history was contained within the pages of the catalog in his hand.

He remembered the day he first pulled it from the old book- case in the small, secluded office at the back of his shop, Hammond Books, in Cambridge, Massachusetts. The lettering on the cover immediately caught his eye, and he marveled at the majesty of the drawings as he flipped its pages. Inside the front cover, he found a hastily written scrawl:

R&S. Caswells Corner. Saturday

He had no idea how the catalog had come to be in the bookcase. The inscription seemed unimportant at first, but after examining the book from cover to cover, Hammond found no other explanation for its inclusion. Then again, the bookcase, a family heirloom passed on to him by his father, Samuel Hammond, was full of such mysteries. It was home to a special collection of books, journals and other printed matter, unearthed over time and saved for the secrets they possessed.

Everything in the bookcase, it seemed, was there for a reason. After months of digging, Hammond hoped that his suspicions about the antiquated catalog were about to be confirmed. His conversations with the owner of the Mansfield General Store, the town librarian, and the postmaster turned up nothing. There was no R&S listing of any kind in the state of Vermont.

It was weeks later, during a chance conversation with the director of the New Hampshire Historical Society in Concord, that he found the answer. R&S stood for Ross and Sheridan, an overland express company that carried tourists and cargo along the Connecticut River on the New Hampshire side.

Caswell's Corner proved even harder to find. It wasn't listed on any map. Eventually, he learned that Caswell's Corner was a nickname given by the locals to a treacherous section of road that skirted the river in Brewster—a road that would be forever known for the tragic events that transpired there in early April of 1864.

What records he could find were buried in the musty basement of the Brewster Town Hall. They recounted how the R&S stage was traveling south along the river on that chilly Saturday in April. When it reached Caswell's Corner, something spooked the horses, sending the coach crashing down the steep embankment into the icy water below, which was running higher than normal due to a record snowfall that year.

Three of the six passengers perished, along with two of the horses. The coach was crushed in the treacherous ice flow and the cargo on board was swept downriver, never to be recovered. Most notable among the losses was the stage driver's seat, or "box," which contained a large shipment of gold nuggets from Cooks River, up near Holden, New Hampshire.

Reading the account of that fateful day chilled Hammond to the bone. Were the Dorsett Brothers the cause of the mishap? What became of the driver's box and the riches it held? Was the gold ever found, or was it buried in the mud at the bottom of the Connecticut River?

The catalog he held in his hand was a possible key to answering those very questions—the only remaining link to a tragedy that was still shrouded in mystery some 80 years later. With his anticipation soaring, he slipped the catalog back in his satchel and pushed his way through the tall grass toward the barn.

When Hammond reached the barn, he went directly to the large sliding door on the end of the building. It was made from wide wooden planks that had grayed with age, held in place by two horseshoe-style brackets that rolled on a long steel track. He pulled on the handle and the massive door resisted momentarily, then opened with a dull rumble.

Inside, the air was cool and smelled of dried wood and old hay. The floor was blackened with oil stains, and sections of it were covered with patches of loose hay. The only light came from above, where gaping holes in the roof let in luminous shafts of sunlight. After a quick check of the first floor, he climbed an old stairway and explored the hay loft. Like the first floor it was empty, but as he stood on the edge looking down, something over in the corner caught his eye.

It was a dark line etched into the floor, beginning at the base of the wall and extending toward a pile of broken hay bales. He returned to the first floor and searched the corner, using his shoe to clear away the spent hay. What he found wasn't a line at all—it was a clean break in the boards, nearly three feet long, much too straight to be a crack. He cleared away more hay and discovered a similar break a few feet away. Together, with the seams in the floor- boards, they formed a small rectangle roughly two feet by three feet. A trap door, perhaps?

Using an old hay hook he found hanging on a nearby post, he worked his way around the edges, loosening the boards on all four sides. It took several minutes, but he was finally able to pry the entire panel free. What he saw beneath it gave him pause. There was no stairway leading to a basement below, no ladder to a hidden room. It was nothing more than a shallow cavity, barely two feet deep, and empty, except for an old carriage blanket balled up in a mound.

He grabbed the edge of the cloth and brought it up into the light. The fabric was heavy and had a velvety sheen the color of root beer. In several areas, it had been chewed clean through by rodents. He was pulling it out of the hole, hand over hand, when he stopped. Hidden beneath the blanket was a large rectangular object. Even in the broken light, he recognized it at once, and seeing it up close sent a cold chill through his body.

Very carefully, he reached down into the hidden compartment and lifted it out. It was roughly three feet long and well over a foot tall. Bigger than he imagined. The sides were pressed metal, faded black, and the leather seat affixed to the top had cupped over time from the weight of the stagecoach driver. The hasp on the front was dotted with rust, as were the metal braces on each corner.

But it was the initials, *R&S*, stenciled in fancy gold script just below the handles on each end, that confirmed his suspicions. The notation in the catalog was no fluke. Someone had anticipated the stage passing through Caswell's Corner on that chilly day in April and noted it in the catalog. As a reminder? Or was it a written instruction, meant for someone else?

The sound of a tractor passing by on the road outside made him turn and look. He waited until it faded into the distance, then turned back to the driver's box. Holding the back of it firmly against his body, he took hold of the hasp and pulled. The hinges creaked sharply and it slowly opened to reveal nothing more than a small booklet, several of which he had for sale in his bookshop back in Cambridge. The cover was worn and had discolored over time, but the signature artwork and lettering were still readable.

No. 82
Farmer's Almanac
1863

by Elijah J. Perkins

At first, it appeared to be nothing more than a historical keepsake. But as he started leafing through it, he discovered a strange drawing on one of the pages, an erratic line that looked like a star constellation. It cut back and forth across the page, zigzagging around a number of curious landmarks before coming to an end next to the sketch of a large rock in the shape of a camel's hump. The drawing was crude, but there was no mistaking its meaning. It was a map.

He quickly climbed to his feet and hurried outside. With the almanac in hand, he walked the property and surrounding woods, looking for a large rock in the shape of a camel's hump. But there was no such landmark to be found.

He returned to the barn and stood next to the open door, eyeing the open field and thinking. *Did they remove the rock when they cleared the field? Or is it on another property? If so, where?*

He opened the almanac to check the drawing again, and that's when he made another startling discovery. Several pages after the map he found another one, much different than the first. It looped around three trees set in a triangle, then snaked back in the opposite direction. It ended at a series of small circles, stacked like rocks in a stone wall.

He flipped more pages and found even more drawings, each different that the one before. One line was completely straight, running along the inner margin of the page. Beside it were two wavy lines, indicating a river or a stream. It came to an end in the bottom corner of the page at the base of an enormous tree, with fat roots that stretched outward in every direction like long crooked fingers.

Once again, he eyed the open field. None of these landmarks were here, he was sure of it. But if the maps in the almanac were any indication, the brothers divided the gold from the driver's box and put it in the ground. But where? Suddenly he was stuck with another thought. The Caswell's Corner mishap took place in early April of 1864. The Dorsett Brothers were killed months later, in July. Did the tractor explosion take their lives before they could dig up what they buried?

He eyed the open field one last time and then calmly tucked the almanac in his satchel. The mysterious fate of the R&S driver's box was now clear, but its contents were another puzzle altogether— one that wouldn't be unraveled until he learned more about the Dorsett Brothers. Did they live here in town? In a town nearby? Were there other family members living in the area? One with a home near a river or stream, perhaps?

Before he left, he went back in the barn and returned the driver's box to its original hiding place. It had survived there for this long, it could stay there until he returned. Once the wooden panel was back in place, he covered it over with hay, just as he had found it. Then he made his way back across the field to his truck.

It was only a matter of time before the riddle of the almanac was solved. And if by chance he wasn't the one to unearth its hidden secrets, it would fall to the one who came after him.

As it has always been.

Those were the words used by his father, Samuel Hammond, in his final hour, when he summoned Nathaniel to his bedside. In their last fleeting moments together, his father revealed the bookcase's veiled past—how it was more than just a collection of shelves, fashioned from an exotic wood in a faraway land, and smuggled to America aboard a brigantine ship.

The bookcase and the books in it were his birthright. A legacy that must be passed on.

As it has always been.

With Nathaniel's solemn promise.

And his father's dire warning.

1

The Getaway

Thursday, 11:00 P.M.

They were famous now. The two most famous 11-year-olds in the entire country. Maybe the world. All because they uncovered an age-old secret, a mystery that had gone unsolved for 150 years. Suddenly, the whole country knew the names Nathan Cole and Gina McDermott, saw their faces, heard about their daring adventure, and learned the gruesome details of what they had found.

What wasn't being reported was how it all began—in Nathan's attic, with an old book he found on the floor, the one from the old bookcase lurking in the shadows; or the strange things the book did, and the person making them happen. The one who had been dead for years. Those were details that Nathan and Gina didn't mention, and would never mention. Not to their parents, not to the press, not even to their friends.

Once the story broke, there was no stopping it. Nathan and Gina became celebrities, the ones everyone wanted to meet.

Everyone.

Everywhere.

Meet them.

Interview them.

Take their picture.

It was in every newspaper from coast to coast. Television stations aired interviews with them, their parents, and town officials. Radio talk shows were flooded with calls, their listeners wanting to know why two young kids would risk their lives like they did. Were their parents deadbeats? How could they let such a thing happen? Others praised the kids for showing some initiative and bravery, noting that unlike others their age, these two had grit. Why couldn't other kids be that way?

Finally, their parents decided that enough was enough. Something had to be done.

"This isn't fair, you know!" Nathan shouted as he crammed clothes into his suitcase.

His mother appeared at his bedroom door. "Are you ready?"

"No," he griped. The truth was, he had only just started packing.

"Well, hurry up. We're leaving."

"Why?" he pleaded. "Why do we have to leave?"

She suddenly remembered something she forgot to pack and darted back down the hallway.

"Wonderful," he mumbled, rolling his eyes. *Why do I bother talking?*

Thirty seconds later she appeared again, holding a thick sweatshirt in her hand. "Come on," she said.

"Mom, look!" he barked, gesturing toward his half-filled suitcase. "I'm not finished."

"Then you need to move faster," she said.

"I still don't understand why we need to leave. We didn't do anything wrong."

"It's not about right or wrong," she said, looking at the sweatshirt in her hand. Before he could respond, she vanished again. This time when she came back, she was holding a small paperback book in one hand and the sweatshirt in the other.

"If we didn't do anything wrong, then why do we have to go?" Nathan demanded.

"You know why," she replied. "This whole thing has gotten out of control. All the reporters calling, ringing the doorbell, following us into town, following us back from town. Your father and I have had it. Gina's parents have had it. We need a break. You and Gina need a break. Now let's go. We need to hurry."

"But—"

He stopped short as she turned and hurried down the hallway. When he heard her footsteps on the stairs, he sighed and went over to his bureau for more clothes. "Your father and I have had it," he said, mimicking her words. "We need a break." He didn't understand what the fuss was all about. It wasn't that bad. Not nearly as horrible as she was making it out to be. It was actually pretty cool. Getting interviewed on camera. Seeing his face, and Gina's, on TV and in newspapers. Even Bianca, the most popular girl at school, was talking to him now.

"Two minutes, Nathan," his mother shouted from downstairs.

His frustration boiled over again and he yelled, "WE DON'T HAVE TO DO THIS!"

Just then he heard a dull thud, muffled and deep, as if a giant marshmallow had bumped against the side of the house. "What was that?" he mumbled, turning around to check his room. In the middle of the floor he saw a book lying on the rug. It was from his grandfather's bookcase, the one in the attic. Ever since he brought it downstairs it had been sitting on top of his bureau, as still as a stone. That was weeks ago, about the same time the first wave of reporters showed up at the front door. After that, as more arrived and took over the neighborhood, he forgot about it. Never opened it. Never even went near it.

"What are you doing on the floor?" he moaned, as if the book could utter a reply. He marched over and picked it up, then slipped it in his bureau drawer for safekeeping. "You'll have to wait until I get back."

He walked back over to his suitcase and latched it shut. Just as he was lifting it off the bed, he heard a long, high-pitched squeak. It began softly and grew so loud that he had to cover his ears. It was followed seconds later by a thunderous crash that sent him toppling over onto the bed.

"Nathan! What are you doing?" his mother yelled from the front hallway.

His heart was racing as he climbed to his feet and turned around. His bureau drawer was on the floor, tipped over on its side. Clothes were everywhere, and sitting in the middle of the heap was the book.

"Nathan?"

"HOLD ON," he shouted.

It felt good to yell.

He stormed over to the drawer and flipped it upright, then tossed his clothes into it without bothering to fold them. "I don't have time for this," he snarled.

"What was that?" his mother called out.

He growled in frustration as he picked up the drawer and slid it back into place.

"NATHAN?"

"JUST WAIT!"

Thinking quickly, he snatched the book up off the floor and carried it over to his bed. He pulled back the blanket and shoved it underneath the mattress as far as he could reach. "Until I get back," he said. Then, with his heart still pounding, he grabbed his suitcase, shut off the light, and hurried down the hallway.

His mother was waiting for him at the bottom of the stairs. "You've got everything?" she asked.

His jaw tightened. "Yes, Mom."

He trudged down the stairs, letting the suitcase clunk loudly on each stair tread.

"Are you sure?" she asked.

"MOM!" *Enough.*

When he reached the bottom step, she opened the door and peeked outside, quickly checking the street in both directions. "Okay," she said. "Your father is waiting in the van with the others. You go ahead and I'll lock up."

His shoulders drooped. "Do we *have* to go?"

"We're not having that discussion again," she said, "and you're wasting time."

"But—"

"GO!" she barked.

He groaned and stepped outside. The front porch light was off and he paused to let his eyes adjust to the darkness. The night air held a chill that gripped his face like a rubber mask and brought back vivid memories of his now-famous adventure with Gina at the courthouse.

One memory in particular stood out.

They were in a narrow passageway. The darkness was barely lit by the small tea light in his hand. Sheets of spider webs hung from the ceiling and walls, full of dead insects—and things that still crawled. They clung to his hair and face. Out of the dark, a hand gripped his shoulder and his body went rigid.

"Let's go," his mother said, nudging him forward. "What are you waiting for?"

The courthouse memory faded as he plodded down the porch steps. His parents' minivan was parked in the driveway, facing the street with the lights off and the engine idling quietly. As Nathan approached the side door, it slid open and he saw Gina's parents sitting in the second row of seats. Without a word, he squeezed past them into the third row.

That's where he saw Gina, puzzle magazine in one hand and a small flashlight in the other. Tucked behind her ear, as always, was a yellow pencil. He often wondered if she slept with it there.

"Hey," he said as he plopped his suitcase down on the seat between them.

"Late… as usual," she mumbled without looking up.

"Early… as usual," he countered.

His mother climbed into the front seat and closed the door. "Let's go," she said, checking the street in both directions.

With that, Nathan's father drove slowly down the driveway.

When he reached the street, he pulled up to the curb and said, "All right, folks, last chance. Have we got everything?"

That brought a resounding "Yes" from everyone in the van.

Everyone except Nathan, who was staring up at the second floor of their house, where the soft glow of his desk lamp filled his bedroom, illuminating a small rectangular object that hung in the middle of the window.

"Nathan?"

The voice broke his concentration and when he turned from the window, he saw everyone staring at him.

"What's wrong?" his mother said.

"I, um, have to go back inside," he stammered.

"Did you forget something?"

"Uh…yeah," he said quickly. "It's important."

His mother muttered something while she dug through her purse for the house key. With every passing second, Nathan tapped his foot nervously on the floor. *Come on, come on.*

His mother finally found the key. "Make it quick, please," she said.

He leaned over the seat and snatched it from her hand, then climbed out of the van.

This isn't happening, he thought as he ran across the front lawn. *I turned that light off, I know I did.* He was just glad he noticed it before his parents did. So far, he'd been able to keep the bookcase a secret from them. The only other person who knew was Gina. Not that anyone else would believe him. An old bookcase on the third floor? *They'd believe that.* Haunted by the ghost of his grandfather? *No. They'd never buy that.*

The house was eerily quiet as he moved through the shadows. When he reached his bedroom, he eased the door open and peered inside. "Are you serious?" he moaned. His mattress was halfway off the bed, the covers were thrown back, and his pillow was on the floor in the corner. Stuck to the middle of the window, as if held there by glue, was the book from the attic.

"Why are you doing this?" he snarled, as he stepped into the room.

That's when everything went haywire.

The second his foot touched the floor, the book flew from the window and slammed into his chest. It happened so fast that it sent him stumbling backwards against the door frame. Using all his strength, he pried it away from his body and held it at arm's length. "What do you want?" he yelled. The book stopped pushing, and he stood there for several long seconds catching his breath. "That's better," he said.

Very slowly, he walked over to his bureau. "All right now," he said, looking at the book as he spoke. "I'm just going to leave you here until I get back. I'll read every page then. I promise."

He set the book on top of the bureau and held it in place with his hand.

Nothing happened.

"Okay?" he said.

The book didn't move.

"Good."

He took his hand off the book and took a step backward. Then another. Just as he took a third step, the book shot off the bureau and straight at him. He tried to duck out of the way, but tripped and fell to the floor. The book sailed over his head and hit the bedroom door so hard it slammed shut.

And there it stayed, on the door.

"All right, that's it," he growled, climbing to his feet. He marched over to the door and took hold of the book with both hands. It wouldn't budge. He put his full weight behind it, pulling with all his strength. "GET. OFF. MY. DOOR!"

Down in the street, he heard a car horn. Two taps, short and sweet. *Hurry up. We want to leave.*

"ALL RIGHT!"

He tried the book one more time. When it still wouldn't move, he gave up. "Fine, stay there," he said, "I don't care."

He grabbed the doorknob and twisted.

It wouldn't turn.

2

The Quick Stop

"You've got to be kidding me," he shouted. He tried the doorknob again, this time using both hands, but it was no use. It wouldn't turn. He stepped back and shook his head in disbelief. "I'm trapped in my own room—by a book."

Then it came to him, and when he spoke again he was speaking directly to his grandfather.

"You want me to bring it?"

People would think he was crazy, talking to a ghost, but they didn't know what he knew. This was no ordinary book. It came from an old bookcase full of secrets. Whatever this one held obviously couldn't wait, which explained everything that happened while he was packing.

And now this.

He stepped toward the door. When he extended his arms, the

book dropped harmlessly into his waiting hands, easy as could be. He let out a sigh of relief and said, "Well, all right, I guess it's coming with me." At the same time, the lamp on his desk slowly dimmed and then turned off completely.

He grabbed the doorknob and turned. This time the door swung open with ease, and he ran from the room. *It's a good thing Gina wasn't here,* he thought to himself as he hurried down the hallway. *She would've jumped out the window.*

When he reached the downstairs hallway, he grabbed his backpack from the bench near the front door and stuffed the book deep in the center compartment. A minute later he was hurrying down the driveway, thinking of what he was going to tell his parents.

"Your backpack? That's what you forgot?" his mother said as he climbed into the minivan.

"Uh, yeah, it's where I keep my homework," he answered, a little out of breath. "I can't believe I forgot it."

When Gina heard that, she put down the puzzle magazine and turned off the flashlight. *Did he just say what I thought he said? His homework? Yeah, right.* She eyed him suspiciously. His hair was a mess and he was out of breath. *He hates homework,* she thought. *HATES it.*

As his father pulled away from the curb, Nathan noticed Gina glaring at him. He quickly looked away as they reached the end of the street and headed downtown.

She poked his shoulder with her finger. Once, then twice.

Very slowly he turned and looked at her. *What?* She didn't utter a word, but he knew exactly what she was thinking.

It was the lowered chin. *I'm waiting.*

And raised eyebrows. *Are you going to tell me?*

The fixed glare. *What are you up to?*

He flashed her an innocent grin. *Who, me?*

And that's when she kicked him in the ankle.

"Oww," he groaned, grabbing his leg.

"What was that, Nathan?" his mother asked.

"Nothing," he mumbled, flashing Gina a dirty look. *I can't believe you did that.*

She shot back a look of her own. *You WILL tell me what's going on.*

"That reminds me," Gina's mother said, turning around in the seat. "Did you pack your schoolwork?"

"Yes Mom, I *told* you I did, remember?"

"Good," her mother replied. "Your teacher was very nice to let you finish it while we're away."

Gina rolled her eyes. *Yeah, real nice.*

Nathan turned back to the window, staring at the storefronts along Main Street. Looking but not seeing. He was consumed by the book in his backpack and the crazy things it did in his bedroom.

Five minutes later they reached the town line. Twenty minutes after that, they were on Route 495 North, blending in with the rest of the late-night traffic.

Just another family.

Out for a drive.

Nothing to see here.

It was a perfect getaway, and when they crossed the state line into New Hampshire, Nathan wedged his backpack down on the floor between his feet and leaned his head against the window. Within minutes he drifted off, lulled to sleep by the dull rhythm of the road.

Sometime later, he was awoken by the sound of a slamming door. The van wasn't moving, and he immediately sat up. "Why are we stopped?" he asked, rubbing the sleep from his eyes.

"Your father wanted to fill the gas tank," his mother said.

They were at a quick-stop gas mart in some remote town he didn't recognize. There were rows of gas pumps, all vacant, and a lone car with New Hampshire plates parked in front of the store.

Gina's mother asked, "Do either of you need to use the bathroom?"

"I do," Nathan answered quickly. He slipped out into the cool night air and hurried across the parking lot.

As Gina watched him go, she got an idea and climbed out of the van and ran after him.

"There's not much to look at here," Elizabeth said, eyeing the businesses up and down the street. No sooner had she spoken the words than a large white box truck pulled into the parking lot. At first it looked like an armored truck making a late cash pickup. But as it came to a stop beneath one of the floodlights that lined the parking lot, she saw the giant satellite dish folded flat on the roof. "You've got to be kidding me," she said.

Two men stepped down from the cab and walked across the parking lot. Nathan's father was pumping gas and talking to Gina's father, who stood nearby. Neither one paid any attention to the news truck or the two men.

Nathan's mother never took her eyes off them. But as she watched them walk toward the front door, it became obvious that they were totally absorbed in their own discussion and were ignoring everything around them. She eased back in the seat and let out a nervous breath.

Sneaking out of town without anyone knowing had her on edge. It was time to relax.

The two men were harmless.

Nathan emerged from the bathroom and found Gina waiting for him. She was standing directly in his path with her arms folded across her chest.

"What's wrong?" he asked.

"You tell me," she shot back. *Or you're not getting by me.*

"Tell you what?"

"What was that nonsense back at your house?"

"What are you talking about?" he replied, avoiding her laser beam stare. He couldn't tell her. Not yet, and certainly not here. He turned his attention to a tall rack of potato chips at the end of a nearby aisle.

"You know exactly what I'm talking about," she said.

He eyed the potato chip display from top to bottom. It had all his favorites.

"That thing about your homework?" she reminded him.

On the top shelf, he saw salt and vinegar chips. *Love those.*

"Since when do you remember your homework?" she asked.

Next to the salt and vinegar chips were sour cream and onion. *Ooh, those are good, too.*

"You're up to something," she insisted.

Below the sour cream and onion were dill pickle chips. *Ewww… whose idea was that?*

"Tell me what you're hiding," she demanded.

Then he saw his favorite—honey barbeque.

She turned to see what he was staring at, and that's when he made his move. He slipped past her and grabbed the chips off the rack.

"Nathan!" she growled. But it was too late. He left her standing there as he darted down the aisle toward the cash register.

The men from the news truck came through the front door and headed straight for the counter that ran along the far wall. It had several tall coffee dispensers, flavorings, cups, lids, sweeteners, and a glass cabinet full of muffins, bagels, and donuts. As they passed the front counter, one of the men said, "Hey Steve."

Steve, the night clerk, was busy cashing in lottery tickets for a woman standing at the register with her teenage daughter. He looked up and gave the two men a nod while the woman drummed her fingers nervously on the counter.

"Not a winner this time, try again," the machine announced. This went on for several minutes.

"Not a winner…"

"Not a winner…"

"Not a winner…"

The woman's daughter grew bored and walked over to a metal rack full of newspapers. The top copy had a story about two kids from Massachusetts. Something about a 150-year old unsolved mystery and their amazing discovery. Included with the story were photos of both kids.

"Nathan," Gina hissed when she caught up with him. "Tell me what you're up to."

"What does it look like?" he said, holding up the bag of chips for her to see.

The girl stopped reading and turned around. When she saw

Nathan and Gina, she stared at each of them momentarily and then quickly looked back at the newspaper story.

"You know what I'm talking about," Gina fumed.

"Not now," Nathan whispered.

"Yes, now," Gina insisted.

The girl walked over to the counter with the newspaper and nudged her mother. "Mom," she said softly, "check this out."

"Just wait," her mother replied. Her eyes were locked on the lottery machine, watching each ticket go past the scanner.

"Sorry, no winners," Steve said, handing her back the pile of tickets.

"Story of my life," the woman groaned.

She turned to leave when her daughter grabbed her arm and showed her the front of the newspaper. "Mom," she said, "take a look at this."

Her mother glanced at the headline and said, "Yeah, yeah, I heard about that. Come on, let's go."

"Wait," the daughter said, staring at her mother with wide eyes.

"What's wrong?" her mother asked.

Her daughter leaned closer and whispered, "Look over my shoulder."

"Huh?"

She nodded at Nathan and Gina. "It's them."

Her mother looked, then did a double take. "OH-MY-GOD! It IS you!" she screamed.

The two men at the coffee counter looked up at once.

"You're those two kids on TV!" the woman shrieked.

"Well, what do you know?" one of the newsmen said softly. He hadn't noticed them when he came in, but there they were.

Ten feet away.

Big as life.

The two most famous kids in the whole country.

He turned to his coworker.

"Go get one of the cameras from the truck. And hurry!"

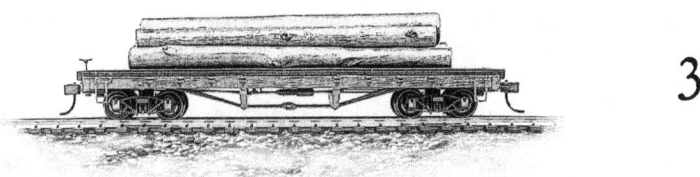

3

The Cottage

"You're famous!" the woman yelled.

Gina tugged on the back of Nathan's shirt and whispered, "Let's get out of here."

"Good idea," he said, tossing the bag of chips on a nearby shelf. The woman and her daughter were blocking the aisle in front of him, so he spun around to go the other way.

And plowed right into Gina.

"Hey!" she blurted out as she tumbled to the floor, pulling him down with her. They landed in a heap, and when they looked up, the woman was standing over them.

"I don't believe it," she exclaimed.

Nathan crab-walked backwards as quickly as he could, but the woman followed him down the aisle.

"Both of you, right here in our town!"

Gina scrambled to her feet, pushed past the woman, and yanked Nathan up off the floor. Together they raced down the aisle and headed for the door, with the woman following right behind them.

"This is taking way too long," Nathan's mother said, watching the front of the store. She expected Nathan and Gina to emerge at any moment, but as the minutes passed, she began to fidget. Suddenly, the front door swung open and one of the reporters slipped out. He sprinted to the truck and climbed in the back. When he appeared again, he was carrying a bulky, shoulder-mount camera.

"No," Nathan's mother yelled. "This is not happening."

She jumped out of the van and made a beeline for the store. Out of the corner of her eye, she saw the newsman running toward the front door.

She ran faster.

Just as she was reaching for the door, it flew open and Nathan and Gina came racing out, followed by the woman and her daughter. "Mom, RUN!" Nathan shouted, as he and Gina bolted toward the minivan.

The newsman saw the kids come bursting out the front door and immediately turned on the camera. He filmed them as they ran past, and had started following them across the parking lot when the woman from the front counter stepped in front of him. "I was the one who found them," she announced. The camera-man tried to step around her, but she moved with him, step for step, blocking his path and keeping her face inches from the camera lens. "It was me," she said, arranging her hair with both hands as she spoke. "I recognized them right away. I've always been good at spotting famous people.

Ask any of my friends."

The second reporter came out of the store and called to his partner. "You getting this?"

"You bet," the cameraman replied, doing his best to aim the camera over the woman's shoulder.

Nathan and Gina reached the van and jumped inside. Nathan's mother arrived right behind them and slid the door shut as hard as she could. "Get in and let's go," she yelled to her husband, who was still at the pump waiting for the gas receipt.

"What's going on?" he asked.

"NOW!" she screamed.

A minute later, and a mile away, Nathan's father asked, "Will someone please tell me what that was all about?"

Nathan's mother was twisted around in her seat, watching the road to see if anyone was following them. When no headlights appeared, she let out a sigh of relief.

"That," she said, "was about our two celebrities."

"Huh?" he replied.

"You didn't see the news crew?"

"There was a *news crew*?" Gina's father bellowed.

"Yeah," Nathan said, "and a *crazy* lady."

"You know," Nathan's mother said, "the whole reason we left town was to avoid situations just like that."

Nathan and Gina said nothing.

"What in the world took you kids so long in the store?" Gina's mother asked.

"*Someone* had to have potato chips," Gina snorted.

"And *someone* tripped me," Nathan replied.

"You tripped *me*," Gina shot back.

"All right, all right," his mother said loudly. "As of right now we're instituting a new rule. For the duration of our trip, no more stores, and no talking to strangers. Is that understood?"

"I like it," Gina's mother said.

"Agreed," Gina's father chimed in.

"You can't be serious," Nathan grumbled.

"Oh, I'm very serious," his mother replied. "Under no circumstances are you to draw attention to yourselves. Is that clear?"

"Whatever," Nathan muttered.

"Fine by me," Gina said, shooting Nathan a dirty look. *Nice going.*

Nathan ignored her and looked out the window. The passing landscape streamed by in murky shades of black and brown—nothing but trees and more trees. *Some vacation,* he thought.

His frustration faded when the van slowed and turned into a narrow break in the woods. It snaked through the forest, to a small, one-story house. Even in the dark, it looked just like he remembered.

Through the trees, he saw the glassy surface of the lake, and overhead, the night sky was a carpet of glittering stars.

"Here we are," his father announced.

"Uh, where exactly *are* we?" Gina asked.

"Crawford, New Hampshire. Why don't you guys wait here, while I go in and turn on some lights."

As he got out of the van, Gina turned to Nathan and whispered, "Where?"

"The cottage."

"The what?"

"My uncle's house," he explained.

He reached down and picked up his backpack, holding it tightly against his chest. Several minutes later the lights in the house came on and everyone piled out. As they began carrying suitcases and supplies inside, Nathan never let go of the backpack—a small detail that didn't escape Gina's watchful eye.

They were coming out of the house for another load when she stopped short in front of him.

"Hey, watch out," he griped, nearly knocking her over.

She stood firm and glared at him. "What are you doing?" she asked. "And don't give me that *what are you talking about* line again."

"Huh?"

"Why are you carrying your backpack in and out of the house?"

"I, um..." he started.

"Na-than?" she said, dragging out his name. "The truth?"

He let out a long breath. "I can't put it down," he said.

"Excuse me?"

He looked over his shoulder to make sure their parents weren't nearby. "There's a book in it."

"A book? In your backpack? What book?"

"From the bookcase in the attic," he whispered.

"The attic?" she said, panic in her voice. "You didn't."

"Kids? Is everything okay?"

"Uh, yeah Dad," Nathan called back. "We're good."

"I can't *believe* you brought it with you," Gina snarled, keeping her voice low. "Don't you remember what happened last time? Have you forgotten all the weird things that first book did?"

"Of course I remember..." he started to say.

She began to pace. "This is really bad. Stuck in this little house with

37

our parents and *you* bring one of those books. Are you crazy? Do you *want* them to find out about the bookcase? Seriously, do you have any idea what they'll do when…?"

"I had to bring it," he said, cutting her off.

For several seconds neither one spoke. She was waiting for him to finish. He was trying to think of what to say next. Recent experience had shown that she didn't react well to books that moved around on their own, or pages that turned by themselves. If he told her how this one trapped him in his room, there was no telling what she'd do, but running into the woods and screaming was certainly a possibility.

"Well?" she said at last, "I'm waiting."

"I can't," he said, stepping around her. He'd have to tell her sooner or later, but now wasn't the time or the place. Not with their parents lurking about.

She caught up with him and grabbed him by the arm. "Tell me," she demanded.

Her mother came out of the house and said, "Come on kids, let's not dilly-dally. It's very late."

"Listen," he said, "I promise I'll tell you, but not now."

"When?" she demanded.

"In the morning."

She gave him her oh-sure face, but he never saw it. He grabbed the last suitcase from the van and went inside. Gina's mother was right. It *was* late. But once they turned in, he had important things to do. And going to sleep wasn't one of them.

A short time later Gina was standing at the end of the hallway, staring into a room that was overrun with stacks of plastic tubs and cardboard boxes. "You've *got* to be kidding me," she said.

"Oh, come on," her mother said as she squeezed past. In one hand she had a pillow, and in the other she had sheets and a blanket. She set the bedding down on top of a tub and removed the thin plastic dust cover from the daybed that was pushed up against the wall.

"You really expect me to sleep on that?" Gina said with a disgusted look. The bed had a thin metal frame and lemon-yellow cushions with blue polka dots, the color of an old denim work shirt.

"Well, you could sleep in the car, I suppose. We could fold down the seat."

"Ha ha, very funny."

"You might want to keep in mind that we wouldn't be here at all if you and Nathan hadn't—"

"Yes, Mom, I know," she shot back, stopping the lecture before it could get started.

Again.

She dropped her suitcase on the floor next to the window and leaned closer to the glass for a look outside into the night. *New Hampshire? Really?*

The moon was shooting splinters of pale light through the dense canopy, creating eerie shadows that covered the ground. She saw one of them move and jumped back, inspecting the window frame from top to bottom.

"What's wrong?" her mother asked.

"This is locked, right?" Gina asked.

"The window?" her mother asked, trying not to laugh. "Relax dear. Nothing slimy is going to crawl in through the window and slither across the floor while you're sound asleep."

"MOM!"

"Sorry," her mother said as she finished with the bed. She plumped the pillow, pulled back the covers, and then gave Gina a hug. "Goodnight dear, pleasant dreams."

After she left, Gina shut the door and sat down on the edge of the bed. She was still stewing about what Nathan had told her. That he would even *think* to bring a book from the attic, from that creepy bookcase. It was beyond belief.

She changed into her nightclothes and climbed into bed, but couldn't get Nathan and the book out of her mind. The last book he found in the attic had taken control of him. He was like a zombie in school, acting like—

What was that?

A high-pitched sound outside her window made her sit up.

Probably just a tree branch.

Her heart began to beat faster.

Yeah, just a tree branch.

She heard it again.

Louder.

Closer.

She ducked back under the covers, burying her head under the pillow. *Pleasant dreams? Yeah, right.*

At the far end of the hall, Nathan was already in bed. He waited until the house was totally quiet before slipping out from beneath the covers. His anticipation grew as he pulled out his backpack, which he'd wedged under the bed. Something his mother told him sparked in his mind like a flash of heat lightning in the night sky. What were her exact words? Something about the bookcase and how his dying grandfather wanted it brought home when his shop closed for good.

"*He asked us to bring it home,*" his mother had told him.

No, that wasn't it.

"*He made us promise we'd bring it home.*"

Yeah, that was exactly what she said.

Promise.

But why?

As he climbed back in bed, he couldn't stop thinking about it. How there were things about the old bookcase that he didn't know. Things about its past that he would never know, because who would he ask? His grandfather was gone. There was no way he could ask his parents. Not after all the things that had happened.

He let out a long breath and turned his attention to the backpack. Once he opened it and took out the book, there would be no turning back. This was no ordinary book. None of them were.

"They're special editions," his mother told him. Special indeed.

He took a deep breath and let it out slowly. Then he opened the backpack and carefully removed the book. In many ways it was similar to the last one. Old. Thick with pages. Unremarkable at first glance. His pulse quickened as he slowly opened it.

And froze.

4

#5401

The knock on the door took him completely by surprise. Before he could hide the book, the door opened and his father peeked inside.

"Nathan, what are you doing?"

"Uh…just some school stuff," he muttered.

His father eyed the backpack on the bed momentarily, then the book. "Well, it can wait until tomorrow," he said.

"Yeah, I guess," Nathan replied, with false resignation. As he spoke, he pulled the backpack toward him to cover the book.

"I mean it. Get some sleep," his father insisted. "I don't want to see that light on again."

Nathan watched the door close and sat there for a moment without moving. Then he pushed the backpack away and picked up the book.

"Nathan?" his father said from across the hall. "What did I just tell you?"

"What?" Nathan asked, annoyed.

"I can see the light under the door," his father said.

"Great," Nathan whispered. He reached over and turned off the light, then waited until he heard the door close across the hallway. That's when he reached into his backpack and took out the small flashlight tucked in one of the side pockets—something he'd kept there ever since his now-famous adventure with Gina.

Sitting cross-legged in his makeshift tent, he switched on the flashlight and took a deep breath. *Here we go.*

The binding gave a weary sigh as he opened the front cover. Outside, the forest stirred from a sudden breeze off the lake, making a tree branch brush against the window. He paid it no mind and turned the page. There, in large black letters, was the title of the book.

A SONG ON THE RAILS
Chronicles of the Railroad Era
By D. Russell Stuart

Just as he finished reading it, the page turned. All by itself. He quickly pulled his hand away and watched as they continued to turn, two, three, four at a time. The first book from his grandfather's bookcase had done the same thing, and it scared the wits out of him. But this time it didn't surprise him or scare him in the least. He expected it to happen. Wanted it to happen. It was his grandfather showing him the way, just like before.

The pages continued turning, then stopped near the middle of the book. Chapter 11. His heart beat faster as he leaned in close and began reading. The chapter had a very unusual name. In fact, it wasn't a name at all—it was a number.

#5401.

Once he began reading, he couldn't take his eyes from the page.

As the late night turned to early morning, the forest outside his window settled into a dead calm. He was in a deep sleep, lost in a dream where he was standing in a dimly lit room. There were no windows and thin needles of light broke through the walls in several places, painting the room in a hazy fog. The floor beneath his feet was unsteady, swaying like a ship at sea, and it was difficult to stand. From somewhere directly behind him he heard a dull scraping sound, like someone was pushing a large piece of furniture across a rough wooden floor.

Before he could turn to see what it was, the whole room was rocked by a powerful jolt that knocked him off his feet. He was thrown against a wall several feet away, like an old shirt, and fell to the floor in a heap. As he struggled to push himself up, he noticed the room had stopped moving. The light that pierced the walls was gone, as was the scraping sound. The room had grown totally dark, and in the dreary silence that followed, someone whispered his name. "Nathan."

He searched the darkness, straining to see, but there was no one there. He was alone. But then something pressed against his arm. Softly at first, like a nudge, then harder, like a jab.

Once.

Twice.

His eyes snapped open and he saw Gina standing beside the

bed, looking down at him. It was daytime. Sunlight was pouring in through the windows, filling the room. But it wasn't his bedroom. He lifted his head and squinted, trying to get his bearings. *Where am I?*

"Get up," she said, poking him again. "If I don't get to sleep late, neither do you."

She turned and looked around the room. There were no stacks of plastic tubs. No outdated daybed. There was furniture. Nice furniture. A desk, a bureau, an old trunk with a quilted blanket neatly folded on top of it. There was no creepy forest outside the windows, full of who knows what. This room had a row of windows that gave a sweeping view of the lake through a row of massive pine trees.

"This isn't fair," she griped. "I get the storage room and you get—"

"What time is it?" he said, cutting her off.

"Time to get up," she fired back. "I'm bored." She walked over to the window and scanned the lake. "What exactly are we supposed to do here, in the middle of nowhere?"

He sat up in bed and rubbed his eyes as the events of the previous day crept back into his memory. Packing his suitcase. The book in the window. The gas station. The long drive north. Carrying supplies into the house with Gina. Staying up late. Reading.

Suddenly he bolted upright and started rummaging through the covers.

"What's wrong?" she asked.

He paid no attention to her and reached down to search the narrow space along the wall.

"What are you *doing*?" she demanded.

"Looking," he mumbled, as he leaned over the edge of the bed to check the floor.

"Yeah, I can see that," she said.

He shook off the bed covers and checked down by his feet. "Where is it?"

"Where is *what*?"

He stopped and took a deep breath. *Think.*

Then it came to him. He jumped out of the bed and darted across the room, to his suitcase propped open on the desk chair. Buried in the tangle of clothes he found it, exactly where he'd hidden it only a few short hours earlier.

"Well? Are you going to tell me what you're doing or not?"

He turned around to face her, book in hand. "You are not going to believe this."

She made a face. *Here we go.*

"Close the door," he said.

She took a hard look at the book in his hands. "Is that it?"

"Yes, and before you get all crazy, let me tell you why I brought it."

"I can't *believe* you," she hissed, her anger from the night before igniting all over again.

"Wait, you need to hear why," he said.

His voice was calm and reassuring, almost pleading, and she stood there for several seconds without speaking. A part of her was screaming, *LEAVE NOW! RUN!* The book was from that old bookcase in his attic. That was all she needed to know. As far as she was concerned, every one of those books belonged right where they were, hidden away on the third floor. Better to padlock the door shut.

But another part of her was whispering, *not so fast... stay.* He was up to something. She knew it the moment he climbed into the van with his backpack. That made it a puzzle, and puzzles were her specialty. For that reason, the soft voice won out and she decided to stick around just a little bit longer.

"Okay," she said, "let's hear it."

"Uh, the door?" he said. "Please?"

"This better be good," she said, then went over to the door and pushed it shut. "There," she said with a phony smile, "it's closed."

He took in a deep breath and let it out slowly. "All right. I had to bring it because—" he began, then paused.

She tilted her head to one side, impatient. "Because?"

He wasn't sure how she'd take it but he told her anyway. He started with the book jumping off his bureau, after sitting there for weeks without moving. Next, he told her how hid it in the bureau, but it pushed the drawer open, then how he stuffed it under his mattress. He confessed to his real reason for going back into the house again. She grimaced when he described how the book flew at him when he stepped into the room, and how it pinned the door shut. By the time he finished, her face was drained of color. If he had looked closely, he would've seen the goosebumps on her arms.

That meant he had to move quickly now—skip to the *real* story— to the only thing that would make her forget her fear of haunted books. It was the thing she liked more than anything.

"But forget all that stuff for now," he said.

"Forget it?" she snapped. She nodded her head slowly and said, "Yeah, sure, no problem. I'll just forget it. Like *that* could happen. Like anything you just said is normal."

"There's more I need to tell you," he said.

47

"I'll bet," she huffed. She'd had enough of his crazy talk. This wasn't a puzzle. It was just creepy. "You have one minute," she said, looking down at her watch.

He ignored her and opened the book. "I stayed up late reading," he explained as he flipped through the chapters. He didn't mention the part where the pages turned by themselves.

"Yeah, yeah," she said. "Fifty seconds."

"And I found this." He held the book up and showed her the chapter titled #5401.

She looked at it briefly and then back down at her watch. "Whatever. Forty seconds."

"Just wait," he said, thinking about how to begin. He had to word it just right or it wouldn't work. She'd walk away and refuse to hear another word about it. And she *really* needed to hear this. He looked directly at her. "Okay," he began, "a train leaves the station just after noontime."

Her shoulders slumped. This sounded like one of those nutty questions from her math homework. "BOR-ing," she said. She tapped her watch and warned him, "Thirty seconds—time's a-wastin'."

"All right, listen. The train travels north and then makes a water stop."

"How nice." She checked the time again. "Twenty seconds."

"While the train is stopped, some of the passengers get out for a breath of fresh air. You know, to stretch their legs and look around." She shook her head and mumbled, "I can't believe this." This time she turned her watch so he could see the sweeping second hand. "Better hurry—ten seconds."

"Then the train takes off again. It travels to its destination further north with no other stops."

"Time's up!" she declared. She rolled her eyes and reached for the door. *I can't believe I just fell for that.*

"And that's when the conductor discovers that one of the train cars is missing."

She stopped short, her hand hovering an inch from the doorknob. "What did you say?"

"One of the train cars was missing," he repeated.

"Missing?" Her voice was laced with doubt.

"Gone," he said.

She spun around to face him. "That's impossible. Train cars don't just disappear."

"This one did," he said.

She marched over to where he was standing. "Didn't happen. You read it wrong, or they made a mistake or something."

"Nope," he said. "It was boxcar #5401. The engineer remembered when they picked it up. So did the conductor."

She thought about that for a moment.

"Let me get this straight," she said, "the train leaves, then it stops for water—"

"And wood," he added. "It was a steam engine."

"Don't interrupt me," she said. "Then it continues on—"

"With no other stops," he muttered.

She glared at him.

"All right, I'll be quiet." He turned and looked out the window. There was a family of Canada geese swimming near the shore, eyeing his uncle's dock suspiciously.

She thought for a second, trying to remember where she left off.

"Okay, so no other stops, and then it comes to… what did you call it?"

"The destination. You know? The last stop?"

"Yeah, I got it," she said, waving him off. "They get to the last stop—"

"West Branch," he whispered.

"Will you STOP?" she growled.

He put his hand over his mouth.

"They get to West Branch, and that's when they find out that one of the cars is gone."

Nathan kept his hand clamped in place and nodded.

"Let me see that," she snapped. She yanked the book out of his hands and skimmed down the first page of the chapter, then the second. *This* was a puzzle. It sounded difficult, but it wasn't. The answer was probably right here in front of his eyes and he missed it. He had a history of missing things, enough to fill an entire page. She'd have this puzzle solved in three minutes. Five tops.

Nathan stood quietly and watched as she searched every word, every sentence.

"There's a perfectly good explanation," she mumbled under her breath.

"What was that?"

"Things don't just disappear," she said without taking her eyes from the page.

"Then how do you explain the fact that it was there when they started out, and gone when they reached the end of the line?"

"Who knows?" she shot back. "But someone would have seen something."

"Nope," he countered. "They interviewed everyone on the train—

the employees, the passengers, *everyone*. No one heard anything, no one saw anything."

"Yeah, well…"she said, only half listening.

"And there's something else," he told her.

"What?" she asked, looking up from the page.

"They never found it."

"What do you mean?"

"To this day, that boxcar has never been found."

When she heard that she turned her head and looked out the window with a blank expression, arranging each of the facts in her mind like a row of dominoes. "Something doesn't add up here," she said.

Before he could respond, the bedroom door swung open and his mother came in. "Well, I see the sleepyhead has decided to get up for the day." She saw the book in Gina's hands and said, "What's this, homework?"

Nathan answered first. "Uh, yeah, I was just showing Gina what she needs to read."

"That's good," his mother said, before addressing Nathan directly. "We're about to clear the table, so if you want breakfast you'd better get a move on."

Nathan heard the word "breakfast" and bolted from the room. When he returned a short time later, he found Gina standing at the window, staring out at the lake. She turned to face him with her arms crossed tightly against her chest, her face the color of chalk.

"What's the matter?" he asked.

"I figured it out," she said.

5

Wynn

G ina never moved from the window as she eyed the book on the floor. It was exactly where she dropped it, after discovering a specific detail in the story. Once it hit the floor she fully expected it to move, open up by itself, or worse yet, fly toward her like it had with Nathan in his bedroom. But it stayed put on the floor, and that was the only reason she was still in the room. Nonetheless, she was keeping her distance.

"You figured what out?" Nathan asked, studying the spooked look on her face.

"Why the book did all those crazy things in your bedroom," she answered.

"Okay," he said slowly. He was still trying to figure it out himself.

"Why didn't you tell me?" she asked.

"Tell you what?"

"That the train left from Concord, New Hampshire."

He paused for a second, thinking about the details of the story. "Yeah, that's right," he said, "Concord. So what?"

"So what?" she fired back. "Don't you remember last night?"

"Last night? What about it?"

"When we were driving up here?" *Hello?*

"I remember getting chased by a crazy lady at a gas station."

She slumped her shoulders. "Do you *ever* pay attention?"

He looked down at the floor and said, "Yes." Then in a softer voice, "Sometimes."

"We went through Concord on the way up here," she told him.

"Huh," he replied. "I guess I missed that when I was *sleeping!*"

She gave him a look. *What else is new?*

"So, we went through Concord," he said. "Big deal."

"Yes, it is a big deal," she said, starting to pace, "because now we're north of Concord."

"Yeah? So what?"

She stopped pacing and stared at him. *Seriously?*

"What?" he asked innocently, turning both palms upward.

She shook her head in disbelief. "The train headed north from Concord," she said.

"So?" he replied.

"So, isn't it possible that it passed by here, or somewhere near here?"

"Nope."

She let out a long breath. "Okay, let me explain it again. The train left Concord and went north. We passed through Concord and went north, which means—"

"Nothing," he blurted out before she could finish.

"Why not?"

"Because it only made one stop, in a town called Stone Point."

"Yeah, Stone Point," she said. "I know, I read that."

"My family has been coming up here ever since I was a baby," he explained. "In all that time, I've never seen or heard of any town called Stone Point. Not around here, anyway. And I've never seen railroad tracks around here, either."

"Fine, think what you want," she said, turning back to the window, "but clearly your grandfather wanted you to bring the book with you. He knew where we were going, and he wanted to make sure you didn't leave without it." Her body trembled as if she'd been hit by a sudden blast of Arctic air. "I can't *believe* I just said that. It's SO creepy."

She's right, he thought. There had to be a reason his grandfather wanted him to bring the book. There was always a reason. A reason why the books fell out of the bookcase. A reason why the pages turned by themselves. *We're in New Hampshire,* he told himself. *The boxcar vanished in New Hampshire.* There was an easy way to prove her right, or wrong. "We need a map," he mumbled under his breath.

"What did you say?"

Without answering, he picked the book up off the floor and shoved it into his backpack.

"What are you doing?" she asked.

He zipped up the pack and said, "Come on, let's go."

"Go? Where?"

"Downtown," he said.

"You're not serious."

54

"I'm completely serious. Come on, I'll explain on the way."

"Whoa, whoa, whoa," she blurted out, hurrying over to the door to intercept him.

"What are you doing?" he asked.

"Stopping you before you do something dumb."

He shrugged his shoulders. "What are you talking about?"

"Did you hear what your mother said in the van, after we stopped for gas? The thing about not talking to strangers?"

"Yeah?"

"Well, you remember how that woman reacted at the counter, right?"

"How could I forget?"

"That's going to happen again if we go downtown. You know it will. And if our parents find out, they'll make us stay inside this house the whole time we're here. Is that what you want?"

"Of course not," he said. "We'll just have to be careful."

She was about to say something when he ducked around her and slipped out the door.

Out in the side yard, their parents were sitting back, soaking in the warm morning sunshine. A thin breeze combed the surface of the lake, giving it the appearance of wrinkled skin. The stillness of the morning was broken when the screen door slammed and Nathan came bounding down the steps two at a time.

Gina followed seconds later. "Nathan! Stop!" she hissed.

"What's up, guys?" his mother asked.

"I want to give Gina a tour of the area," Nathan said.

"A tour?" Gina's mother asked.

"Yeah, I figured since Gina's never been here before…"

"I don't like it," Gina's father said. "What if someone recognizes you?"

Nathan's father nodded his head. "I agree."

"Oh, come on," Nathan groaned.

"They're right," his mother said. "After that episode last night, you two need to keep a low profile."

"A low profile?" Nathan countered. "Why? There's nobody around. It's the same every time we come here. The town is deserted."

"All right, all right," his mother said, holding up her hand for him to stop his rant. She looked over at the others and said, "He's right. It's early in the season. The summer people don't show up for another couple of weeks. This time of year, Crawford is basically—"

"A ghost town," Nathan cut in.

For a moment none of them spoke. Then his mother said, "If we let you go, and I'm still not convinced it's a good idea, you're to talk to no one. Is that understood?"

"Yes," Nathan grumbled.

"If people look at you, look the other way," Gina's mother said.

Gina cocked her head. *Look the other way? Really?*

"What you need is a disguise," her father said. "Did you kids bring hats? How about sunglasses? You should get them and put them on. In fact, every time you go outside you should—"

"Dad!" Gina exclaimed.

"All right, everyone calm down," Nathan's mother said. She looked over at Nathan. "What I said last night still stands. Are we clear on that? No stores, and no talking to strangers."

Nathan shrugged. *Whatever.*

"If there's a repeat of last night..." she started to say.

"Don't worry," he said. "We won't talk to anyone. We won't look at anyone. We'll stare at the ground everywhere we go."

"All right, wise guy," his mother said. "Just be careful. Try to remember why we're here."

"Yeah, yeah, yeah," he mumbled.

They turned and walked up the dirt driveway until they came to the main road.

"I have a bad feeling about this," Gina muttered.

"Relax," he said. He pointed to the right. "This is Jewel Lake Road. The boat landing is up that way about a half a mile."

"Wait a minute," she blurted out, "we're going somewhere in a boat? "

"No," he replied. "That was the tour. I hope you liked it." He pointed in the opposite direction. "We need to go that way."

"That way?" she said, looking down the road. It was long and straight, the shoulder on either side a mix of hard pack gravel that fell away down a slender bank overgrown with tall grass and wildflowers. Beyond it was nothing but woods. "How far?"

He started walking. "Not very," he called back over his shoulder.

"Wait!" she said, running to catch up. "Tell me where we're going."

"You'll see."

They had walked for nearly ten minutes when Gina looked up and saw an intersection in the distance. Unlike the busy streets back home, where there was always a seemingly endless line of traffic, there wasn't a car in sight. "This place is too quiet," she muttered.

"Sure it is," Nathan said, "but wait till this summer."

"Why, what happens this summer?"

He stopped walking and pointed back toward his uncle's driveway. "You see that stretch of road?"

She turned to look. The road behind them extended well into the distance. "What about it?" she asked.

He didn't answer.

"What about it?" she asked again. Still no answer.

"Did you hear me?" she said, turning back toward him. "Nathan?" She turned in a full circle. "NATHAN?"

The road was deserted in both directions. "Okay, very funny," she yelled.

There was no reply.

She listened for a moment and then spun around again, looking in every direction.

He had completely vanished.

To her left was a swath of tall grass. It covered the embankment that sloped downwards and eventually leveled out at the tree line. She peered into the tangle of trees and yelled, "If you're hiding in the woods, I hope you get stung by a bee!"

She waited for a reply but all she heard was the buzzing of bugs in the tall grass.

"Fine," she yelled, "I'll go by myself." She started to walk away when she saw a small section of the grass sway, as if brushed by the wind. But there was no wind. It was only ten feet away, but the grass was too tall and she couldn't see what was causing it. She took a half step closer. "I can see you, you know."

Again, there was no answer.

She took another half step. "Nathan?" called out, her voice

breaking. That's when she saw the top of his head. "Nice try," she said as she marched down the slope.

He was sitting upright in the grass, rubbing the back of his neck.

"Ditching me?" she said. "Really? What are you, five years old?"

He shook his head and blinked hard. "I didn't *ditch* you," he said. He touched the side of his jaw, flexing it back and forth.

"Yeah, right," she shot back. *Tell me another one.*

"I was standing there next to you and then I got pulled sideways."

"You got pulled sideways? That's a new one. Remind me to write it down in the *Nathan Cole Book of Stupid Excuses.*"

"I'm serious," he said.

"Uh-huh. Pulled sideways. By what, exactly?"

"Beats me. One minute I was standing up there in the road, then something grabbed my arm and sent me flying. I tripped and landed here."

She began to laugh.

"What's so funny?"

"You," she said. "You ditch me. I find you. And the best you can come up with is 'I got pulled sideways?" She laughed even harder.

"It's the truth."

"Yeah, sure," she said, nodding her head. *Whatever you say.*

"Fine. Don't believe me, but that's what happened." He stood up and brushed flecks of dirt and broken bits of grass off his blue jeans, the brushed past her.

He was halfway up the embankment when she said, "Um, aren't you forgetting something?"

He stopped and turned around. "What?"

"Your backpack?"

He touched his shoulder, feeling for the strap, but all he felt was the smooth fabric of his shirt. "That's weird," he said as he walked back toward her, "I must've dropped it when I fell."

"You mean when you ditched me and hid in the grass."

"I got pulled sideways," he said through clenched teeth.

"Just get your backpack and let's go," she said. "We're supposed to be going somewhere, although you still haven't told me where."

He waded through the tall grass, eyeing the ground around him. When he reached the spot where he fell, he pushed the grass aside with his foot. After several passes back and forth, he stopped.

"What's the matter?" Gina asked.

"It's not here."

"It has to be there," she said in her *don't-make-me-come-down-there* voice.

He scratched his head and started again, this time crouching low to the ground and using both hands to part the grass. A few minutes later, he stood up and frowned, scanning the area from the road to the tree line in both directions. "This is *crazy*. I just had it, now it's…"

Suddenly he froze.

"What is it?" Gina asked.

He had his back to her, staring at a spot on the edge of the woods, back in the direction they had come from. "Come here a minute," he said, motioning to her with his hand.

"Why?" she asked nervously.

He turned around and looked at her, all the while trying to sort something out in his mind.

"Are you going to tell me what it is?" she asked.

"Just come here," he said.

She stood up straight and folded her arms. "Not until you tell me."

"Suit yourself."

He pushed his way through the tall grass and headed toward the woods.

"Hey, where are you going?" she yelled. "Wait for me."

She sprinted down the embankment and nearly collided with him when he came to a sudden stop.

"What's wrong?" she asked, slightly out of breath.

"Look," he said, pointing to a small tree set back in the woods. Sitting on the ground at the base of it was his backpack.

"Great, you found it, now let's go," she said impatiently.

"That's strange," he said slowly, looking back at the matted grass where he fell. It was at least 30 feet behind him.

She looked back too. "Wait a minute. If you fell back there," she said, pointing to the tall grass, "then how did your backpack get over here next to that tree?"

He was lost for words as the truth revealed itself in a series of slow motion flashes.

We were walking… we stopped… something grabbed me… and spun me around.

Then he figured it out.

I never saw it coming because it didn't come from the front. It came from behind me.

An eerie sensation plucked at his nerves, like fingers tugging on the taut strings of a guitar. It was the same feeling he got when he saw the book suspended in his bedroom window.

"I know what happened," Gina said, breaking the silence. "You must've thrown it when you fell. I mean, it only makes sense, right?"

"Yeah, I guess," he mumbled, even though he knew it didn't happen that way.

"Well, just get it and let's go," she said impatiently.

"Right," he said softly. But he didn't move. He just stood there, staring at the backpack.

"Well? GO!" she said, pushing him from behind.

"All right, all right," he said, stumbling forward.

Years of harsh winters had taken their toll, and the tree was draped in a thick tangle of broken branches. He reached down to grab the backpack when he paused. There was something odd about the bottom of the tree.

"Uh, any day now would be nice," Gina called out.

"Just hold on," he said, pulling away some of the broken branches.

"What are you doing?" she yelled.

"Come over and see," he said, peeling away more branches.

She exhaled loudly and plowed through the grass, grumbling the whole way. "A tour, you said. You were going to show me around. But no, you want to play lumberjack."

He was removing the last branch when she came up behind him and stopped short.

"Uh, Nathan? That doesn't look like a tree."

"It's not," he said.

She stepped closer, and for several seconds she didn't say a word.

What they thought was the narrow trunk of a tree was, in fact, a thick steel post. The original black paint had bubbled and cracked over the years and in the shadow of the larger trees it looked like tree bark. Perched at the top was a large rectangular sign. Forest green with white lettering. At the top was the official state seal of New Hampshire.

"It's a historic marker," he said.

"Yeah, no kidding," she replied. *I can see that.*

He looked up at the surrounding trees. "A branch broke off up there," he said, pointing to a jagged stub of splintered wood on the side of a nearby pine tree. "And when it fell it brought those other branches down with it."

"Thanks for the news flash, Paul Bunyan. Now move." She edged him out of the way and started reading the dedication aloud. "Lakeside Station, built in 1871 by the New England Central Railway, was a popular stop on the Lakes Region Line."

She stopped reading. "A railroad line," she said, astonished.

"Here in this town," he added, with equal amazement.

In unison, their gaze slowly shifted to the backpack that was propped up against the bottom of the marker.

"You put the book in your backpack, didn't you?" she said. Her voice was just above a whisper, like she was speaking for the first time ever.

"Uh-huh."

She felt goosebumps forming on her arms. "I was afraid of that," she murmured.

He stared at the backpack in awe. It all made sense now. The book, the backpack, the tree. It was his grandfather, giving him another clue. "Go ahead," he said, his eyes still fixed on the backpack, "read the rest of it."

She took a deep breath and continued.

"It operated for several years until it was completely destroyed—"

"By the worst storm of the century."

"That's *not* what it says," she snapped.

"I didn't say anything," he replied.

They turned at the same time and saw an old man standing at the top of the embankment, partially obscured by the tall grass. His voice was thin but carried the weight of age and experience.

"Tornado flattened it like a pancake," he said.

Nathan and Gina looked at each other, not sure what to say. They never heard the man approach; he just appeared out of thin air.

"Took out the whole street," he said, gesturing with his hand. He hobbled closer and pointed at the historic marker. "I've been telling those boys down at the state barn about that mess for months now. I guess they got better things to do than pick up old tree branches."

"Uh, I didn't mean to cause a problem," Nathan said.

"Never you mind, son," the old man replied. "Now, I'd climb out of there if I were you. This whole stretch of road is crawling with poison ivy."

Gina immediately checked the ground around her feet, but all she saw was matted grass. Nathan grabbed his backpack and together they climbed up the slope to the road. Only then did they get a good look at the stranger.

He wasn't much taller than they were and he hadn't shaved in days. His plaid shirt was untucked and torn in places, and his baggy pants were wrinkled like an old paper bag. He sized them up for a moment and then pointed at each of them. "I know you," he said in a high shrill voice. "You two were on television."

Gina elbowed Nathan in the arm. *Nice going.*

"It's all they've been talking about," the old man mused.

"We're not supposed to discuss it," Gina said abruptly.

"I don't doubt it," the man said. He started to walk away when he stopped and turned back around. "The name's Barrett, but most folks call me Wynn. Short for Winslow." He did a quick check of the road in both directions. "Winslow C. Barrett," he said in an official voice, "according to U.S. Post Office, that is." He checked the time on his watch. "Which, by the looks of things, has decided to take the day off."

"Uh, I'm Nathan and this is my friend, Gina."

"Right," Wynn said, eyeing each of them carefully for the second time.

Gina glared at Nathan. *Why did you tell him that?*

"I was headed out to check the mailbox when I saw you walk by," Wynn said. "Knew right away you weren't from these parts."

"You did?" Nathan asked. He glanced over Wynn's shoulder and saw the mailbox on the opposite side of the road. It was perched atop an old wooden post that was tilted backwards, fighting to stay upright. Just to the left of it was the opening of a dirt driveway that snaked back into the woods.

"Wasn't that hard," Wynn said. "Schools around here don't let out for the summer until next month. So unless you're skipping class, you must be from out of town."

"We're staying at my uncle's place on Pine Point," Nathan said.

Gina cleared her throat. *Stop telling him everything!*

"It's a pleasure to make your acquaintance," he said with a tip of his cap. Then he motioned toward the historic marker. "Don't see many folks stopping to read that. Are you kids railroad buffs?"

Gina made a face. *Buffs? Who says 'buffs'?*

"Well, um…" Nathan stammered.

"We're doing a project for school," Gina blurted out. It was her one-size-fits-all excuse, the one she used on her parents all the time.

"I see," Wynn said, eying the two of them suspiciously.

"Actually, we were just on our way into town to find a map," Nathan explained.

"Is that so?" Wynn said.

"We're looking for a place called Stone Point."

Wynn blinked hard. Then he took off his baseball cap and scratched the top of his head. "Stone Point. That's a name I haven't heard in a long, long time."

"I've never seen signs for it," Nathan said.

Wynn chuckled. "I don't imagine you have." He put his baseball cap back on his head. "Good luck finding it on any map," he said. "Especially the ones they sell downtown."

"Do you know where it is?" Nathan asked.

"Sure do," Wynn said. "It's here."

"Here?" Nathan and Gina blurted out at the same time.

"That's right. You're standing on it."

6

Janet French

There was a brief moment of silence as the old man's words hung in the air.

"What did you say?" Nathan asked.

"Come on, let's go," Gina whispered, pulling him by the arm. *This guy is nuts.*

"No, just wait," he said, pushing her hand away.

"Well, let's see now," Wynn said, scratching the back of his head. "Stone Point..."

The sudden blare of a car horn stopped him before he could continue. It came from directly behind them, and when they turned to look they saw a dark blue minivan coming up the road.

Nathan closed his eyes and slumped his shoulders. *I don't believe this.*

"Now you've done it," Gina said.

The minivan came to an abrupt stop and Nathan's mother climbed out of the driver's-side door. "Nathan, come over here," she said sharply. The words came out so fast that they sounded like one word. *Nathancomeoverhers.*

"Hold on a minute," he groaned, holding up his hand. He turned back to Wynn, anxious to hear what he had to say.

"Nathan!" his mother said again. Louder.

"You best go, son," Wynn said softly.

Nathan shook his head and sighed, then trudged over to the minivan.

"What are you doing?" his mother demanded. "You told me back at the house that you wouldn't talk to anyone. Did those words come out of your mouth or was I just hearing things?" Before he could answer she said, "Won't talk to anyone, won't look at anyone. Yes, I'm quite sure those were the words you used."

"Mom, relax," he said, "everything's fine."

"Is it?" she snapped.

Wynn walked over to where they were standing and tipped his cap. "Winslow Barrett, ma'am, but most people just call me Wynn. Nathan tells me you're staying out on Pine Point."

"Yes, that's correct," Nathan's mother said reluctantly. "Nathan's uncle has been kind enough to let us use the cottage for the week." Then she slid the side door open and motioned inside. "Let's go, kids." Her face was still tight with anger.

"Mom, no," Nathan protested. Five more minutes, that's all he needed.

"Nathan?" she said sternly. Her tone made it clear that there would be no negotiation. The matter was settled.

"You go on now," Wynn said. "I expect we'll be seeing each other again before too long. This town's not that big."

Nathan kicked at the gravel and then reluctantly climbed into the minivan. *Five more minutes,* he thought, *that's all we needed.*

Wynn watched them drive off, shaking his head in disbelief. *How do you like that?* He hadn't heard anyone mention Stone Point in years. Decades even. Most of the old timers who knew the name had died off years ago. As far as the new residents in town, even if they did hear about it, what would they care? They were too busy racing their fancy speedboats across the lake and shooting off fireworks at all hours of the night. So how was it that two young kids from nowhere near here knew about it? Not only that, they were actually looking for it.

Curious.

Nathan slumped back in the seat. His arms were folded across his chest and his jaw was clamped shut. What he really wanted to do was shout at the top of his lungs. *He was about to tell us everything!*

His mother was the first to break the silence.

"I thought we made it clear that you weren't to talk to anyone."

"Actually," Gina replied, "Mr. Barrett started talking to us first."

"That's right," Nathan sniped. *So there.*

"It would've been impolite to ignore him," Gina added.

"Yeah," Nathan said. *Take that.*

"Okay, okay, I get it," his mother said. "I guess Mr. Barrett is harmless enough."

Gina gave Nathan a dizzy look. *Harmless? More like crazy.*

"But what we told you before still applies," Nathan's mother said.

"While we're here, you are not to draw attention to yourselves."

"You know, I think my husband was right," Gina's mother said as they turned at the traffic light. "They should be wearing hats and sunglasses."

Gina shook her head, annoyed. *This again? Really?*

"I think you're right," Nathan's mother said as she pulled into the grocery store parking lot. She found a vacant spot near the front of the store and turned off the engine. "Shall we?" she said.

"I'll stay here," Nathan grumbled.

"Me too," Gina chimed in.

"All right then," Nathan's mother said. "You two wait here. We shouldn't be too long."

They were barely out of the van when Gina turned to Nathan. "What is your problem?"

"He was just about to tell us about Stone Point! Then *they* have to show up. We were that close," he said, pounding the seat in disgust.

She rolled her eyes. *Oh brother.*

"What?" he asked.

"I wouldn't believe a whole lot of what that old man says," she replied. "Did you see his clothes? It looked like he just crawled out of a dumpster."

"There was nothing wrong with his clothes."

"Well, how about his crazy voice?" she asked.

"What are you talking about? His voice is fine."

"Nathan," she said, staring at him intently, "the man cackles."

"Cackles?"

"Like a chicken."

"He does not sound like a chicken."

"Fine, don't believe me," she said, turning to look out the window, but the guy is a wacko."

After that they didn't talk. Gina stared at the grocery store, wondering if she'd made a mistake by not going inside. Nathan was looking in the opposite direction, his attention drawn to a building across the street.

"I can't believe they want us to wear hats," Gina mumbled.

Nathan was still glued to the window and didn't reply. In the back of his mind an idea was forming.

"Hello?" Gina said, snapping her fingers at him. "Anybody home?"

Again he didn't respond. Maybe coming to the grocery store would pay off after all.

Gina sighed and looked the other way again. "I should've gone in the store."

Suddenly, Nathan turned away from the window and slid his backpack under the seat.

When Gina saw that she said, "What are you doing?"

He took one more look across the street, then pushed his hair back behind his ear.

"Hold on," she said. When he did the hair thing she knew he was about to do something foolish, something that would likely spell trouble for both of them. "What are you up to?" she asked suspiciously.

"You say the old man is a wacko? Well, there's one way to find out." Without another word, he opened the side door and jumped out.

"Hey," she yelled as he slammed the door shut. "Wait."

She climbed out of the van and raced after him. He was four parking spaces away when she finally caught up with him. "Where are you going?" she demanded.

"Over there," he said, pointing to the small building across the street. It was built from thick logs that gave it a rustic frontier look, like something out of an old western movie.

"I don't think we should be doing this," she said. "You heard what your mother said, right?"

"Don't be such a worry wart," he replied as they reached the sidewalk. There was a long line of morning traffic and he had to wait to cross the street.

"A what?" she asked.

He looked both ways, and then darted across the street.

"I definitely should've gone into the store," she said.

Wynn Barrett stood at the mailbox, surveying the street in both directions, hoping to see the postal delivery truck. "Reading a historic marker. Who does that?" he mumbled to himself. Certainly not any of the kids he knew. If the news stories he'd seen on TV were true, maybe they really were brighter than the rest of the kids their age.

Or just lucky.

Making a discovery like they did? Unraveling a secret that had gone unsolved for over 150 years? Luck or no luck, it was all very interesting. He finally gave up on the mailman and walked back down the driveway.

Those two kids had given him an idea.

Nathan was almost to the front door of the building when Gina caught up with him.

"Stop," she said, grabbing him by the arm. "You're going to get us in big trouble."

"Relax, will you?"

"How can I? You haven't told me what you're doing."

"I'm going to prove to you that Wynn Barrett isn't crazy," he said.

"And just how are you going to do that?" she demanded. "*You're standing on it,*" she mimicked in a squeaky voice. "What kind of nonsense was that?"

"What if it's true?" he countered.

"If it's true—and I don't think it is—didn't you hear what he said? About not finding it on any map?"

"Correction. He said we wouldn't find it on any map they sell downtown."

"Exactly. Now, let's go," she said, pulling him toward the street.

"But that's not what I'm looking for," he said, yanking his arm free.

"Wait, what?"

"Think about it," he said, then opened the front door and slipped inside.

"Nathan!" she yelled, as the door closed in her face. She blew out an angry breath, then stormed into the building and found Nathan standing several feet inside, staring at something on the wall to his left. "Nathan!" she growled. "What are you doing?"

"Excuse me young lady, is there a problem?"

She turned and saw a plump woman with bushy blond hair standing behind the counter that ran along the back wall. Her head was tipped down slightly so she could see over the gold-rimmed glasses perched on the tip of her nose.

"No," Gina replied very matter-of-factly. Then she turned to Nathan. "We need to go. Now."

He ignored her and drifted further into the room, studying the giant framed photographs that decorated the walls. Each one showed a nearby lake, or mountaintop, or raging river.

She spun around and raced back to the front door. The minivan was sitting empty in the parking lot, and a slow stream of people were sauntering in and out of the grocery store. There was no sign of her mother, but she knew that could change at any moment. Nathan's mother said it herself. *"We won't be long."*

She turned away from the door and did a double take.

Nathan had vanished.

"Now where did he go?" she griped, scanning the rows of long wooden cases that filled the middle of the room. Some were open shelves with piles of brochures and magazines, others had glass fronts and held nature artifacts and stuffed wildlife from around the region. "What is this place?" she mumbled.

Out of the corner of her eye, she noticed the woman at the counter watching her over the top of her glasses. This time, she stared back, and that's when she noticed the long wooden sign hanging on the back wall.

Crawford, New Hampshire
Vistors Center

"Visitors Center? Great!" she grumbled. "I can buy a pine cone."

She darted into the maze of cases, searching for Nathan. As she came around a case filled with old tools, she spotted him. He was standing perfectly still, staring at something on the wall.

"Hey," she said, as she came up behind him. "I am *not* going to wear a hat."

"That's strange," he mumbled.

"And I am *not* going to wear sunglasses."

"I don't believe it."

"But that is exactly what's going to happen if we don't... wait a minute... what did you say?"

He turned around and looked her in the eye, his face free of expression.

"What's wrong with you?" she asked.

"It makes no sense," he replied.

"What are you talking about?"

"Look at this," he said, turning back to the wall.

She sighed and stepped around him. "We don't have time for this."

Mounted on the wall was a large map of central New Hamshire. It was a relic, printed so long ago that the paper had started to buckle and crack. It was dotted with small colored tacks that marked various landmarks and tourist attractions. As she stood there looking at it, the cryptic comment Nathan made outside suddenly became clear. He wasn't looking for a new map—he was looking for an old map.

"All right," she said. "What am I looking at?"

"This," he said, pointing to a dot that identified Concord, New Hampshire.

She leaned closer and saw the tiniest of black lines. "What is it?"

"A railroad line," he said.

The line started at the dot and meandered northward with a number of curious twists and turns.

"Is this the same railroad line we read about on the historic marker?" Before he could answer she said, "Wait, never mind, it doesn't come anywhere near Crawford."

"Yeah, I noticed that," Nathan said in a troubled voice. "Which means either the historic marker was wrong..."

Gina chuckled. "Or whoever drew this map got it completely wrong."

"They most certainly did *not* get it wrong, young lady."

Gina spun around and saw the woman from the counter standing directly behind them. "Oops!" she whispered, then quickly looked away.

Nathan turned to the woman and read the name on her nametag. Janet French.

"Uh, excuse me, Miss French?" he said politely. "Do you think you could help us?"

Janet, who was still glaring at Gina, turned to Nathan and smiled. "Why certainly," she said, in a voice that was syrupy sweet.

Gina cringed. *Yuck.*

"Thank you," Nathan said, bowing his head slightly.

Gina rolled her eyes. *I'm gonna be sick.*

Nathan ignored her and said, "We were wondering...there was a train station in this town a long time ago, right?"

"That's correct," Janet replied, "Lakeside Station."

Nathan pointed to the map. "Well, according to this map, there were no tracks around here. There's this line here, near Concord, but it doesn't come anywhere near Crawford."

Janet adjusted her glasses and stepped forward. "Actually," she said, examining the map closely, "there was a time when those tracks *did* come to Crawford."

"The Lakes Region Line?" Nathan asked.

Janet's face lit up like a jack-o-lantern. "Very good. I can see you've done your homework."

Gina frowned. *Oh please.*

Nathan pretended to be embarrassed. "Well," he said with a shrug, "most kids hate to do homework, but not me."

Gina's jaw dropped open. *WHAT?*

"Well, I'd say that you're a very special student, then," Janet beamed.

Gina threw her hands up in frustration. *That's it, I'm outta here!* She stormed back to the front door before Janet French could utter another sappy comment about The Amazing Nathan Cole, Student of the Century.

"Now, what you probably don't know," Janet said, "is that the Lakes Region Line was eventually torn up. That explains why the tracks on this map don't go to Crawford. When this map was printed, the Lakes Region Line was already long gone." She paused and looked over at Gina, who was staring out the front door. "So, the person who drew this map," she said, speaking loud enough for Gina to hear, "got it completely correct."

Gina wasn't listening. She was too distracted by what she saw across the street. Her mother was standing outside the front door of the grocery store with a cart full of groceries. Nathan's mother was standing nearby, reading the shopping list. "I knew it," she fumed, "I knew this would happen."

She ran back to where Nathan was standing and said, "We need to leave, right now."

Nathan ignored her and addressed Janet. "Could you answer one more question for me?"

"Why, of course," Janet replied.

Gina grabbed a hold of his arm. "I mean it," she said. "We have to go!"

Nathan peeled her hand off his arm and eased her away. She stumbled backward and then glared at him in disbelief.

Really?

She took a step toward him, but he put his hand up to keep her away. That was the last straw. "Fine, have it your way," she said, waving him off. She turned and marched back to the front door, muttering the whole way.

"What is it you'd like to know?" Janet asked, once Gina was gone.

"Can you tell me about Stone Point?"

"My, my," Janet said. "You really have done your homework."

He offered an innocent shrug. *What can I say?* He didn't bother to mention their conversation with Wynn Barrett.

"Stone Point was the original stop on the Lakes Region Line," Janet explained. "That was well before Lakeside Station."

He nodded slowly as her words sank in. *Of course.* It was right there in the book. The train stopped at Stone Point for wood and water. His grandfather must have known that. What else could possibly explain the crazy events in his bedroom as they were getting ready to leave? "The fuel stop," he muttered under his breath.

"I'm sorry, what did you say?" Janet asked.

This time he played dumb. "Uh, Stone Point... that was a train station, right?"

"Actually, no," Janet said. "It was a fuel stop. In those days the trains were powered by steam, so they had to stop every so many miles for wood and water."

"I see," Nathan replied, nodding his head like she was telling him something he didn't already know.

Janet shook her head sadly. "It was such a pity," she said.

"What was?" Nathan asked.

"That Stone Point was destroyed in that terrible storm."

When she got outside the Visitors Center, Gina looked across the street and stopped short. Her mother had turned the grocery cart around and was going back into the store with Nathan's mother. "I don't believe it," she muttered. She spun around and ran back inside the building, where Janet French was still rambling on.

Nathan was about to ask another question when Gina latched onto his arm and dragged him across the floor, trying to break free the whole way. When they reached the front door, she pushed it open with her shoulder and heaved him outside before he could utter a single word.

Wynn Barrett went back inside the house, straight to the living room. Sitting in the far corner near the window was an old roll top desk. It was a family heirloom, passed down to him by a distant uncle. Over the years, it had become a dumping station for numerous important papers, bills and other things he didn't burn in his wood-stove.

He reached down and took hold of the carved wooden handle

on the bottom drawer. It squeaked in agony as he wrestled it open. From beneath the heap of old letters, Christmas cards and outdated catalogs, he took an old three-ring notebook. In its worn pages was a painful story, one filled with many unanswered questions, and tragedy.

"LET GO OF ME!" Nathan shouted, once they were outside the building.

"We have to get back to the car, right now," Gina said as she released his arm.

"But I wasn't done asking—"

"Too bad," she said, cutting him off. She turned and charged down the walkway. "You can come back later," she shouted over her shoulder.

He ran after her and yelled, "Janet told me about Stone Point."

She kept walking. *I'll bet she did.*

"Wynn Barrett wasn't wrong," he called out.

She reached the curb and paused. Seconds later, Nathan appeared at her side.

"The map wasn't wrong, either," he said.

When she heard that, her shoulders slumped. *I can't believe I'm going to do this.* "All right," she said, "I want to hear all of it, but we just dodged a bullet, and right now we have to hurry."

A town truck stopped and motioned for them to cross. She waved to the driver and then bolted across the street.

"Bullet?" he yelled, "what bullet?"

On the way back to the van she explained what she saw. She also reminded him of what would happen to them if they were discovered out of the minivan, talking to complete strangers. Exactly what they were *not* supposed to be doing.

First, they'd get a lecture.

From all four adults.

And it wouldn't be pleasant.

Then, they'd receive some unbearable punishment.

That would be even worse.

"Will you slow down?" he groaned, trying to keep up with her.

"No," she shot back. "Come on, I'll race you."

She took off running across the parking lot. They were halfway back to the van when something came rolling out from under a green Subaru on her right. It looked like a can of soup and she jumped over it with ease.

Nathan never saw it.

When she heard him yell, she looked back and saw his legs go out from under him, sending him crashing onto the pavement.

"Are you all right?" she called out as she doubled back.

As he grimaced and pushed himself up off the tar, a middle-aged woman appeared, holding an empty plastic grocery bag. "I am so sorry," she said. "Are you hurt? This flimsy bag ripped while I was unloading my cart and my groceries went everywhere."

"I'll live," Nathan muttered, brushing dirt off his shirtsleeve.

The woman's young son emerged from between two nearby cars, holding a slightly dented can of baked beans. "Found it, Mom," he said.

He took one look at Nathan and Gina and his eyes lit up.

"What's wrong, dear?" his mother asked.

"Look," he said, pointing.

"Look at what?"

"It's those two kids, the ones on TV."

The mother took a long look at Nathan, then Gina. "It *is* you," she said, her voice growing louder. "On the news!"

Thinking quickly, Nathan said, "I think you've got us confused with someone else."

"Impossible," the woman said, "I never forget a face."

"No, really," Gina insisted. "This happens to us all the time. We're not who you think we are."

"Ooh, just wait until I tell all the girls at the salon," the woman exclaimed. She dug in her pocket for her phone.

"Uh, there's really no need to—" Nathan began.

"Are you kidding me?" the woman gushed. "Celebrities, right here in Crawford?"

"We're really not," Gina said.

"Wait, I know," the woman said, pulling out her phone, "I'll call my sister. She works for the TV station in Manchester."

Nathan and Gina shouted in unison, "NO!"

Just then they heard a noise that stopped them cold. It was the clatter of wobbly wheels and the jostling of groceries.

It came to a stop directly behind them.

7

Ernie Bell

A woman's voice said, "What's going on here?"

Nathan's head flopped forward. *We've had it now.*

Gina felt all the energy drain from her body. *We almost made it.*

The woman holding the soup can stepped forward and smiled. "Hey, Norma."

Nathan and Gina perked up.

Norma?

"Hello, Susan," came the impatient reply.

Nathan and Gina spun around and saw a woman in a crumpled gray business suit. She stood behind her grocery cart, drumming her fingers on the handle. Her wrinkled face sagged like it might fall off at any moment.

"Look who we just met," Susan said, beaming from ear to ear.

She pointed at Nathan and Gina with the dented soup can.

Norma glanced at them briefly. "Wonderful," she muttered, then began rummaging through her pocketbook. Her stringy gray hair fell into her face and she had to push it aside to see what she was doing.

"They're celebrities," Susan told her.

"Is that a fact?" Norma said, wrestling a key ring from the inner pocket. "This is all very interesting, but if you don't mind I'd like to get into my car." She nodded at the green Subaru behind them.

"Oh, sorry," Nathan said, stepping out of the way.

She thumbed the fob on her keyring and the car emitted a soft beep. Without another word, she opened the rear hatch and began loading in her groceries, while Susan stood nearby, soup can in hand, explaining how she discovered the two young celebrities.

Gina took Nathan by the arm and whispered, "Let's go."

They backed away and then zigzagged through the parking lot until Susan or Norma were out of sight. Once they were safely back in the van, Gina sat back in the seat, relieved. "That was close," she said.

"Too close," Nathan replied.

Before he could say another word, Gina gave him a look.

"What?" he asked.

"Most kids hate homework?" she said, mocking his words from the Visitors Center. "But not me?"

"Hey, make fun of me all you want," he said, "but it worked, didn't it?"

She made a sour face. *You are so pathetic.*

Nathan smirked. "Do you want to hear about Stone Point or

not?"

"Of course, I do."

He gave her the short version: Stone Point the fuel stop, Lakeside Station, and Janet's curious remark about a terrible storm. When he was done, the same spooked look he'd seen on her face at the historic marker was back again.

"What's wrong?" he asked.

"Doesn't it freak you out?" she asked.

"Which part?"

"All of it," she said. "The book in your bedroom window just as we were leaving; the backpack next to the tree that wasn't really a tree; now we find out that Stone Point was actually here." She stopped and took a breath, then stared out the window. "That train was here," she mumbled. "It came through this town."

She spoke as if she were standing trackside on a hot summer afternoon, watching the train rumble down the track, its steel wheels sparking on the rails, black smoke billowing from the smokestack, and the caboose slowly fading from sight as the train rounded a gentle turn in the distance.

Her whole body shook. "It's creepy," she said. "Just creepy."

Nathan was busy connecting everything that had happened, starting with the book falling out of the bookcase, up to their discovery at the historic marker. "You were right," he said. "It's my grandfather."

Gina bit her lip. *You mean, your dead grandfather.*

"Somehow he knew we were coming up here. He waited until I was about to walk out the door to—"

"Stop," she said, putting her hand up. Hearing him relive it was giving her chills.

"I know that freaks you out," he said, "but there's a reason he's doing it, and until I can figure out what that reason is, he's going to keep doing it. I just know it." He paused for a moment and then said, "It's weird."

"What's weird?" she asked.

"It's hard to explain, but it feels like I'm supposed to look at those books in the attic. Me, Nathan Cole." He turned and stared out the window, as if the answer was written on the glass. "Why me?"

Just then, the rear hatch of the minivan popped open.

"Wait 'till you see all the yummy food we bought for everyone," Nathan's mother said as she began piling grocery bags into the back.

"Great," Nathan mumbled. "I can hardly wait."

Gina's mother opened the passenger door and climbed in. She set her pocketbook on the floor and then turned around. "Yes, *lots* of yummy food," she said, "and these, just for you." She smiled and handed Gina a plastic grocery bag.

Gina opened it and took a look inside. When she saw what it was she tossed it on the floor. "Very funny, Mom."

Nathan leaned forward and picked it up. Inside the bag were two baseball hats and two pairs of cheap plastic sunglasses. He pulled them out one by one and examined them. "These are cool," he said, holding up a silver pair of wrap-around sunglasses. A black spider web was printed across the front. The second pair had thick, fluorescent green frames with no designs or markings at all. "Eww," he said as he stuffed them back in the bag and dropped it on the floor.

Nathan's mother closed the hatch and returned the cart.

Moments later she climbed in the front seat and backed out of the parking spot.

That's when Nathan saw them.

The green Subaru was gone, but in its place a crowd of people had gathered. They formed a half circle around Susan and her son as she gestured toward the spot where Nathan had fallen.

He felt a sudden jolt of panic. They were going to pass right by the group, and that had disaster written all over it.

They'd turn.

They'd look.

They'd see.

"I wonder what that's all that about?" his mother asked.

"It looks like something happened," Gina's mother replied.

Nathan and Gina exchanged a worried look.

"Do you think we should stop?" Nathan's mother asked.

"Nah, they're fine," he said, trying to stay calm.

"I don't know," his mother countered. "Maybe we should see if they need help."

"Mom, they're just some friends talking. Hey, is it lunchtime yet? I'm starved."

"I don't know," his mother said. "They do seem to be worked up about something." She slowed to a crawl and rolled down the window.

"Seriously, there's a restaurant right up the street," he said. "Is anyone else hungry?"

They were almost to the group when he grabbed the plastic bag off the floor. He pulled out one of the baseball caps and shoved it on his head. The other one he handed to Gina, who quickly slipped it on her head and wrenched it into position.

Next came the sunglasses.

Nathan handed her the ugly green pair and kept the spider web glasses for himself.

"No way," she whispered, snatching them from his hand. She tossed him the ugly green pair just as the minivan came to a stop.

Wynn Barrett sat in the corner of his living room, studying the pages that had been pieced together years ago by one of his relatives. As he looked at each of the pages for what seemed like the hundredth time, old feelings of anger began to surface. He closed the notebook, but this time he didn't put it back in the drawer. The faint glimmer of an idea was forming in the back of his mind.

It was those kids.

Everyone was talking about them. Day after day, another story, another telling of their deeds, each time with a new twist. From the desk drawer, he took out another relic—a shiny piece of paper that had been folded and unfolded so many times over the years that it now felt like a piece of velvet cloth. He unfolded it and examined it from top to bottom. "Oh yeah," he said with an approving nod. "This might just do it."

"Is everything all right here?" Nathan's mother called to the crowd.

A man from the group came walking over to the minivan. "Yeah, we're fine," he said. "We just had our first celebrity sighting of the year."

"Oh?" Nathan's mother replied. She glanced over the man's

shoulder and saw a woman holding up a dented can of soup. She was showing it to the crowd and gesturing wildly with her other hand.

"Yeah, the summertime brings them in from all over," the man explained. He gave them a friendly wave and said, "You folks have a good day now."

Nathan and Gina were slouched down in the seat and breathed a sigh of relief as he walked away. They slowly sat up as Nathan's mother drove away, and that's when Nathan saw Susan's son. Soup can boy. He was standing outside the circle of adults, watching the minivan with the same look of shock, his expression set like dried plaster as they drove toward the exit.

"I wonder what he meant by that?" Gina's mother said. "'Our first celebrity sighting?'"

Nathan's mother looked in the rearview mirror and saw Nathan and Gina wearing the baseball hats and sunglasses. "Yeah," she said, eyeing them both suspiciously, "I wonder."

Ernie Bell sat in the Lakeside Diner, reading the local newspaper. The smell of bacon and fried eggs hung in the air, and the last of the breakfast crowd was sitting at a table in the corner.

"Can I freshen up that coffee for you, Ernie?" the waitress asked, holding a coffee pot over his half empty mug.

"No thanks, Sally," he said, covering the mug with his hand. He reached into the back pocket of his uniform and pulled out his wallet. "My cruiser awaits."

"Gotta keep the streets of Crawford safe," she joked.

"Yeah, right," he said with a chuckle, throwing some bills on the counter.

After he left the diner, he drove toward town and turned onto Jewel Lake Road. He hadn't gone far when he saw a figure in the distance, walking in the road. "Barrett, you old kook, what are you up to now?" he muttered, stepping on the gas pedal. He had to get the crazy old codger out of the road before someone ran him over—a calamity that had nearly happened on several occasions over the years.

Wynn was in full stride and didn't stop when Bell pulled up beside him and lowered the window. "Barrett, what are you doing in the road?" he said, not hiding his annoyance.

"Taking my morning walk," Wynn answered, eyes straight ahead.

Bell rolled along slowly beside him, keeping pace. "Where to this time?" he asked.

"Pine Point."

Bell pulled ahead, then leaned across the seat and opened the door. "Get in," he said, "I'll drive you."

Wynn stopped walking, considered the offer for a moment, then climbed in the front seat.

Nathan and Gina were sitting at the picnic table in the side yard. It was set next to a grove of tall birch trees, their trunks the color of new-fallen snow. Gina was reviewing the notes she'd scribbled in her notebook, the one her grandmother had given her years ago. It was the size of a paperback book and bound in soft deer hide, the color of a caramel candy. On the front, a small rose had been hand-tooled into the leather. Her notes included everything from their episode at the historic marker, to what Nathan had learned at the Visitors Center.

Each clue was like a giant piece of furniture packed in a tiny room, hard to get past, and blocking the view of the next. Only by writing them down could she sort them out and try to make sense of them.

Nathan sat across from her, his back to the lake, staring at the pockets of dark and light in the forest. He began drumming his fingers on the tabletop.

Gina looked up and said, "Stop that."

He didn't.

"Stop it, I said."

This time he stopped, exhaled loudly and said, "We're wasting time."

"What are you talking about?"

"Sitting here," he said.

"And what exactly are we supposed to be doing?" she asked.

"Looking."

"Looking for what?"

He closed his eyes and flopped his head forward. *Must I explain everything?*

"Hey," she said, snapping her fingers at him. She'd been doing that a lot lately. "Looking for what?"

"The boxcar, of course."

"No," she said flatly.

"No? Why not?"

"Because we can't just go charging off into the woods looking behind every tree. We need to think this through."

"But we know it was here. The train came through this town."

She wrinkled her brow. "And?"

"And that means the boxcar vanished somewhere between here and West Branch."

"How do you figure that?" she asked.

"In the book, it says the train stopped at Stone Point, right?"

"Right."

He turned both palms up. "There's your answer."

"Huh?"

"The boxcar was still attached," he said.

"How could you possibly know that?" she demanded.

He rolled his eyes. "Because they interviewed everyone on the train. Remember?"

"Yeah… and?"

"And not a single person saw anything suspicious."

"So what?" she said, shrugging.

He flopped his head forward again. When he looked up, he spoke slowly and in short fragments. "If they got to Stone Point… and the boxcar was gone… someone would have noticed… they would have said something."

"All right, all right, I get it," she said. Sometimes he could be such a pain. "So you think we should just start looking somewhere between here and West Branch?"

"Yes," he exclaimed, smacking both palms on the tabletop.

"And you know where this West Branch is, I take it?"

"Actually…" he started to say.

"Wait. You don't know where it is?"

He looked down at the tabletop. "Uh, not exactly."

"Okay, well, that's kind of important, don't you think?" She took the pencil from behind her ear and scribbled the name West Branch in her notebook, under the "Possibilities" heading.

Just then, the sound of a speedboat powering across the lake caught her attention and she looked up. In the midday sun, the surface of the lake sparkled like millions of tiny diamonds.

"Is that why they call it Jewel Lake?" she asked.

Nathan glanced over his shoulder. "Yeah, you just figured that out?"

She gave him a look. *Don't start with me.*

"Well, it's kind of hard to miss," he said.

"Whatever you say," she replied slowly. As she spoke, her eyes remained fixed on the lake.

"What is it?" he asked.

"Hard to miss," she mumbled.

"Huh?"

She watched the speedboat fade in the distance, then said, "After I read about the missing boxcar, I was convinced someone on the train made a mistake."

"What do you mean?"

"Someone wrote something down wrong, or not at all."

"Go on," he said, not sure what point she was trying to make.

"But there's no way that could have happened."

"Because?" he said, motioning for her to finish.

"Because, sooner or later, they would've caught something like that. It would've been hard to miss. Even if they forgot to pick it up in the first place, they would've found it sitting in a railroad yard somewhere, or on one of those side thingies."

"A sidetrack?"

"Yeah, one of those," she said. "Or, let's say they dropped it off at the wrong place. Sooner or later, someone would've found it. I mean, everyone was looking for it, right? For years? Again, it would've been impossible to miss."

He nodded his head and stared at her in amazement. *She IS the puzzle master.*

"So, we can rule out human error," she said, crossing that off the top of her list of possibilities. She thought for a moment and then asked, "Boxcars are big, right?"

"Right."

"Not the kind of thing they could just stash in the woods."

"They?"

"Yes, they," she snapped. "Haven't you been listening?" She leaned forward and looked him directly in the eye. "That boxcar wasn't lost in the paperwork. It wasn't mistakenly left somewhere. That leaves only one possibility. It was stolen."

For several seconds he just sat there, thinking. Up until now he'd been totally focused on tracks and fuel stops and railroad stations. How the boxcar could simply vanish into thin air like steam rising from a tea kettle had never crossed his mind.

She saw the realization slowly dawn on his face. "Somebody wanted it and they took it," she said. "Where it is now is anybody's guess."

The sound of an approaching vehicle made them both turn and look.

"We've got company," he said, as Ernie Bell's cruiser rolled to a stop in the yard.

"The police? What do they want?" she asked.

"Beats me."

Ernie climbed out of the vehicle and immediately began surveying the property. Wynn Barrett emerged seconds later. When he saw Nathan and Gina at the picnic table, he waved. Nathan immediately jumped up from the table and hurried over to talk to him. Gina muttered something under her breath, then slowly made her way across the yard.

"Hey, Wynn," Nathan said.

"Hey to you," he replied. Then he looked at Gina. "And to you, too."

Gina nodded and flashed a weak smile, like she was eating a sour pickle.

The screen door squeaked open and Nathan's mother stepped outside, then came down the steps, a confused look on her face. Gina's mother followed right behind her. They weren't expecting anyone, and when they saw the police cruiser pull in, they didn't know what to think. There was that older fellow from this morning, too.

"Good afternoon," Wynn said, as they came down the steps.

Ernie Bell's curiosity piqued. He wasn't sure who the women were, but there was something very familiar about the two kids.

Nathan's father came up the steps from the dock, wiping his hands on an old cloth rag. "What's going on?" he asked. Gina's father was with him, eyeing the two visitors intently.

"Social call," Wynn said, coming over to shake his hand. "The name's Wynn Barrett. I'm your neighbor…live just down the way." He motioned to Ernie. "Officer Bell here took pity on me and offered me a ride."

Ernie stepped forward and extended his hand. "Ernie Bell," he said.

"David Cole," Nathan's father replied, as they shook hands.

"Jack's brother?"

"Yes," David said. "He's letting us use the place for the week. This is my wife, Elizabeth, and our good friends Bill and Laura McDermott."

Ernie nodded slowly as the pieces fell into place. "Wait a minute," he said, pointing at Nathan and Gina. "On TV, right?"

Nathan and Gina looked at Wynn.

"Hold on now," he said, "I didn't say anything."

"Actually," Ernie said, "I've been following your story since it broke. That was a nice piece of detective work."

Nathan and Gina looked sheepishly at the ground.

"Officer Bell? Wynn?" Elizabeth said. "We were just about to have lunch. Would you care to join us?"

Ernie Bell shook his head. "No thanks, ma'am. Maybe some other time, when I'm off the clock."

"I'd better take a rain check too," Wynn said.

"Let me know if there's anything you need while you're here," Ernie said to Nathan's father. Then he turned to Wynn. "You need a lift home?"

Wynn looked up at the cloudless sky. "No, it's a beautiful day. I think I'll hoof it back."

Gina looked away and made a face. *Hoof it? Who says that?*

Ernie Bell walked back to the cruiser as all four parents went into the house to get ready for lunch. Gina was halfway up the steps when she noticed that Nathan had stayed behind. She glared at him and gestured toward the screen door. *Let's go!*

He shook his head. *Not yet.*

He turned to talk to Wynn just as the old man reached into his shirt pocket. "I have something for you," he said, pulling out the folded sheaf of paper. He pressed it into Nathan's hand. "This may help you."

"Huh?" Nathan said.

"You know, with what you're looking for," Wynn said, with a wink. Then, he turned and walked across the yard.

Nathan's eyes went wide. *What we're looking for?*

Gina saw the exchange and hurried back down the steps.

Ernie Bell saw it too, along with the spooked look on Nathan's face. *What was that all about?* he wondered.

As he drove down the driveway, he eyed Wynn in the rearview mirror. When he reached the tar road, he couldn't shake the uneasy feeling in the back of his mind, the one that told him he should keep a close eye on the kids while they were here in town. Wynn Barrett too. It was early in the season and things were still quiet. A few extra patrols of Jewel Lake Road wouldn't be a problem.

Nathan watched Wynn shuffle across the lawn, all the while trying to make sense of what just happened.

"What did he say to you?" Gina asked.

"Something about this," he said, opening his hand to reveal the folded paper.

"What is it?"

He unfolded it and skimmed it briefly. "It's a magazine article."

"A magazine article? About what?"

He finished reading and looked up at her without speaking.

"Well, tell me," she said impatiently.

"You're not going to believe this."

8

Cora Whittier

Wynn hobbled down the driveway and stopped at the main road. All around him the woods were alive with movement and sound. He stood upright and took a deep breath of the morning air, sweet with the aroma of the forest in early summer. It was a good day. The kind of day when he could take a long walk and think. And there was a lot to think about.

"Flowers?" Gina asked. "Let me see that." She pulled the paper out of his hand and read it quickly from top to bottom. "Crazy old man," she mumbled as she thrust it back toward him.

Nathan ignored the dig, folded the paper, and slipped it into his back pocket.

"What did he say to you?" Gina asked.

"Something about this helping us find what we're looking for."

"What? she blurted out, eyes wide. "How could he possibly—?"

"Relax," he cut in. "I was wondering the same thing at first, but it's nothing."

"What makes you so sure?"

"Something you said at the historic marker."

"I said lots of things at the historic marker."

Nathan's mother appeared at the screen door. "Kids, come on in, lunch is ready."

He started up the steps when she grabbed his arm. "What was it?"

"He asked if we were railroad buffs, remember?"

"Yeah?" she replied, trying to remember that moment in time.

"And you told him we were working on a school project?"

"Oh, right," she said. "And you think that's what he was talking about when he slipped you that useless piece of paper?"

"Yes," he said, pulling his arm free. "Trust me, he has no idea what we're doing." He started up the steps and said, "Why would he care anyway?"

"Because he's a creepy old guy with nothing better to do," she mumbled.

"I heard that."

Lunch was served on the screen porch. As the parents jabbered on and on about the lake and the boat, Nathan tuned them out as he rehashed the things Gina said at the picnic table, about the boxcar, how it had been stolen, and was too big to hide.

He was staring down at his plate, breaking potato chips into little pieces with the tip of his finger, when Gina kicked him under the table. "Oww," he muttered, shooting her a nasty look.

She nodded to her left, and when he looked over he saw his mother staring at him. "What?" he said as he rubbed his shin.

"I asked if you were okay," his mother said.

"I'm fine," he replied, throwing another dirty look at Gina. "At least I was," he added, under his breath.

"For a moment there, you looked a little lost."

"Me? Lost? Never."

Gina cleared her throat and muttered, "Yeah, right." *What about our first day at the new middle school?* she was tempted to ask. *When you sat in the wrong class for half the morning? Or the class trip to the Science Museum, when you got locked in the basement?*

"Would you like another sandwich?" his mother asked.

"Or some more potato chips?" Gina asked with a smirk.

"No thank you," he replied, ignoring Gina's comment, "but can I ask you a question?"

"Of course," his mother said.

"Do you know where West Branch is?"

Gina was putting an olive in her mouth, but when she heard his question, she lurched forward and spit it out. Everyone turned and looked as it bounced off her plate and rolled across the table. It didn't stop until it hit the salt shaker.

"Sorry about that," she mumbled, her face a bright shade of red, as she reached over and picked it up.

Nathan glared at her. *What is wrong with you?*

She glared right back. *ME? What's wrong with YOU?*

"West Branch," Nathan's mother said, trying to locate the name in her memory. "Is that a town?"

"Couldn't tell you," Nathan said, shrugging.

"I've never heard of it," his father said. "Are you sure it's in New Hampshire?"

"Pretty sure," Nathan muttered.

"Why do you ask?" his father said.

"Uh, no reason," he replied, staring at the pile of potato chip crumbs on his plate. Suddenly he wasn't hungry anymore. First Stone Point and now this? Another mystery stop on the Lakes Region Line? He excused himself from the table and went down to the lake to think. As he sat on the edge of the dock, letting his sneakers dangle several inches above the water, he watched a small sunfish dart in and out of its nest, fending off any intruders.

Eventually he got bored with that and pulled the folded paper from his back pocket. The name *Harper's* was printed at the top of the page. Right below that was the title of the article. "Saving the May Flower," he said, reading it aloud. "How nice." Curious, he began reading.

> *One of the first flowers of the spring, the Trailing Arbutus, may very well owe its existence to a single person—a resident of the small town of Crawford, New Hampshire.*

The sound of a passing motorboat made him stop reading and look up. The boat's wake sent a torrent of waves rolling toward the shore, rocking his uncle's boat back and forth. It banged against the dock with a hollow thud as he continued reading.

> *This pungent posy, with oval leaves that keep their green*

throughout the year, may have lost its heavenly scent for good, due to the fanatical flower vendors of the day. The pinkish-white leaves and sweet aroma made them an attractive cash crop during the early spring months, so much so that it was nearly harvested out of existence. Before that could happen, however, Cora Whittier decided to take action.

He stopped reading. "What is this, a joke?" Maybe Gina was right. Maybe Wynn really was a crazy old man. He took a deep breath and let it out. "I might as well read all of it. I'm almost to the end."

Cora scoured the woods in her small town of Crawford, New Hampshire, for these flowers that she loved so well. Then, setting up a makeshift nursery in her backyard, she started a crop of Arbutus that would not only survive the ravages of the street vendors, but, as it turned out, Mother Nature as well.

The sudden call of a loon startled him and he nearly dropped the paper in the water. The loon swam past the dock, inspecting him closely. When it was gone from sight he turned his attention back to the story.

In early May of that year, under blackening skies and near hurricane force winds, Cora set out to save the massive nursery, which would have been an impossible task if not for the help of a timely passerby. "Those poor flowers would be gone for sure if not for my nephew, Seth, who helped me move the plants inside. Lord only knows what would have happened to them if he hadn't stopped by that day."

To this day the Trailing Arbutus adorns flower gardens and lines walkways throughout the town of Crawford, New Hampshire, all thanks to Mr. Carson's chance visit on a stormy day in May.

"Well, that was exciting," he muttered as he began to fold the paper. Out of the corner of his eye he saw Gina coming down the steps to the dock.

"What are you doing?" she asked.

He held up the magazine article. "Reading this."

"You can't be serious," she said. She came over and sat down beside him. "You should've given that thing back the minute the old man gave it to you."

"Well, for some reason he thought I should have it."

"Oh, there's a reason all right," she replied. "He's nuts!"

Nathan gave her a look. *Enough.*

"So," she said, changing the subject. "Do you want to tell me what that was all about?"

"What was *what* all about?"

"At the table? Asking about West Branch?"

"I wanted to find out where it was," he said defensively.

"Yeah, I got that, but keep asking questions like that and they'll start asking questions too. The kind you don't want to answer."

She was right. He needed to be more careful. The last thing he wanted was his parents asking about the book, where it came from, or what they were doing with it.

Especially what they were doing with it.

The sound of heavy footsteps on the dock made them both turn and look. Nathan's father was coming toward them with Gina's father following close behind. "There you are. Just the person I need."

"Huh?" Nathan replied.

"We're taking the boat motor down to the marina," his father said. "We could use your help."

"Sure," Nathan said in a flat voice.

"Don't sound so excited," Gina joked.

"Very funny," he replied. As he got to his feet he whispered, "If you're not too busy, try to find out where West Branch is."

Nathan's father removed the motor from the boat's transom, and then Gina's father helped him load it in the minivan. While they were doing that, Gina went back up to the screen porch and plopped down in one of the rocking chairs.

After they pulled out of the yard, she thought about Nathan's comment. "Find West Branch," she said aloud. "Yeah, right." What did he expect her to do?

Go back to the Visitors Center? *Not gonna happen.*

Go ask the crazy neighbor? *As if.*

Then it hit her.

Even if they figured out where it was, and they somehow managed to get there, what would they find after all these years? Answer: nothing. *Why are we even talking about West Branch?* she wondered. *Nathan said it himself. When the train arrived there, the boxcar was already gone.* Meaning: whatever happened to it occurred well before that.

"Oh, I am so good," she beamed as she rocked back and forth in the chair. Nathan was convinced they needed to search the whole area from Stone Point to West Branch, but he was wrong. She thought back to the giant map at the Visitors Center with acres upon acres of land—vast stretches of woods, mountains, and lakes. "We don't need to search the whole region," she said. "Just a small piece of it."

She stood up and pumped her fists in the air. "Yes! Who's the puzzle master?" Then, on instinct, she said, "I need to write this down." She raced into the house, repeating the same words under her breath as she walked down the hallway to her bedroom. "Just a small piece, just a small piece..."

She found her notebook where she had stashed it before lunch, tucked under the pillow on her bed. She flipped it open and was about to start writing when an alarming thought surfaced in her mind.

Just a small piece.

"No," she said. "Not that."

Despite her attempts to push the thought out of her mind, it grew more believable and more disturbing with each passing second.

Nathan's father pulled into the marina and found a vacant spot next to the Service Department entrance. While he and Gina's father hoisted the motor out of the van, Nathan sat in the back seat staring out at the boats that lined the edge of the property, his mind overrun with questions about West Branch. *Where was it? Had the name been changed to something else? If so, how will we find it? And how are we supposed to get there?*

"Nathan, close the hatch for us, would you?" his father said.

"Huh?" he mumbled, letting the thought go. He turned around in the seat and saw them holding the motor. "Oh, right," he said. "Sorry about that."

He hurried around to the back of the van, and was reaching up to close the hatch when a car pulled into the next space. The driver was a tall man with graying hair, wearing a powder blue bathing suit and a faded Jimmy Buffet tee shirt. The woman with him had a *Bride of Frankenstein* tangle of hair that pointed in every direction, like she'd just been electrocuted. She was wearing oversized sunglasses with thick white frames that reminded Nathan of a giant bug.

"It was really them?" the man said to the woman as he got out of the car. "The boy *and* the girl?"

"Yeah, how wild is that?" the woman replied. "She said it was definitely those two kids they've been talking about on the news."

When Nathan heard that, he froze.

"And she saw them at the grocery store?" the man asked. He opened the trunk and pulled out a small boat propeller. The fins were scratched, and one of them was nearly bent in half.

"Actually, her son was the one who recognized them," the woman explained.

Nathan turned his head away and stood perfectly still, hoping they wouldn't notice him.

"I wonder what they're doing in Crawford?" the man asked.

"Who knows?" the woman replied.

Nathan took a deep breath and tried to calm himself. *Relax. Any second now they'll walk away.* But as he stood there listening, he noticed something peculiar: they had stopped talking.

Very slowly he turned his head, and saw them both staring directly at him.

"Is everything all right, son?" the man asked.

Nathan wrinkled his brow. *What kind of question is that?*

Then it came to him. For the past minute he'd been standing there like a statue, with his arms fully extended over his head, holding up the rear hatch.

"I'm fine," he said, pulling the hatch halfway down.

The woman stepped closer. "Excuse me, but have we met before? You look very familiar."

"Uh, no, I don't think so," he said, then slammed the hatch shut and darted around the side of the van. Once he was inside, he slid the door shut as hard as he could and crouched down on the seat. Maybe if they didn't see him, they'd just forget about him and go away. But as he sat there hunched over, he saw something slither out from under the front seat and he bolted upright.

That's when the front door opened.

9

The Sidetracks

G ina went back out to the screen porch, unable to shake the troubling thought. The wind chimes were clanging softly, and the gentle breeze blowing off the lake carried the sweet aroma of the pink lady slippers that carpeted the nearby forest.

But she was too deep in thought to notice.

She sat down in the chair, tapping her foot nervously. Ever since the Visitors Center, she'd believed that they would find the boxcar sitting on an old rail bed, buried under a heap of old dead trees. But there was another very real possibility. It was pure genius, and at the same time devastating, because it would explain why the boxcar had never been found.

What if they took it apart?

What if it was broken into hundreds of small pieces—maybe more—and scattered from one end of the county to the other? She tossed her notebook on the coffee table and buried her face in her hands. *We're never going to find it,* she told herself. She shook her head to try and clear her mind. When that didn't work, she got up from the chair and started pacing back and forth.

"They didn't do it," she said, trying to make herself believe. "They *wouldn't* do it."

"Wouldn't do what?"

She spun around and saw her mother standing on the lawn. In her hands was a bunch of freshly-picked wildflowers.

"Mom!" she shouted. "Don't do that!"

"Do what?" her mother asked.

"Sneak up on me."

"I didn't sneak up on you," her mother said calmly.

Gina snatched her notebook off the coffee table and stormed outside.

"What was it you were talking about?" her mother asked.

"Nothing," Gina yelled as she tromped across the yard. She got to the edge of the woods and resumed pacing. "What are we supposed to do now?" she muttered under her breath. "Give up?"

Something told her they might not have a choice.

The front door of the minivan opened, and Nathan's father slid into the front seat. "Forgot the checkbook," he said. When he looked in the rearview mirror and saw the look of shock on Nathan's face, he immediately turned around. "Is everything all right?"

Nathan's heart was racing. "Uh, yeah Dad, I'm good," he managed to say.

"Well, we shouldn't be too much longer," his father assured him.

He fished around in the center console until he found the checkbook, then hurried back inside the building.

Nathan let out a nervous breath, then slowly leaned forward to see what was moving on the floor. If it was snake, he'd open the side door and let it out. But how could a snake get in the minivan? He leaned a bit closer and stopped. Then leaned closer still. "You've got to be kidding me," he exclaimed, when he saw what it was.

He reached down and grabbed the strap of his backpack. With everything that had happened, he had completely forgotten that he'd stashed it under the front seat when they were at the grocery store. "Thanks for scaring me to death," he said as he pulled it onto his lap. Then it came to him: if the strap was moving around on the floor all by itself, it could only mean one thing. He quickly unzipped the pack and pulled out the book. When he had it open to Chapter 11, he said, "Okay, what is it?"

Nothing happened.

"Well?"

Still nothing.

He turned the page, and just as he pulled his hand away it turned back, all by itself. "Hey!" he said, then turned the page a second time. Just like before, it flipped back. "All right, all right, I get it," he said. "You want me to look at *this* page." He shook his head in disbelief. *I'm talking to the book again.*

Very slowly he scanned the page from top to bottom, reading each sentence carefully. "Yeah, yeah, yeah," he said. "I already saw this. Did I miss something?" When he was done reading he started again, going even slower, staring intently at every word. Halfway down the page, something caught his eye. It was very small, so small that he didn't notice it when he read the chapter the night before. He slid closer to the window and angled the book to catch the light just right. "What is that?" he said, the book inches from his face.

Gina was still pacing along the edge of the woods when the minivan pulled into the driveway. It had barely come to a stop when the side door opened and Nathan jumped out.

"Nathan," she shouted, as he raced toward the porch.

He turned and saw her, then made an immediate U-turn and headed for the picnic table.

"Come here," he called out, waving her over with his left hand. When he got to the picnic table, he sat down and opened his backpack.

At first Gina didn't move. Then, slowly, she walked over and sat down across from him. He sensed something was wrong when she folded her arms and leaned forward on the tabletop. When she sat there without saying a word, he knew it was bad.

"What's the matter?" he asked, studying her face. The light was gone from her eyes.

She looked down and sighed.

"Gina?"

She closed her eyes and shook her head.

"Hey, that's okay," he said. "We can just sit here and—"

"We're never going to find it," she blurted out, before he could finish.

"Excuse me?"

"The boxcar," she said. This time she looked up from the table. "I know why it's never been found." She shook her head again and sighed, "Why it will *never* be found."

"All-right," he said slowly, waiting for her to explain.

"We've been so *stupid*," she hissed, staring down at the tabletop again.

He said nothing.

"We never saw it," she sighed. "Never even *considered* it." Her frustration boiled over and she pounded her fist on the table.

Nathan was lost for words. She was talking in riddles, and he really needed to show her what he found in the book. It was time to move this along. Gently. "You said something about the boxcar?" he said softly. "Something about not finding it?"

"Yeah," she said, nodding slowly. "I've been trying to think of a way to tell you."

"Tell me what?"

"That there's no way we're going to find it. We're wasting our time."

"What makes you say that?"

She hesitated for a moment and then said, "Because they took it apart."

"Huh?"

"They broke it into pieces and scattered them halfway across the state, or buried them, or tossed them in the lake. Who knows?" She turned and stared into the woods, her face twisted in anger. "From the very start, we've been talking about looking for the boxcar—the whole boxcar. Well, we're never going to find it because it's in a thousand small pieces."

"Wait," Nathan said. "*That's* what you're upset about?"

"Yes, I'm upset. I really wanted us to find it."

He fought back a smile.

"What?" she said. "You don't believe me?"

"No," he replied, with a pitiful look.

Her eyes locked on his. "Nathan, this is serious."

"It didn't happen," he said.

"No?" she fired back. "Think about it. A boxcar is something everyone can identify. It's long. It's tall. It has lots of wheels. But take it apart? That's completely different."

"How so?"

"Because, when you remove part of it, like a door? And you lay it on the ground? And you pile junk on top of it? Or take a wheel, throw it in a scrap heap with a million other pieces of metal? They're invisible."

"You're right," he said.

"Yes, I know I am."

He smiled and said, "But you're wrong."

"So how did it go?" Elizabeth asked. She and Gina's mother were in the kitchen skewering chicken chunks and veggies for the evening barbeque.

"Great," David answered. He snatched a chunk of bell pepper from the platter on the counter before Elizabeth could slap his hand away.

"Can they fix it?" she asked.

"Yeah, it won't take long. We can pick it up tomorrow."

As they spoke, Gina's father was watching Nathan and Gina through the window. "What are they doing now?" he muttered.

Gina's mother went to the window and looked across the yard.

"Homework would be my guess."

Gina's father mumbled something under his breath.

"What's wrong with that?" his wife asked.

"Nothing," he said. "I just figured they'd be swimming or climbing trees or something."

"They can climb trees when their school work is done," she replied. "If they want to work, let them work. They're far enough behind as it is."

Elizabeth finished the chicken and went over to the sink. As she rinsed her hands, she watched the kids through the window. There was something about the way they were talking. Their hand gestures. The looks on their faces. They were up to something, and it didn't look like homework. A troubling thought flared momentarily in the back of her mind, but she quickly pushed it away and dried her hands.

Gina glared across the table at Nathan. "What do you mean, I'm wrong?"

"I mean, they didn't take it apart. Why would they?"

"I don't know," she replied. "To destroy the evidence?"

He raised both eyebrows. "Evidence? What evidence? Did they sign their names on it?"

"This isn't funny," she snapped. "Maybe they wanted the parts."

"Wanted the parts? For what? Another boxcar?"

"I don't know!" she shouted.

"Look," he said, calmly. "If they needed parts, why would they take a boxcar in the middle of a moving train? I mean, how would they even do that?"

She looked away, her mind busy processing his words.

"The only evidence they would need to hide is whatever was inside the boxcar. Did you think about that? Why they chose *that* car?"

She nodded ever so slightly. "Because there was something inside it they wanted?"

The light was slowly returning to her eyes.

"Exactly," Nathan said. "What happened to the car after that didn't matter. Why would it? Once they got what they were after, they probably got out of town as fast as possible." He gave her a knowing look. "I know I would."

"That's right," she said, her words coming faster now. "Why stick around and risk getting caught?"

Nathan smiled and nodded his head. *She's back.*

"There was no time," she said, seeing the fault in her thinking. "Taking a boxcar apart would take days. Maybe longer."

"Okay," he said, "so we're all good on that?"

The tiniest of smiles crossed her face. "Yes," she said softly.

"Good, because I need to show you something." He pulled the book out of his backpack and opened it to Chapter 11. "Right here," he said, turning it around so she could see. He pointed to a rectangular diagram in the middle of the page. It was very old, very simple, and clearly hand-drawn. The whole thing was no bigger than a bar of soap.

"Yeah, I saw that," she said. "It's an old map, and not a very good one, if you ask me."

"Did you look at it closely?"

"Not really. It's pretty basic."

"Look again," he said, pointing.

She gave the page a half-hearted glance, then shrugged her shoulders. "What am I looking at?"

"Closer," he said.

"I'm telling you, I already saw—"

"Closer," he insisted.

She bent down, closer, staring intently at the image. It took her several seconds but then she saw it. "What's this line?" she asked, tracing across the page with her finger. It was very thin, and it cut across the map from the lower left to the upper right.

"When I first saw it, I thought it was a town boundary," he told her.

"But it's dotted," she said.

"Yeah, that means it was a railroad line. It has to be the Lakes Region Line."

But that's not what caught his eye at the marina. There was more, and Gina saw it seconds later.

"What are those two things?" she asked, pointing at two smaller lines. They were mirror images of each other, breaking off the main line like a two-pronged fork. They ran parallel to it for a short distance before snaking away in opposite directions.

"My question exactly," he replied. "At first, I thought they were creases in the paper...you know...from people bending the page."

"But...?"

"They have to be side tracks," he said.

"Are they important?"

"I have no idea. We could try to find them, but we have no idea where to look. For starters, we'd have to find the main line, and we don't know where *that* was."

Gina was busy studying the diagram and didn't respond. Seconds later, she smiled and slowly nodded her head. "What is it?" he asked.

She closed the book and slid it back across the table to him. "I know exactly where to look."

10

The Reference Room

Early the next morning, Gina was sitting at the breakfast table. Nathan was across from her with his head resting on top of the table. The sun had been up for some time, but the house was totally quiet. Outside, the lake was perfectly still. The surface was mirror-smooth, reflecting the puffy clouds overhead. In the soft pink glow of the morning sky, they looked like cotton candy.

"You better not be sleeping again," she warned him.

"I'm not," he mumbled, "but I should be. Tell me again, why are we doing this?"

Gina rolled her eyes. *Seriously?* She reached across the table and grabbed his backpack. "Sometimes, Nathan Cole, I swear." She pulled the book out of the middle compartment and opened it to Chapter 11. "Hey," she said, pounding her fist on the table. "Wake up."

He raised his head slowly and opened his sleepy eyes.

"*That* is why we're going," she said, pointing to the bottom of the small map they had inspected the day before.

He squinted at it briefly. "Oh, right."

Her eyes bore into his. "Do you even remember what I told you about this?"

"Uh, sort of," he grunted. "Then what did I say about it?" "What are you now, my teacher?"

She shoved the book at him. "Right there," she said, pointing to the map. "What does it say?"

He frowned and pulled the book close to his face. Just below the map was a tiny line of print. "Courtesy of The Lakes Region Gazette."

"Very good," she said, clapping her hands. "And what do we think that is?"

"An old newspaper," he sighed. The conversation they had the night before was coming back to him now—the tiny listing below the map; what it meant; how there might be more information about the railroad line, and the two mysterious sidetracks.

"And where do they keep old newspapers?" she asked.

He exhaled loudly. "At the library."

"Exactly!" she said, yanking the book away from him. As she slipped it into his pack, she said, "Any more questions?"

Before he could respond with one of his usual zingers, his father came padding into the room. "What are you two doing up so early?" he said, rubbing the sleep from his eyes.

"We need a ride," Gina replied.

David stopped walking and gave them both a look. "A ride? At this hour?"

Gina looked over at the clock on the stove. "In 47 minutes to be exact."

"And where do you two need to be in exactly 47 minutes?"

"The library," Gina said.

"We have some research to do," Nathan added.

Gina glared at him. *Careful.*

He smirked. *Relax.*

"I assume this would have something to do with your homework?"

"Something like that," Nathan replied.

"Well, we have to pick up the boat motor anyway. But I need you two to do me a favor."

"Uh-okay," Nathan said carefully.

"You're on vacation. That means you're supposed to, I don't know, relax a little? Have some fun? Maybe go swimming? Exploring? Things like that?"

"Oh, don't worry, Dad. We will."

Exactly 47 minutes later, they all piled into the minivan, along with Gina's father, who came along to help with the boat motor.

"How long are you two going to be?" David asked.

"Um," Gina said, trying to think. "An hour?"

"And how do you plan on getting home?" her father asked in his sharp drill-sergeant voice.

"We can walk," Nathan suggested.

"Absolutely not."

"How about this?" David offered. "You call us when you're done and we'll come get you."

"Call?" Nathan asked. "With what? You and Mom won't let me get a cell phone, remember?"

"That's enough," David said as he pulled out onto Jewel Lake Road. "Let's not start *that* argument again. Here's what you do. Tell one of the library employees who you are, and I'm sure they'll let you use the phone."

Gina's father cleared his throat.

"Oh, right," David said. "Just ask if you can use the phone to call for a ride home."

"Do *not* tell her who you are," Gina's father said.

"Dad!" Gina groaned. "We get it."

"Hey look," Nathan said, pointing at the road up ahead, where Wynn Barrett was standing on the shoulder, staring into the woods.

"Oh, goody," Gina whispered sarcastically.

"He's up early," David said as he tapped on the horn. He rolled down the window and came to a stop just as Wynn was turning around. "Good morning," he called out.

"And a fine good morning to you," Wynn croaked. When he saw the kids sitting in the back seat, he shuffled over to the open window.

"Hi Wynn," Nathan said.

Gina gave a one-handed wave, a quick left-to-right swipe, like she was clearing a spot to see through a steam-covered window.

"What brings you out so early today?" David asked.

"I've been hearing noises," Wynn said.

Gina stifled a laugh. *I bet you have.*

Nathan elbowed her. *Quit it.*

"Right there in that patch of trees," Wynn explained, pointing at the woods next to his driveway.

David craned his neck to see. "What do you suppose it is?"

"Hard to say," Wynn replied. "This time of year, it could be just about anything."

Gina smirked. *Like a squirrel?*

"Probably some deer, or a bear," Wynn explained.

Gina frowned and looked out the window, scanning the trees. *Yeah, right.*

"Every now and then we see a moose passing through."

Gina rolled her eyes. *Enough, already…can we GO?*

"Well, thanks for the heads-up," David said. He gave Wynn a nod and then drove off.

As they pulled away, Nathan looked back and waved.

"Really?" Gina said.

When they reached the Crawford Public Library, David pulled up to the curb near the front door. Two blocks down the road, on the same side of the street, was the Visitors Center. As Nathan and Gina climbed out, he called out, "Don't forget to call us when you're done."

"Just a minute," Gina's father said. He reached into the back seat and grabbed the plastic grocery bag that was sitting on the floor. "You forgot these."

He tossed the bag through the open window to Nathan, who snagged it out of mid air with one hand.

"Oh yeah, thanks," Nathan said, when he looked inside.

As the minivan drove away, he pulled one of the baseball hats from the bag and stuck it on top of his head. Next came the sunglasses.

"Are you serious?" Gina asked.

"I think you're forgetting something," he said, pointing at the grocery store further down the street. The lot was packed with cars and people were coming and going through the front door in a steady stream.

"Oh, right," she said, remembering their run-in with Norma and her son. "Give me that hat."

Across the street, in the parking lot of the Crawford Municipal Building, Ernie Bell was sitting in his police cruiser. He recognized the blue minivan as it stopped at the curb briefly, then pull away. When he saw Nathan and Gina don their baseball hats and sunglasses, he laughed out loud. "Those two," he said as he pulled out of the parking space. "They are too funny."

Once they were inside the library, Nathan pulled Gina aside. They were standing in a large foyer lined with tall windows that faced the street. Twenty feet away, behind the counter, the librarian was stamping books. A high school student was standing next to her, taking the books and loading them on a push cart with angled shelves. The librarian looked over at Nathan and Gina briefly and then continued her work.

"So what's the plan here?" Nathan whispered.

Gina took off the hat and sunglasses and said, "It's simple. That map came from an old newspaper. If we find a copy of it, we might be able to find out about the sidetracks."

As she spoke, Nathan glanced out the front window and saw a white news van drive by. He peeked over the tops of his sunglasses and read the words painted on the side in large red letters. *Channel 5 News.* His mind flashed back to their late-night visit to the Quick

Stop, to the moment when he and Gina exploded through the front door. There was a man standing there, with a camera, filming them as they raced across the parking lot.

"Hey," Gina said, elbowing him. "Are you listening?"

He snapped out of his funk and said, "Uh, yeah."

"What did I say?"

"Old newspapers," he replied, scanning the first floor. All he saw were bookcases packed with books. "But I don't see any. Are you sure they have them here?"

"It might help if you take *these* off," she said, pulling the sunglasses off his face.

"Easy!" he exclaimed, grabbing them back from her.

"Just let me do the talking," she said. She started walking toward the front desk when she stopped and turned around. "And take off that dumb hat."

Behind the counter, the librarian was busy stamping books but stopped when Nathan and Gina approached. "Good morning," she said, in a pleasant voice. "How can I help you?"

"Do you keep copies of old newspapers?" Gina asked.

"Yes, we do," the librarian replied. She placed the book she was holding atop the pile in front of her, then pushed it down the counter, where a high school student stood waiting. "You can put these away now, Jeffrey," she said.

Jeffrey arranged them, spine up, on a wooden push cart and was just about to wheel it away from the counter when he glanced over at Gina and did a double take. He adjusted his glasses and looked again.

"What is it, Jeffrey?" the librarian asked.

"Uh… nothing," he replied. He took hold of the cart with both hands and quickly wheeled it out onto the main floor of the library.

"Was there a particular newspaper you were interested in?" the librarian asked.

"*The Lakes Region Gazette*," Gina answered.

"Ah, yes…we have quite an extensive archive of *Gazettes*," the librarian said. "We keep them down in the basement. Are you looking for a particular date?"

Gina hesitated, then turned to Nathan and shrugged. *Date?*

He turned to the librarian and said, "Could you excuse us for just a moment?" He pulled Gina away from the counter and whispered, "I thought you said this was going to be simple."

"Well, maybe I exaggerated a little," she said, "but relax, we know the map was printed by *The Lakes Region Gazette*. And you heard what she said. They have a bunch of them here, so all we have to do is—"

"Wait," Nathan said, picturing the map in his mind. It wasn't dated, but it did show something else just as important—the main line. And the main line was still in use the year the boxcar disappeared. *That* was a date he knew all too well.

"What are you thinking?" Gina asked.

"Come on," he said, leading her back to the counter. "Sorry about that," he told the librarian. "We'd like to see copies of *The Lakes Region Gazette* from 1870."

"Any particular topic?" she asked.

"The railroad," Nathan replied.

The librarian set her stamp down on the counter and eyed them both, one at a time. Nathan felt a knot form in the pit of his stomach.

It was going to be the grocery store parking lot all over again.

"Wait a minute! You two look very familiar...I know, you're those two kids...the ones they've been talking about on TV."

"Very well," the librarian said at last. "Since you know the subject and the year, I can show you an easy way to find what you need."

Nathan let out a sigh of relief.

"Follow me, please," the librarian said, stepping out from behind the counter. She led them down the length of the main floor, past tall bookcases on either side of the aisle. They were set at 90° angles, creating even more aisles.

When they reached the far end of the building, she walked them through an arched entryway and stopped. "This is the Reference Room," she said. The outer walls were lined with bookcases, and spread throughout the center of the room were tables and chairs and low bookcases. Directly across from the entryway was a large picture window that overlooked the lot next door.

"Are you familiar with microfilm?" she asked.

"Uh, I've heard of it," Nathan said, "but I've never actually seen it."

"Very well." She spent the next five minutes explaining the use of the microfilm machine and the metal cabinet in the corner of the room, where they kept the reels. When she was done she said, "You can look through the reels one by one, but if you want to save time I recommend the indexes."

"Indexes?" Nathan asked.

"Right over here," she said, stepping around him. She walked over to a bookshelf that ran beneath the large picture window and took out the index for 1870. "The index is a listing of newspaper stories by topic and the page they appeared on. It also tells you every story on that topic for that year."

Nathan's eyes lit up. "Why didn't we think of this before?" he whispered.

"Shhh," Gina said. *Pay attention.*

"Okay," the librarian said, as she walked back toward them. "Right here I see a listing for Railroad Express and Stage Stories." She handed the index to Nathan and went over to the metal cabinet. She came back to the table seconds later holding a small metal canister. "This is the reel with the story I just mentioned. Let me show you how to use it."

She stepped up to the machine and showed Gina how to load the reel, then how to maneuver through it. The whole process took less than a minute. All the while, Nathan was totally absorbed in reading the listings in the index.

"Now, if you want, you can make a copy of what you're viewing," the librarian said. She showed Gina how to center the image, and then how to work the copy machine. "Copies are ten cents," she said, "and you'll need exact change."

Gina cleared her throat to get Nathan's attention. *Are you hearing this?*

He ignored her and kept reading.

"Any questions?" the librarian asked.

"No, I think we're all set," Gina replied.

"Well, good luck. I'll be at the main desk if you have any questions."

Gina thanked her and waited for her to leave. Once she was gone, she turned to Nathan and said, "What are you doing?"

This time he looked up from the page. His jaw hung open and, for several long seconds, he stared at her without speaking.

"What is it?" she asked.

He didn't respond.

"Will you *say* something?" she told him. "You're freaking me out."

Without taking his eyes from hers, he pulled the folded magazine article from his back pocket and thrust it toward her.

She eyed it suspiciously. "Is that the stupid magazine article about flowers?"

"Take it," he said softly.

"What for?" she asked, "I already saw—"

"Take it," he said again.

She sighed and then plucked it from his hand. "I thought we came here to find out about those sidetracks."

"Forget the sidetracks," he said.

"Forget the sidetracks?" She looked away, sighed, then looked back. "The whole reason we came here was to—"

"Read it," he said before she could finish.

She made a face. "Fine," she said as she unfolded the paper. "I can't believe you're making me do this."

"Just read," he said.

"All right, all right."

She held the paper close and began reading aloud. "Saving the May Flower." She rolled her eyes. *Seriously?* Then she read the rest, skipping through it quickly. "Cora Whittier, longtime resident, yeah, yeah… Crawford, New Hampshire, blah, blah, blah… Trailing our buttus—"

"Arbutus," he said.

"Our what?"

"Are-BU-tuss," he repeated, pronouncing each syllable slowly. "The flower? It's all right there in the article."

"Whatever. May I finish, please?"

He extended both hands, palms up, at the paper. *Be my guest.*

"First flower of spring... pungent posy—who cares?—cash crop... blah, blah, blah... makeshift nursery... Mother Nature... blah, blah... hurricane..." She stopped reading and looked up. "Okay. What's the big deal?"

"Cora Whittier," he said.

"What about her?"

"I found a story about her," he said, pointing to the index. "It's listed under *Stories about Crawford, New Hampshire.*"

"Well, yeah," she said, waving the magazine article back and forth. "That's kind of a no-brainer, don't you think?"

"Then I found a story about her nephew," he said.

"The guy who helped her save the flowers?"

"Yeah, Seth, but this one's under a different category."

"What did he do this time, rescue a cat from a tree?"

Nathan shook his head slowly, awestruck, like he'd just seen a ghost.

"So?" she asked impatiently. "What's the category?" "Railroad Stories," he replied.

"Huh?"

He nodded toward the microfilm reader. "Turn on the machine."

11

Jeffrey

Gina powered up the microfilm machine and the screen instantly lit up with a faint blue glow. Nathan checked the listings in the index and said, "Go to the issue of June 16th. Page 1."

She pressed the forward button on the tray, just as the librarian had instructed, and the reel spun forward. Images of old newspaper pages flew by in a blur. She stopped every few seconds to check the date, then advanced the reel again. In the back of her mind she kept asking herself what little pink flowers had to do with the railroad. Seconds later, she stopped and pressed a second button on the tray. The reel moved again, but this time the pages went by at a slow crawl.

"Okay, here it is," she said. "Page 1, June 16th."

The front page looked nothing like any newspaper they'd ever seen. *The Lakes Region Gazette* was written across the top in a fancy Old English font. Below that, the page was divided into eight even columns. The news stories were set in small type that was difficult to read. Nathan leaned in and studied each of the headlines. "There," he said, pointing to one of the columns at the top of the page.

ROBBERY TRIAL
POSTPONED

AP – The Central Ohio Railroad trial was unexpectedly postponed on Monday when key suspect Seth Carson failed to appear. Carson has been charged as an accessory in the robbery along with three other men. According to local officials, Carson was last seen in a Cleveland-area restaurant on May 23. A full investigation is under way.

When they were done reading, Gina turned to Nathan, confused. "You're sure this is the same guy? The one who helped Cora Whittier?"

"It has to be," he replied.

"So, you're telling me that a known train robber was in town just before the boxcar vanished?"

"Well, it says he was a key suspect."

"Excuse me," she said, "a suspected train robber shows up in town right before the boxcar disappears? H-E-L-L-O."

"Not so fast," he said, "there's more." He checked the index. "Go to June 23rd."

This time it only took a few seconds, because it was the following week's edition. Just like before, they found what they were looking for at the top of the page.

SETH CARSON HEADED WEST

AP – According to law enforcement officials, suspected train robber Seth Carson was seen boarding a westbound Central Pacific Railroad train headed to San Francisco, on the afternoon of May 24. Several eyewitness reports confirm that a man matching Carson's description, and using the same name, bought a ticket and boarded the train.

Gina stared at the screen as she processed this new information. "What day did the boxcar disappear?" she asked.

"June 24th," Nathan said.

"Is that accurate?"

"Go to the next issue," he told her.

She advanced the reel and stopped at the issue of June 30th. The headline was set in a three-column box in the top right corner.

BOXCAR VANISHES!

She leaned closer and began reading the story. Nathan was about to do the same when he noticed they were no longer alone. The librarian's helper, Jeffrey, had slipped into the room and was standing over in the corner, restocking books in one of the tall bookcases.

"It looks like the book was right," Gina said. "It *was* June 24th." She stopped reading and thought for a moment. "That was a month after Seth Carson got on the train to San Francisco."

Nathan didn't reply. He was too busy watching Jeffrey, who was taking books off the cart one at a time and sliding them onto the shelf. In between each one, he stopped and looked over at them. A few minutes later, he slowly wheeled the cart out of the room, looking back as he went.

Nathan turned back to the screen. "You were saying—" he began.

"Shhh," she said, cutting him off. She had finished reading the original story and had already advanced the reel to the next week, following what had become a full-blown investigation by local and railroad authorities. "Do you have any change?" she asked, without taking her eyes from the screen.

"No, just a dollar bill," he answered.

"Go get change," she told him. "And hurry." He started to walk away when she called to him. "And Nathan?"

"Yeah?"

"Just dimes."

Wynn Barrett was wedging stones into the ground behind the mailbox post when he looked up and saw the minivan approaching. He climbed to his feet as the van slowed but didn't stop. Both men in the front seat waved, and that's when Wynn noticed that the back seat was empty.

He stood there for a moment, thinking.

Where are the kids?

There was only one way to find out.

Nathan hurried to the front desk and got dimes from the librarian. He was walking back when he spotted Jeffrey watching him from behind one of the tall bookcases. When he got back to the Reference Room, Gina was leaning forward, studying something on the screen.

"What's the deal with that kid?" he said.

"What kid?"

"The librarian's helper. Jeffrey?"

"Forget about him," she said. "Give me the change."

He dropped the coins in her hand and picked up the index. "I'll read you the issue dates."

"Not so fast," she said as she fed the coins into the copier. "There's something I want to show you." She slipped the last coin into the machine and sat down at the microfilm reader. As the images on the screen flew past, Nathan looked up and saw Jeffrey slip into the room again.

He walked over to one of the low bookcases, where he had a direct view of the microfilm machine, and began arranging books on top of the bookcase, his eyes never leaving Gina.

As Nathan watched him, something didn't seem right—he was only using one hand. Suddenly, he brought his other hand up from behind the bookcase. In it was his cell phone, aimed directly at the two of them.

"HEY!" Nathan shouted.

"What is it?" Gina asked.

Nathan dropped the index on the table and charged toward Jeffrey, who pocketed his phone and bolted from the room. Nathan raced after him, weaving through the maze of tables and chairs in his way. When he reached the entryway, he continued down the center aisle, checking between the bookcases on either side.

He was almost to the front counter when he heard someone talking. The voice was very faint, coming from somewhere off to his left. He eased down one of the side aisles, and when he reached the end he stopped and looked between the bookshelves. Jeffrey was standing ten feet away, in a stairwell that led to the bottom level. His cell phone was pressed to his ear. "Sure I'm sure," he said softly, "they were right in front of me. Dude, I saw them up close. It's definitely them."

Nathan turned his ear toward the opening between the shelves, straining to hear.

"Yeah, I tried to, but they saw me," Jeffrey said. As he spoke he peeked around the corner watching for Nathan. "Don't worry," he whispered, "I'll get it, and when I do we're going to be famous."

Nathan felt a surge of panic.

"I already told you why," Jeffrey said, his voice growing louder. "Don't you watch the news? They vanished, and everyone's looking for them. But *we're* the ones who found them. We'll be on TV. *We're* the ones they'll be talking about."

When Nathan heard that, he jumped to his feet and raced back to the Reference Room. Gina was still working at the microfilm reader, centering another story on the screen.

"We have to go," he said, grabbing the index off the table.

"No," she said pointedly. "I'm not done." As she spoke, she pressed the print button and the copy machine began to hum.

Nathan ran to the window and slid the index back on the shelf. Then he hurried back to the table and grabbed his backpack. "I'm serious," he said. "We need to leave right now."

She turned from the screen. "What's wrong?"

"No time to explain. Come on, I mean it, we have to go."

There was a look of alarm on his face, and when he slipped his backpack on his shoulder and started to leave, she knew he wasn't kidding around. "Hold on, wait for me," she said, quickly rewinding the microfilm.

He walked past her and stopped at the end of the table, his eyes trained on the entrance. If what Jeffrey said on the phone held true, he was sure to appear again, camera in hand.

Gina packed the microfilm and returned it to the cabinet, then went back to the table. "I wasn't finished, you know," she griped, as she gathered the photocopies.

Nathan ignored the comment. "All set?" he asked, still watching for Jeffrey.

"Yes," she said in a huff.

"Good, let's go."

They zigzagged across the room, around the tables and chairs, and when they reached the arched entryway Nathan paused.

"Where are we going?" she asked.

"Quiet," he whispered.

He checked the main walkway and then turned left and hurried down the side aisle. When he reached the end, he stopped and peeked around the corner of the tall bookcase. Halfway down the back wall, he saw the stairs that led to the lower level. Jeffrey was nowhere in sight.

"Come on," he said.

They crept along the back wall, and when they reached the stairs, he paused again.

"Why are you stopping?" Gina asked.

"Wait here a second," he said, then hurried down the steps to a small landing. From there, he had a full view of the room below.

There was a coat rack on one wall and a donation box for used books directly across from it. Straight ahead was a door that led outside to the parking lot. "This way," he called back to Gina, motioning with his hand.

"Nathan, wait!" she hissed as he hurried down the stairs two at a time. When she reached the bottom floor he was nowhere in sight. It was only when she pushed through the back door that she found him waiting for her.

"This way," he said, heading toward the street.

"Wait," she said. "Why are we running?"

"I'll tell you when we get around the corner. Now come on, let's go. And stay close to the building."

"Why?"

He pointed to the large windows overhead. "Someone's looking for us."

"What are you talking about?"

"Just follow me."

She glanced up at the windows briefly and then followed him along the back wall. When they reached the sidewalk, he turned right on Bow Street and walked briskly toward Main Street. They were halfway up the street when she caught up with him, and that's when her patience finally ran out.

"All right! Enough!" she blurted out, cutting in front of him.

"Hey, watch out," he said, nearly bowling her over.

"I'm not going any further until you to tell me what this is all about," she demanded.

He straightened up and looked back to see if they were being followed. When he saw that the sidewalk was clear, he said, "You remember that kid, Jeffrey?"

"The librarian's helper? What about him?"

"He recognized us."

"What? No way."

"It's true. He was spying on us. You were busy making copies, you didn't see him. But that's not all..." His words fell short when something at the corner caught his attention and his eyes went wide.

"What're you talking about?" she asked. "And why are you—?"

"This way," he said, cutting her off before she could finish. He grabbed her arm and pulled her into the lilac bushes that skirted the end of the library building.

"What are you doing?" she shouted as he yanked her into the thicket.

"Quiet!" he said. "They'll hear you."

Wynn Barrett reached the traffic light at Main Street and stopped. *Hmmm, let's see now,* he thought as he looked to the right. In the distance, he saw the diner and the card shop. Further down was the front lot of the marina. *No, they wouldn't be down there.*

He turned and walked the opposite way. As he was approaching the library, he saw the kids walking up Bow Street. Thinking quickly, he ducked behind one of the large maple trees that lined the park. From there, he watched them approach Main Street. *The library,* he thought. *Of course.* They seemed to be in a hurry, and the girl was carrying a handful of papers.

Ernie Bell finished his patrol of Jewel Lake Road and drove back into town. There was no sign of Wynn Barrett anywhere, which meant he was probably cooped up inside his house, or maybe he had wandered into the woods and gotten lost. Either way, he was going to find him. Everything he'd witnessed told him the old man was up to something. But what?

When he reached the Main Street intersection, he turned left and pulled over to monitor midday traffic. He was watching the stream of oncoming cars when something in the distance caught his eye. He studied it for several long seconds, then he reached for his personal duty bag on the front seat and pulled out his binoculars.

Gina wrenched her arm free from Nathan's grasp. "Have you completely lost it?"

He put his finger to his lips...*quiet!*...then pointed through the bushes at the Channel 5 News van parked 20 feet away at the corner.

When Gina saw it she quickly ducked down beside him. "What are *they* doing here?"

"Looking for us," he replied, watching the van closely. The front windows were down and the driver was talking on his cell phone.

"You don't know that," she said.

"It's true," he replied. "A little bird told me."

"What is that supposed to mean?" she asked.

He gave her a brief rundown of what happened when he chased Jeffrey from the Reference room, and what he overheard him saying on the phone. When he told her the part about their disappearance being on the news, and everyone looking for them, her eyes went wide. "Does your uncle have a television?"

"Yeah, it's in the living room. Why?"

"We can't let our parents turn it on. If they see a news report about us being here in Crawford, they'll lock us in our rooms, or worse yet, pack up and take us somewhere else."

After that, neither one spoke, as the precarious nature of their situation sank in.

"What I want to know is how they found us," Nathan said, breaking the silence.

"Well gee, I don't know," she replied sarcastically. "Let me think." She counted on her fingers as she spoke. "There was the crazy woman at the gas station. There was the guy with the camera there too, then that old crab at the Visitors Center—"

"Her name is Janet," he said, "and she was very nice."

"Yeah, real nice," she snickered. *Like a rash*. "There was the lady in the grocery store parking lot. And didn't she say something about her sister working for a television station?"

"All *right!*" he said. He hated it when she made lists. "We'll just have to wait here until they leave."

"You think?" she snapped. She watched the van for a moment and then turned back to him. "What was that you were saying before about Jeffrey?"

"He was watching us the whole time we were in the library."

"No," she said, "the other thing, when you chased him out of the room."

"He snuck into the room and tried to take a picture of us with his…"

He stopped short.

"Now what?" she asked.

He closed his eyes and sighed. "The phone. We were supposed to call for a ride."

"Forget about that," she said. "Are you saying he took a picture of us?"

"He tried to, but I scared him away."

She shook her head and sighed. "A picture of us on his phone? Do you know what will happen if he does that? If anyone does that? The whole world will see it. Our *parents* will see it. Then we're cooked. They'll ground us for sure, and then you can say goodbye to finding the boxcar."

"Now you know why we needed to get out of there."

"It's too bad," she said in a somber tone.

"Too bad? That we got away before he could take our photo?"

"No. Too bad that we can't go in the library again."

Ernie Bell couldn't believe his eyes. "Found you," he mumbled, as he watched Wynn Barrett peeking out from behind the tree. "But what are you doing?" He moved the binoculars to the right. The only thing of interest was a news van parked at the curb. "I don't get it," he mumbled, turning the binoculars back to Wynn. "What are you looking at?" Then a series of images from earlier in the morning flashed through his mind. *The blue minivan...the kids going into the library...the minivan driving away.*

Suddenly, his suspicions grew darker.

He's not watching the van.

He's not watching anything.

He's waiting.

Gina bit the edge of her lip as she watched the van idling at the curb. *This is bad.* She turned to Nathan and said, "From now on we need to be more careful. We have to assume that everyone we see knows who we are."

Nathan shook his head and frowned.

"What?" she asked. "You think I'm wrong?"

"No, I think you're absolutely right. It just makes me mad, that's all."

"What does?"

"People. Why can't they just leave us alone?"

"Uh, I think it's a little late for that."

"What do you mean?"

"The days of people leaving us alone are over. They ended the moment we snuck into that old courthouse."

Nathan didn't reply. He knew she was right, but what was he supposed to do, ignore everything that happened? The book falling out of the bookcase? The strange things it did? The clues his grandfather had shown him? He couldn't, even if he wanted to. Based on what had happened so far, it was clear that his grandfather wasn't going to let him quit.

His concentration was broken when he heard the squeal of car tires. He looked up and saw the news van pull away from the curb and make an abrupt U-turn in the street. After it drove away, he opened his backpack and pulled out their baseball hats and sunglasses.

"Come on," he said, scrambling to his feet. "Let's get out of here."

Ernie stashed the binoculars in his personal duty bag and flicked a switch on the dashboard. The light bar on the roof came alive in a burst of flashing blue light, immediately slowing traffic in both directions to a near stop. He pulled away from the curb and sped down the street just as the news van sped past him in the opposite direction. He paid it no mind. He drove until he was directly across from Wynn, then pulled to the curb.

At that very same moment, Nathan and Gina emerged from the bushes. They didn't look back, they didn't slow down, they just ran across Bow Street.

Ernie was getting out of the cruiser when he saw them running toward him. He recognized the baseball hats and sunglasses at once.

"Are you all right?" he shouted as they approached.

Nathan stopped running and looked back over his shoulder to see if anyone was following them.

"What is it?" Ernie asked. "Is something wrong?"

"We need to get home," he said, slightly out of breath.

"You need a ride?" Ernie asked. "Come on, I'll take you."

He walked to the side of the cruiser and opened the back door. Nathan climbed in and slid across the seat to make room for Gina. But just as she stepped off the curb, her ankle gave out and she collapsed against the side of the car.

"Whoa, easy there," Ernie said, helping her to her feet. "Are you okay?"

"I'm fine," she replied, stepping back up on the sidewalk. She tore the hat and sunglasses off her head and flung them in the back seat of the cruiser, then knelt down and gathered the papers that were scattered on the ground.

Once she was inside the car, Ernie closed the door and stood there for a moment looking across the street.

The old man had vanished.

On the ride back to Pine Point, the police radio squawked and chirped. Ernie turned it down so they could talk, but the kids were saying nothing. As he drove past the library, he eyed them in the rearview mirror.

"So, here's what I don't understand," he said, breaking the silence. "You guys are on vacation, right?"

Nathan was staring out the window, thinking about Jeffrey's troubling phone conversation.

"They vanished... Everyone's looking for them... Don't you watch the news?"

"What was that?" he asked.

"You guys are on vacation," Ernie repeated, as he pulled into the grocery store parking lot and turned the cruiser around.

"Something like that," Nathan muttered. He turned back to the window. After their recent adventure at the courthouse, they'd done all the TV interviews, met with all the reporters, answered every question, and posed for all the pictures. It was fun then, but now it was time for everyone to leave them alone. He hadn't been near a television since they left home, but if what Jeffrey said was true, then their situation was worse than he originally thought. *We're not being followed*, he thought. *We're being hunted.*

Ernie waited for a break in traffic and then pulled back out onto Main Street. "So you're on vacation," he said, trying to get them talking, "and you go to the library?"

"Yeah," Nathan said, only half listening. He was thinking about what he was going to tell his parents when they saw the police cruiser pull into the driveway. What he could possibly say to explain why they hadn't called for a ride like they had originally agreed.

Ernie slowed to a stop at the traffic light, watching them in his rearview mirror. These kids were spooked. He could hear it in their voices and see it in their blank expressions. Something had happened back at the library—something that spooked them. The light changed and he pulled forward. As he turned onto Jewel Lake Road, he tried a different approach.

"How's the ankle, Gina?"

Gina was slumped back in the seat with her head resting against the side window. "Fine," she replied. The truth was, her ankle was sore and her head felt like it was begin squeezed in a vice. She looked down at the stack of papers in her hand. It was only a small sampling of what she found on file, but each page held a critical new clue to the puzzle.

She thought about the microfilm reels and all the pages she'd seen. All the stories. So much information had been right there at their fingertips. But not anymore. The library was now off limits. With Jeffrey lurking behind every bookcase, they couldn't risk going back.

She stared out the window and tried to put their crazy morning behind her. What she needed was time to think, time to sort out the new information. There was more to the story than what they read in the book. Lots more. When they got back to the cottage, she'd write it all down in her notebook, filling in more pieces to the puzzle. But first, she had to tell Nathan what she found.

Wynn Barrett crouched down behind the Civil War monument in the park. It was set back behind the trees where he'd been hiding when Ernie Bell showed up. Once the cruiser was gone from sight, he made his way back to the sidewalk. As he walked, he noticed a single sheet of paper lying in the street. He picked it up, giving it a quick read as he returned to the sidewalk.

It was a page he'd read before. Many times. Reading the words again stirred old feelings of anger buried deep inside. A moment later, those feelings faded and a smile crossed his lips. He folded the paper into a neat square and slipped it into his back pocket. As he started down the sidewalk, he felt the warm sun on his face. He could smell the newly mowed grass in the park across the street, mixed with the scent of wild roses.

"Ah, yes, another beautiful day," he said, as he made his way up the sidewalk.

Everything was proceeding quite nicely.

Even better than he first imagined.

Ernie Bell tried a few more questions as he drove up Jewel Lake Road, but the responses he got were the same every time.

"Good."

"Fine."

"Yeah."

After that he gave up. The person he really wanted to question was Wynn Barrett, and the next time he saw him they'd have a serious talk. The old man might've slipped away today, but sooner or later, he'd catch up with him. It was only a matter of time.

Up ahead he saw a break in the trees that marked the driveway to the Cole property.

"Okay," he said. "Here we are."

Nathan and Gina didn't respond.

As he slowed to a stop at the mouth of the driveway, he said, "You guys take it easy now, you hear? You're on vacation for crying out loud."

When there was still no answer, he checked the rearview mirror and did a double take.

The kids were gone.

12

The State Park

E rnie twisted around in the seat and looked through the steel cage divider. "Guys?"

His attention was diverted when he heard the toot of a car horn. When he spun back around, he saw a vehicle stopped in the road beside the cruiser. It was the news van from the front of the library. He lowered his window and said, "Can I help you?"

"The Sunset Inn," the driver said. "Is that around here somewhere?"

"Follow this road," Ernie said, pointing over his shoulder toward town. "When you get to the traffic light, turn right. The first left is West Lake Road. That'll take you right to the Sunset."

The driver nodded and then drove off. That's when Ernie heard someone whisper.

"Are they gone?"

He spun around in his seat. "Yeah, they're gone," he said. *But where are you?*

Nathan's head slowly appeared. He scanned the road in both directions and then sat up.

Gina appeared seconds later. "You know, you really should clean back here," she said. "It smells funny."

"I don't doubt it," Ernie said under his breath. Then he asked, "What were you doing on the floor?"

"Hiding," Nathan said.

"From those reporters?"

"Yup."

Ernie considered that for a moment, then shook it off. "All right then," he said, climbing out of the cruiser. He opened the back door and Nathan jumped out, followed by Gina, who was only too happy to get out of the cramped and foul-smelling back seat.

"Thanks for the ride," Nathan called out over his shoulder as he and Gina darted around the back end of the cruiser.

Once they were gone, Ernie turned and looked down the long expanse of Jewel Lake Road. The white van was a small speck in the distance.

Nathan raced down the driveway, trying to get out of sight as quickly as possible. With the luck they'd been having, it wasn't out of the realm of possibility that the news van might make another surprise appearance. He was just glad he spotted it in time to pull Gina down behind the front seat. If he hadn't, they would've been recognized for sure.

"What's the big rush?" Gina huffed, struggling to keep up.

Nathan stopped and looked over her shoulder at the main road. "Getting out of sight," he said.

"Relax," she replied. "The news guys are gone. Didn't you hear the driver? They're looking for the Sunrise Inn."

"The Sunset," he said, correcting her.

"Whatever. It's not important." She held up the copies from the library. "*These* are important."

He eyed the papers in her hand. In all the confusion, he had completely forgotten about the old newspapers at the library. "Did you find out about the sidetracks?" he asked.

"I most certainly did, but that's not what I need to show you."

His eyes lit up. "You found something else?"

She nodded her head slowly. *You bet.*

He made a face. *Well?*

Before she could answer, an approaching vehicle drew their attention. The tires of the blue minivan made a curious popping sound they rolled across the gravel driveway. Seconds later, the van came to an abrupt stop beside them.

"What's going on?" Nathan's mother demanded.

Nathan looked at Gina, then back at his mother. "Uh, we're standing here?"

"Yes, I can see that," she snapped. "I thought you were going to call for a ride."

"We couldn't," he said. "We didn't have any money for the phone."

"No money for the phone? Your father said you were going to ask the librarian to use the phone."

"We were," Gina explained, "but then we saw Officer Bell and asked him for a ride instead."

"Officer Bell?" her mother asked. "Who is Officer Bell?"

Gina rolled her eyes. "Really, Mom? You met him yesterday."

"Oh, yes, now I remember. The nice man with the short hair."

"How many times are we going to talk about this?" Elizabeth asked. "We agreed that you wouldn't call attention to yourselves."

"Mom! We didn't call attention to ourselves," Nathan protested. "We had to hide—"

Gina poked him in the back. *STOP!*

"You had to *what?*" his mother asked.

"What Nathan is trying to say," Gina said, before he could say another word, "is that we stayed in a separate room at the far end of the library to do our work, so no one would see us."

"I see," Elizabeth said, eyeing them both suspiciously. "And then you got a ride from Officer Bell."

"Yes," Nathan and Gina said at the same time.

"So where is he?"

Nathan pointed toward the main road. "He dropped us off at the end of the driveway and then left. If you hurry, you can probably catch him."

"This isn't funny, Nathan. I was told you were going to be at the library for an hour. It's almost noon. Gina's mother and I were on our way downtown to look for you."

"We're here. We're fine," he said, shrugging. *Relax, already.*

She stared straight ahead for several seconds, then let out a heavy breath. "All right, let's go."

"Where are we going?" he asked.

"The state park."

His shoulders sagged. "Really? Do we have to go?"

"If you want lunch, then yes, I suggest you get in."

When Nathan heard the mention of food, he quickly opened the side door and jumped in.

Gina shook her head in frustration and looked down at the papers in her hand. "So much for these," she muttered under her breath.

"What was that, dear?" her mother asked.

"Nothing."

She folded the papers and jammed them in her back pocket. *We're never going to solve this puzzle,* she thought, as she climbed into the van and shut the door.

Wynn Barrett walked into his house and stopped in the front hallway. The midday sun was streaming through the front windows, throwing long ribbons of light onto the floor. He stood perfectly still, staring at an old photograph that hung on the wall, as he had done many times before. The image was very old, and the photo quality was poor, but it held a place of honor in his home, and his heart. "Soon, Josiah," he said softly, wiping a thin layer of dust off the frame. "Soon."

They drove for almost a mile when they came to the entrance for the state park. It wasn't hard to miss. There was a large sign on the right, made from heavy wooden planks, the color of mud. The words *Jewel Lake State Park* were carved into it and painted squash yellow. The whole thing hung from a tall L-shaped brace made from heavy wooden logs.

Elizabeth pulled in and followed the gravel road to a small

parking area.

"Where's Dad?" Gina asked her mother.

"He and Nathan's father are meeting us here."

"They're *meeting* us here?" Nathan asked.

"That's right," his mother replied.

"How?"

"You'll see."

They gathered the lunch supplies and followed a stepped path that twisted and turned down a gentle slope through the forest. The woods were cool and still, and the air held the musky scent of earth and pine. Soon, they came to a small beach and picnic area on the edge of the lake. Nathan was at the front of the procession and was the first to see his father sitting at one of the picnic tables. "Hey, how did you get here?" he called out.

His father pointed to the motorboat anchored several feet off shore. Gina's father was standing on the beach nearby, scanning the distant shore through a pair of binoculars. When he heard Nathan, he turned and waved to the group.

A short time later, they were all seated around the picnic table. Lunch was spread out before them on a series of platters and plates, with a small army of bowls and plastic containers for salad, chips, cookies, and slabs of watermelon.

"So how did you guys make out at the library?" Nathan's father asked.

"Good," Nathan managed to say with a mouthful of food. His mother looked off into the forest and said nothing.

"Were you able to find the information you needed?" Gina's mother asked.

Gina was picking at the potato salad on her plate. "Yes and no," she answered, without looking up. *I would've found even more,* she thought, *if Jeffrey hadn't ruined everything.*

"That must be some homework assignment," her father said. "It's the only thing you've been doing since we got here."

"Why don't you tell us what it's about?" Gina's mother suggested.

"Mom," Gina groaned. "Can we just eat?"

"You know, I think your dad's right," Nathan's father said. "You two have been working nonstop on your schoolwork since we arrived."

Nathan was chewing a mouthful of food and shrugged. Maybe if he didn't answer they would drop the subject and move on to something else.

"I can't believe I'm about to say this," his father said, "but I think it's time you both took a break."

Nathan and Gina looked over at him at the same time.

"I know, I know," he said quickly. "It sounds crazy, telling you not to do your homework, but we're on vacation." He turned toward the lake and swept his hand in a wide arc. "Look at this beautiful lake, this amazing forest. I say go. Explore. Climb a tree. Skip rocks across the water. Search for hidden treasure."

Nathan and Gina looked at each other, nodded in agreement, and then jumped up from the table.

"I'll race you," she said, sprinting toward the beach.

Gina's mother called out, "Don't touch any poison ivy...or snakes...or any strange looking mushrooms."

"Don't worry," Nathan's father said as the kids ran off. "We're in the middle of nowhere. What possible trouble could they get into?"

They got as far as the beach and stopped. From there, the path forked to the left and right, following the shoreline in each direction until it eventually got swallowed up by the forest.

"This way," Gina said, choosing the path to the left. She led the way, walking quickly, until they were out of sight of their parents.

"How awesome was that?" Nathan asked. "My dad telling us not to do our homework?"

"It was great," Gina replied. "Remind me to send him a thank you card."

"Very funny."

"I'm serious," she said. "Did you really want to hang out with your parents all day? In the woods? Answering questions about what we're working on?"

"Not really."

He looked past her and stopped. "Hey look."

Fifty feet up the trail was a long wooden footbridge. It arched over a slow-moving river that fed into the lake. Before Gina could respond, he brushed past her and ran full speed toward it.

"Wait up!" she shouted.

When he reached the bridge, he ran halfway across it, then stopped to catch his breath. With every step he took, the heavy planks beneath his feet made a dull clunking sound that echoed across the water and into the woods. From that vantage point, he could see the cove, and beyond it, the main channel of the lake. Lining the horizon were jagged mountaintops in deep shades of green and brown. He turned and went to the opposite railing, just as Gina came up behind him.

She stopped and glanced down at the river. "Very nice," she mumbled, then walked to the far end of the bridge. When she looked back, he was still leaning on the handrail, staring down at the slow-moving water below. "Well, come on," she yelled. "Don't you want to see what I found at the library?"

"Oh, right," he said, pushing off the railing. He was turning to go when he noticed something in the weeds further up the river. He squinted hard, trying to see what it was, but it was masked by the shadows of the overhanging trees.

"Uh, today?" Gina called out.

"Alright already," he replied, hurrying across the bridge.

They continued up the trail for a short distance and stopped where a second trail split off to the left and zigzagged up a steep rise.

"This way," Nathan said.

They followed the trail to the top of the knoll and discovered an open wooden structure built from heavy logs.

"What do you suppose that is?" Gina asked.

"It's a lean-to," he told her. "Come on, let's go check it out."

"A what?" she asked.

"Lean-to," he shouted as he sprinted toward it.

She hurried after him, trying not to trip on the tree roots and rocks that jutted out from the ground. When she finally caught up to him, he was standing inside the lean-to, surveying the view.

"Lovely," she said, eyeing it from top to bottom. It had three walls and a single-pitched roof. Several feet in front of it, half buried in the dirt, was a circle of large blackened rocks that formed a fire pit. "What's it for?"

"Camping," he replied.

She gave him a doubtful look. "Camping? Are you serious?"

"Yeah, why wouldn't I be?" he asked.

"Because it's facing the wrong way."

"What are you talking about?"

"You can't even see the lake," she snorted.

Nathan laughed. "They did that on purpose."

She made a face. *Yeah, right.*

"Seriously," he said. "People camp here, even in the winter."

"Why would they do that?" she asked.

"They just do, alright?"

She rolled her eyes. *What is wrong with people around here?*

"They faced it this way to protect the campers from the winds off the lake."

"Oh really. And you know this how?"

"My grandfather told me."

"Speaking of your grandfather," she said, as she wrestled the folded copies from her back pocket. She waved them in the air and said, "That book of his only told part of the story."

"What are you talking about?"

She sat down on the front edge of the lean-to.

"Have a seat and I'll show you."

157

13

Storms

Gina unfolded the wad of papers and smoothed them out on the floor of the lean-to. "These are just some of the stories I found while you were chasing Jeffrey around the library."

"I still can't believe he was trying to take our picture," Nathan said. *Creep.*

"Yeah, well, forget about him. This is way more interesting, I promise." She arranged the papers into a neat pile on her lap. "Let's see," she began, examining the top copy. "The boxcar was picked up in Concord."

"We know that," he said.

"Don't interrupt."

"Sorry."

"The train left on schedule and made excellent time." She paused, as she continued to scan the copy. "Okay, right here, records show that it got to Stone Point on time, and, it arrived at West Branch right on schedule."

"So, there were no mechanical problems," Nathan said.

"That's right. And the conductor keeps something called a Delay Report."

"What's that?"

"It's a record of where they stopped, for how long, and for what purpose. There were no delays listed."

"Which means they didn't make any unscheduled stops," Nathan said. "And like you said in my bedroom, if they did, someone would have mentioned it during the investigation."

"Exactly." She went to the next page. "They talked to everyone, some more than once. They even did background checks on anyone who seemed suspicious."

"Let me guess," he said. "They found nothing."

"That's right. Everyone checked out fine."

Nathan let out an exasperated breath. "What else?"

"Oh, we're just getting started," she said. She sorted through the next few pages until she found the one she wanted. "The search area was huge. It went from Stone Point all the way to West Branch."

"Wherever that is," he mumbled.

"Relax," she said. "I found it."

His eyes lit up. "You did?"

She handed him the paper and pointed to a small map. It was set in the middle of the investigation story. "Right there," she said.

He took the paper and studied the map closely. "Look, it's just north of Alton Bay," he said. "That's not far from here. Twenty miles, maybe less."

"Oh, the search area was much bigger than that," she said.

"Huh?"

"They didn't just check the tracks. They checked the woods on both sides, too."

His shoulders drooped. "Oh, right."

She saw the dejected look on his face and said, "Don't worry about that." She flipped to the next page and said, "This is the information we went to the library for in the first place."

He straightened up. "The sidetracks?"

"Yes. Between Stone Point and West Branch there are only two other sets of tracks." She handed him the copy of another map of the search area. This one showed the area around Stone Point, the last known location of the boxcar. In the middle of the map he saw the same two dotted lines he discovered in the book, only these were much clearer. "There's a logging sidetrack here," she said, pointing to one of the dotted lines. "And one directly across from it, right here."

"What's that one?"

"It leads to a small group of granite quarries called The Three Sisters."

He studied the map, waiting for her to continue.

"Both sidetracks, and the land around them, were searched more than once. Obviously, they found nothing."

"Well," he said, handing her the paper, "it was worth a shot, right?"

"Not so fast," she said. "There's more, and here's where it gets interesting."

"Go on," he said.

She went to the next page. "That whole month, the weather in

New Hampshire was crazy."

"Right," he said. "There was that whole Cora Whittier flower thing."

"Yes, in May," she said. "That was the first storm."

"Wait. What?"

"There was another storm. It hit weeks later. June 24th to be exact."

"The same day the boxcar vanished."

"Correct." She flipped more pages, reading bits and pieces as she went. "It was a monster tornado. It ripped up everything and made a huge mess." She stopped and looked over at him. "That's the storm that took out Stone Point Station."

Nathan thought back to something Janet French said when they were at the Visitors Center.

That terrible storm.

"Now, are you ready for this?" she asked. The look on her face was one he'd seen many times before. The hint of a smile. The wide eyes, full of anticipation and light. "This is the last thing I copied," she said. "Check it out."

She handed him the stack of papers. The top sheet had a copy of a newspaper article that appeared in *The Lakes Region Gazette* after June 24th. He glanced at the headline briefly and then read the story out loud.

INVESTIGATION SLOWED

Crawford, NH – The ongoing investigation by authorities from the New England Central RR has been slowed by recovery efforts in the wake of the recent tornado. A spokesman for the rail line expressed concern that "Additional manpower is needed and until that help becomes

available,
(continued on next page)

He came to the end of the story and flipped to the next page. He glanced at it briefly, then turned back to the previous page.

"What's wrong?" Gina asked.

"Where's the rest?"

"The rest of what?" she asked.

"The story."

"It's right there," she said.

"No, it's not."

"Let me see those," she said, yanking the copies out of his hand. She checked each one to make sure they were in the right order, then said, "Something isn't right here."

"What are you talking about?"

She thought back to the Reference Room. "You had a dollar, right? In the library?"

"Yeah."

"And you gave me ten dimes." It wasn't a question.

"Yup," he said. "I watched the librarian count them out on the counter."

"And I used every one of them," she said. "I made ten copies."

"Yeah?"

"There are only nine copies here."

"Did you leave one at the house?" he asked.

"How could I? We never went in the house. We only got as far as the driveway, remember?"

"Oh, right. Did you leave it at the library?"

She thought back to the moment he came into the Reference

Room and told her they had to leave. "No," she said. "I grabbed all the copies, I'm certain of it."

"Wait a minute," he said. "Remember how you tripped on the sidewalk? When you were getting into the cruiser? You dropped the papers on the ground."

"Yeah, but I picked them all up."

"Then I don't know what to tell you," he said.

For several seconds, they sat without speaking. When Nathan looked over at her, she was staring down at the ground, deep in thought.

"What is it?" he asked.

"There was something on that last page."

"What do you mean?"

"I can't remember what it was, but it was important."

"Well then, there's only one thing to do."

"And that is?" she asked, expecting the usual Nathan Cole wisecrack.

"We need to go back to the library."

"You're not serious."

"I'm completely serious," he replied. "If what you found was that important."

"I think you're forgetting about Jeffrey."

He stared off into the forest, thinking, then planning. "We'll just have to sneak in," he said.

"What?" she fired back. "You want to sneak into a public building, in broad daylight?"

"Why not?" he said. "We've done it before."

He was right. And with that decided, she refolded the papers and tucked them in her back pocket.

On the way back down the hill neither one spoke. When they reached the main trail, they continued along the shoreline until they came to another beach. This one was much smaller than the one by the picnic area. The rippled sand was the color of wheat and dotted with small stones that tickled their toes as they waded out from the shore. With the lake shimmering in the afternoon sun, they took turns skimming flat rocks across the water. There was no talk of boxcars, tornadoes, missing papers, or people hounding them with cameras.

After that, they walked further up the trail, where they discovered another side path. It wound up and around a gentle hill to a second lean-to that was smaller than the first, and surrounded by a forest of steel-gray beech trees. Just beyond it was a massive rock ledge that overlooked the entire lake. They sat with their feet dangling over the edge, watching sailboats glide up and down the channel. A seaplane appeared out of nowhere, sailing gracefully down length of the lake like a giant heron, before touching down at the far end. A short time later, the sun began to sink lower in the sky.

It was time to head back.

That night, as Nathan lay in bed, he couldn't stop thinking about the information Gina shared with him at the lean-to. *What now?* he asked himself. Other than the lost photocopy, and whatever clues it might hold, he had no idea what they should do next. *Should we start combing the woods? Where would we start?* Many people had done it before them, with zero results. What possible chance did they have of finding anything?

Gradually, his eyelids grew heavy and he drifted off to sleep. That's when the stillness of the room was shattered by a loud thump. His eyes snapped open and he bolted upright in bed, listening in the dark. Something was moving on the far side of the room, inching across the floor with a soft scraping sound. *What is that?*

He turned on the bedside lamp and it stopped. For several seconds he sat there, listening and letting his eyes adjust to the light. When he finally looked across the room, he saw his backpack, but not on the chair where he'd left it. It was halfway across the floor. "Not this again."

He climbed out of bed and went over to pick it up. But just as he plunked it down on the chair, it lurched forward and landed at his feet. "Stop that," he whispered, picking it up again. He was about to put it back when he remembered the ordeal in his bedroom, as he was packing to leave. His grandfather was trying to tell him something then—was he trying to tell him something now? There was only one way to find out.

He carried the backpack over to his bed and climbed under the covers. With his curiosity on high alert, he pulled the book from the pack, along with his flashlight. What could his grandfather want him to see that he hadn't already seen? He turned on his flashlight, opened the book, and sat there, waiting and watching. *Well?*

This was normally when the pages would turn by themselves. Like a giant flashing road sign, his grandfather would show him the way. But not this time. He turned the pages to Chapter 11. "What is it?" he whispered, pulling his hand away. Suddenly the book slammed shut. *Huh?* He tried again, opening to Chapter 11, but the same thing happened. *Okay, not Chapter 11.* Clearly his grandfather wanted him to see something else, but he was going to have to find it on his own.

He opened the book again and fanned through the chapters with his thumb. As they flew past in a blur, something caught his eye. *Whoa, what was that?* It happened so fast that he only saw it for a split second. He turned back a few pages. Then a few more. "Where was it?" he muttered under his breath.

He took a breath to calm himself and then went back to the front of the book. He went page by page, carefully scanning each one from top to bottom. He saw pictures of the first locomotives, elaborate railroad stations, railcars of every size and shape, photos of work crews and famous railroad tycoons. *It wasn't a picture,* he told himself as he turned the pages.

At one point he stopped to examine a diagram showing different wheel configurations of locomotives. *No, not a diagram either.* He kept going, turning pages faster and faster as he neared the final chapters of the book. More pages. More photos. Then maps. Lots of maps.

"No, no, no," he whispered. "It wasn't a map, it was ...wait!"

He stopped turning pages.

THERE!

14

The Ride

The next morning, Gina was awakened by the sound of a motorboat doing figure eights in the cove. The sound of the bow, slapping the surface of the water as it crossed its own wake, echoed into the forest outside her window. "Don't people sleep on Sunday morning in this town?" she groaned, as she sat up in bed. Her stomach made a deep rumbling sound, and she eased out of bed and got dressed.

As she stumbled down the hallway toward the kitchen, Nathan's bedroom door suddenly flew open. He ducked his head out into the hallway and waved her inside. "Come here," he said. "Hurry."

She brought her hand up to her mouth to smother a yawn. "What is it?"

"You'll see," he said. "Just get in here."

"All right, all right, relax," she muttered.

He waited for her to step into the room and then quickly closed the door.

The sun was bright in his room and she had to squint. "Did you eat yet?" she asked.

"No, I've been waiting for you."

"Well, I'm starving, so make it quick." As her eyes adjusted to the light, she noticed he was keeping one hand hidden behind his back. "What's wrong with your arm?"

"Nothing," he replied. "I need to show you something." At first, he was going to tell her about the backpack falling on the floor, but things like that were a sore subject with her. Best to tell her later. Or never.

She fought back another yawn. "Well, what is it?"

He brought the book out from behind his back. "Check this out," he said, pushing it toward her.

She glanced at it briefly without taking it from him. "Why are you giving me that? I've already seen it."

"Look inside the front cover."

She flopped her head to one side. "Yeah, right."

"What's wrong?"

"Like I'm going to fall for that again."

"Fall for what?" he asked.

"You know."

He shook his head. *Sorry, I don't.*

She stared at him without speaking. *Nice try.*

"What?" he demanded.

"Last year? In homeroom?"

"What are you talking about?"

"You shoved that book at me? Told me to look inside the front cover?"

"What book?"

"The one with the snake in it?"

"Oh, that," he said, fighting back a grin as the memory returned.

It was a small rubber snake, more like a worm actually, but her scream was legendary. Scared the wits out of Mrs. Carpenter and made the whole class explode in laughter. *Classic.*

"Yeah, that," she said, seeing the recognition on his face.

He pushed the book at her again. "It's not that, I promise."

She studied his face for several long seconds, then took the book and slowly pried it open, all the while holding it away from her body.

Just in case.

But there was no snake. No dead flies. Only a folded piece of paper, no bigger than a book of matches. "What is this?" she asked. *And why are you wasting my time with it?* she nearly said.

"I'm not sure. I was hoping you could tell me"

She gave him a this-better-not-be-a-joke look, then removed the paper and handed him back the book. The paper was old and thin, the color of a dried orange peel. Unfolded, it measured roughly six inches long and two inches wide. On one side there was nothing but faded newsprint. The other side was part of a diagram, drawn in fine black lines.

"So, what do you think?" he asked.

"Well, it's from a newspaper, obviously," she said. "And judging by the straight edges, it wasn't torn out, it was cut out."

"O-kay," he said slowly, waiting for her to continue.

"Where did you find it?" she asked.

169

"In here," he said, holding up the book. "But it was strange."

"What do you mean, strange?"

"It wasn't in the chapter about the missing boxcar."

"Where was it?"

"It was in a different chapter."

"A different chapter," she repeated, casting him a doubtful look.

"Yeah, toward the back of the book. There was a whole chapter about some guy from the Civil War. Major Eli something."

"So, what does it have to do with the boxcar?"

He shrugged his shoulders. "I have no idea."

"Then why are we looking at it?" she groaned.

"Because it's connected."

"And what makes you think that?"

"It just is," he said.

"But you have no idea how?"

"Look," he replied, "I can't tell you how, but it's related. I'm 100% sure."

Now she was really curious. "You're 100% sure." *Do tell.*

"Yes," he said.

"But you can't tell me how."

He exhaled loudly. "It's bookcase stuff, all right? Do you really want to hear it?"

The very mention of the word "bookcase" made her shiver. "Don't bother," she said, thrusting the newspaper clipping at him. The bookcase in his attic, and the books in it, had done things she wouldn't have believed possible if she hadn't witnessed them with her own eyes. Clearly, something else had happened, something haunted and creepy, and whatever it was, she didn't want to hear about it.

He pushed her hand away. "Will you relax? Just take another look at it. If anyone can figure it out, it's you."

She shook her head slowly and said, "I can't believe I'm doing this," then pulled the clipping back and gave each side a closer inspection. "Well, for starters," she said, holding it up for him to see, "this diagram is an advertisement for a sewing machine."

"How do you know that?"

"I just do," she replied as she turned the paper over. She scanned the newsprint side briefly then said, "This side looks like a news story or maybe—"

"Or maybe what?"

She pulled the paper closer and stared at a grouping of words at the bottom of the page.

"Did you see this?" she asked, ignoring his question.

He stepped forward and glanced at the paper briefly. "Yeah, I saw it. It's gibberish."

"Look again," she said, handing it to him.

He took the paper without complaint, or the usual wisecrack, and inspected the last four lines of copy. It was a jumble of broken words, along with a few he recognized.

illiam F. Brooten, age 38
at St. Clara's Infirmary
veland, January 11, 1871,
rounded by his family.

"See it?" she asked.

"No," he said, shaking his head. "What exactly am I looking for?"

She reached over and stabbed at the bottom of the paper with her finger. "Right, *there.*"

He looked again. Just above the grouping of words he saw two thin lines drawn in pencil. "Someone drew on it," he said. "So what?"

"They did more than that," she said.

"What are you talking about?"

"Those two lines, see how they cross?"

"Yeah, what about it?"

"They're the beginning and end."

He looked up at her, eyebrows raised. "Excuse me?"

She made her what's-wrong-with-you face. "They're the beginning and the end...of a circle."

"Okay, now you lost me."

She rolled her eyes and exhaled. "You know when you circle something with a pencil?"

"Yeah?"

"The beginning and end of the line don't always meet. Sometimes they cross."

"Oh... right," he said, staring at the two lines again. "I totally missed that."

"You *think?*" she fired back. "You can't see the rest of the circle because it got cut off."

"The question is," he said, focusing his attention on the jumble of words, "why did they circle it? These words make no sense."

"Not so fast," she said, leaning in. "See that word, 'Infirmary'?"
"Yeah?"

"You know what that is, right?"

"Not exactly."

"It's a hospital."

"O-kay," he replied slowly. *If you say so.*

"And the first word, 'illiam'" she said, pointing as she spoke, "is probably William."

"Go on," he said, looking at her, astonished. *How does she do that?*

"That word 'rounded'? He wasn't 'rounded' by his family. The word is probably 'surrounded,' as in, he was surrounded by his family."

"Of course," he exclaimed. "Surrounded by his family in a hospital. That means he was sick."

"Or dead," she offered. "What you're holding in your hand is an obituary."

"What's this word 'veland?'" he asked.

"It's probably part of a town name, like Groveland or Cleveland, or something like that."

He was about to respond when there was a sharp knock on the door.

"Nathan? Are you up?" his mother asked.

He fumbled with the newspaper clipping then shoved it back in the book. "Uh, yeah, I'm up," he called out as he hurried over to the bed. He had just tucked the book under the blanket when the door opened a crack.

"Your father is taking us all on a boat ride," his mother said. "So I suggest you shake a leg."

"A boat ride?" he grumbled. "What time is it?"

"It's a little after nine o'clock."

"We can't go on a boat ride," he told her. "We haven't eaten breakfast yet."

"We?" she said, opening the door all the way. "Oh, good morning, Gina."

Gina smiled sheepishly but said nothing.

"Well, we can't very well leave the two of you here alone," his mother said.

"Uh... Mom... we have homework to finish, remember?"

She eyed them both. "If we leave you here, you're going to finish it?"

"I certainly hope so" Nathan said.

"It's not an option, Nathan," she said sternly. "You stay here and finish your homework, or you come with us. That's your choice, take it or leave it."

"We'll stay," he said, without hesitation.

Gina nodded her head in agreement.

"All right, then," his mother said. "There's cereal on the table and juice in the fridge. Your father is anxious to go, so I guess you two will just have to wait until next time."

Nathan made a face. *Oh darn.*

His mother ignored him and said, "When you're done eating, please remember to clean up."

"Yes, Mom," he groaned, with a tired look.

"Okay, well, I'm not sure how long we'll be gone," his mother said.

"Why, where is Dad taking you?"

"He wants to show Gina's parents around the lake. I'm guessing he'll take us down to the Marina, maybe stop at Little Bear on the way back."

"Little Bear?" Gina asked.

"It's an island," Nathan explained.

"Oh."

"It's shaped like a bear," he said.

She made a face. *No kidding.*

From down at the dock came the blare of a boat horn. "Time to go," his mother said. "We'll see you in a little bit." As she closed the door, she said, "Finish your homework!"

A short time later, Nathan and Gina were sitting at the kitchen table eating breakfast. Gina was refilling her juice glass when she grimaced.

"What's wrong?" Nathan asked.

"My shoulder hurts," she said, "thanks to you."

"What do you mean, thanks to me?" He raised the cereal bowl to his mouth and drank what was left of his second helping.

"Throwing stones at the State Park?" she said. "That was your idea, remember?"

He set the bowl down and wiped his mouth. "We weren't throwing them."

"No? Then what were we doing?"

"We were skipping them," he said. "There's a difference."

"Yeah, right." *Whatever you say.*

"And I won," he said, getting up from the table. *So there.*

"You did not."

"Ten skips," he announced proudly as he walked over to the sink. "That's a new Jewel Lake record."

"I seriously doubt that," she snickered. "And by the way, it was only eight."

He rinsed his bowl and spoon and set them in the dish rack, then he came back to the table and sat down. "All right," he said, rubbing his palms together, "this is perfect. We have two hours, possibly three."

"What are you talking about?"

"That's how much time we have until our parents get back."

"Time for what?"

"To go to the library. If my dad is taking your folks on a tour of the lake, it's going to take at least that long. Trust me. The lake is huge. Down to the Marina and back? That's two hours easy. And that doesn't include the time they'll spend on Little Bear."

She closed her eyes and sighed. "Not this again."

"What?" he asked.

"You're not worried about Jeffrey? And his phone? With the camera? What will happen if he takes our picture? And then posts it on—"

"Stop!" he cried out. "I haven't forgotten about Jeffrey. But what if he's not there? Did you think about that?"

She looked at him for several long seconds as she considered the possibility. "So, you think we can just waltz into the library without anyone seeing us?"

"I never said we were going to waltz," he said.

"I'm serious," she shot back.

"So am I. This couldn't have worked out better. We need to get the rest of the story about the tornado. You know, the copy you lost?"

"I didn't lose it," she said. "It disappeared."

"Right," he said, making a face. "We also need to find out about that clipping I found last night."

"The obituary?"

"Yeah, that."

"I think you're forgetting something else," she said. "How are we going to get there? And don't say we can just walk, because I am not doing that again."

He stared across the room, thinking. As the seconds passed, he began to nibble on the inside of his lip. "If only we were back home, we could use our..." Then it came to him. "I know!" he blurted out. Without another word, he jumped up from the table.

"Where are you going?" she demanded, but he was already out the door. When she heard the screen door slam on the porch, she yelled, "Hey! Wait for me..."

She ran outside and found him on the far side of the yard. He was standing in front of an old wooden shed set back in the pines. It was a rickety building that looked like the slightest wind might cave it in. There were no windows, just two large doors on the front secured by an old rusty hasp, and the roof was carpeted with a thick layer of pumpkin-colored pine needles.

"What are you doing?" she asked.

He didn't reply as he wrenched back the hasp and pulled the door open. Then he grabbed the other door and did the same. For several seconds he just stood there, looking into the shed, staring at the curious collection of tools, spare tires, and broken lawn furniture. The narrow path down the center was blocked by an old barbeque grill that was missing a wheel.

"What are you looking for?" she asked.

Again, he said nothing as he stepped into the shed and disappeared into the shadows. When he came out moments later, he was carrying a bike on his shoulder. It was the one his uncle bought him—a mountain bike with all-terrain tires.

Gina raised both hands in the air. "Stop right there."

He propped the bike up against the shed door and gave each tire a squeeze.

"I mean it," she said. "I know what you're thinking."

He went back into the shed and came out seconds later carrying a tire pump.

"You're making a huge mistake," she said.

One by one he inflated each of the tires.

"Someone is going to see you."

When the tires were rock hard he set the pump down and went back into the shed.

"They'll take your picture," she shouted.

From inside the shed she heard a loud crash, and seconds later he appeared with his uncle's mountain bike, which was similar to his but larger. He leaned it up against the other shed door and checked the tires. They were fine.

Gina crossed her arms. "Go ahead, ignore me," she said. "I'm not going anywhere."

He went back into the shed for a third time and came out with an old cloth rag.

"I mean it," she said.

He wiped down the seats and the handlebars of both bikes. When he was done, he walked straight past her and into the house.

She stood her ground.

A minute later he came back with his backpack slung over his shoulder. She stood and watched as he took his old bike by the handlebars and walked it away from the door.

"So, you're really going to do this," she said, like he had lost his mind

He climbed on the bike and pedaled around the yard in a wide loop.

"How are you going to work the microfilm machine?" she called out. "You don't know how to use it."

He was almost to the driveway when he heard her shout, "All right, all right. I'll go!"

He stopped riding and looked back over his shoulder. "Come on then."

"You expect me to ride that?" she said, pointing to his uncle's bike. He rode back to where she was standing and dismounted.

"Here, you can ride my bike."

She took hold of the handlebars, then looked at him and smirked. "Just remember," she said. "I warned you."

Wynn Barrett sat at his kitchen table reading the photocopy Gina had dropped in the street. When he was done, he set it down and stared out the window, questions racing through his mind. He tapped his finger nervously on the tabletop, then stood up and went outside. The whine of a boat motor out in the cove got his attention and he walked down the path toward the lake to see who it was. When he got close to the shoreline he saw them.

Nathan's father was at the helm. The girl's father was seated next to him. The two women were facing them, sitting on the bench seat at the stern. They were cruising out toward the channel, chatting, pointing, and soaking in the sun. *Where are the kids?* he wondered.

He made his way back up to the house, and when he reached the front steps, he paused to think. Then, he turned around and started down the driveway toward the road.

Gina went first. Nathan followed behind her at a close distance. When they reached the end of the driveway, the road was deserted in both directions.

"Go ahead," Nathan said. "I'll watch the back, you watch the front. If we see any cars coming we yell, okay?"

Gina rolled her eyes. "We yell? What are we trying to do, scare them away?"

"No," he said patiently. "If you hear me yell, you pull off the road and hide in the woods."

"Oh, that'll be fun."

"I have the hats and sunglasses in my backpack if that would make you feel better."

"No, thank you," she shot back. The memory of tripping on the sidewalk when she was getting into the cruiser was still fresh in her mind. "I'll take my chances with the woods," she said under her breath.

Wynn got to the end of his driveway and stopped. In the distance, he saw Nathan and Gina emerge from their driveway and start riding toward him. He stepped back behind a massive pine tree and waited. Moments later the kids rode by. They were on the opposite side of the road and didn't see him, but he heard them.

Every word.

"You have a plan, I take it?" Gina called over her shoulder. As she rode, she kept her eyes glued to the long stretch of road up ahead.

No cars in front.

"A plan for what?" he called back. He was keeping his distance and checking over his shoulder every few seconds.

No cars in back.

"For getting into the library without anyone seeing us," she yelled.

"Oh, right," he said.

"Well?" she shouted.

"We'll figure it out when we get there."

Wynn waited until they were a good distance down the road and then stepped out from behind the tree. "Well, how do you like that?" he said. "A gorgeous day and they're going to the library— again."

This was a good sign.

He walked out to the street and started walking toward town. With any luck, someone would drive by and offer him a ride.

Nathan and Gina rode for the next ten minutes without seeing a single car. As Gina was approaching the main intersection, she crossed to the other side of the street. At the light, they'd turn left and follow Main Street to the library, two blocks down on the right. She was riding past the tall hedge of forsythia bushes that lined the park when she heard Nathan shout.

"GINA, STOP!"

She slowed to a stop and turned around just as he pulled up next to her. He dismounted and looked over at the intersection, fifty feet away, then moved in front of her, blocking her view with his body.

"What are you doing?" she asked.

"Wait here for a minute."

"Why?"

"Look over my shoulder," he said.

There was something about his voice. He wasn't joking around. It was all over his face, too. Very slowly, she stood up off the bike seat and peered over his shoulder. The intersection was quiet, except for a few vehicles that were passing by from left to right, headed downtown. "Yeah?" she said.

She eyed the short line of cars waiting for the light to change. "Yellow sports car, a big blue pickup truck, and, wait a minute, is that...?"

The third vehicle in line was the Channel 5 News van. It was mostly hidden by the pickup truck, but there was no mistaking the small satellite dish folded flat on the roof, or the red lettering on the side.

She ducked down behind him and said, "What do we do now?"

Nathan was busy sizing up their options and didn't reply. Because the pickup truck was blocking the van, he had no idea if they'd been spotted. Even if they had been seen, did the driver know who they were? Maybe yes, maybe no. It was a risk they couldn't take.

There was something else to consider as well. When the light changed, the cars in line would turn left, turn right, or come straight through the intersection, directly at them. For the time being, however, the news van was blocked in by the truck in front of it and the cars behind it. And that gave him an idea. It was crazy, but they had no choice. All the other options would end badly.

He took a deep breath and pushed his hair back behind his ear. "All right," he said. "Here's what we're going to do."

"Uh, Nathan?"

"What?"

"The light just turned green."

15

The Back Way

"Let's go!" Nathan yelled. He jumped on the bike and pedaled toward the intersection.

"Nathan, wait, what are we doing?" Gina shouted as she raced to catch up with him.

At the traffic light, the yellow sports car's emergency flashers were on and the driver was out of the vehicle. Everyone behind him had no choice but to sit and wait.

"Follow me," Nathan shouted over his shoulder. He rode toward the intersection, pedaling as fast as he could, but he didn't turn left toward the library—he went straight across onto Lake Street.

Past the yellow sports car.

Past the blue pickup truck.

Past the news van.

The words *Channel 5 News* flashed bright red in the corner of his eye as he flew past. At the same time the driver looked over and pointed. And he wasn't alone. There was a woman in the passenger seat. When she saw them ride by, she stuck her head out the window and shouted for them to stop.

Nathan ignored her and sped down the sidewalk. There was no turning back now. Part one of his plan was fully underway. Now it was time for part two. Up ahead was Emerald Street, a road he remembered from years ago when he was riding with his uncle. If memory served him right, it would provide the perfect escape route.

He pulled up to the corner and stopped to look back. The yellow sports car still hadn't moved. The driver of the blue pickup truck had grown impatient and was inching his way around it.

"Where are we going?" Gina called out as she approached.

"To the library, just like we planned."

She jammed on her brakes and came to a stop next to him. She was breathing hard and her hair was a mess. "The library is that way," she said, pointing back toward the traffic light.

"I know that, but we have to lose them first," he said, pointing at the news van.

Gina looked back over her shoulder. The woman in the van had also grown tired of waiting. She had gotten out and was hurrying down the sidewalk toward them. Gina recognized her at once. "Uh, Nathan?" she said, "You'd better think of something fast. That's Catharine Chase."

"Who?"

"The woman on the evening news? The one that breaks the really *big* news stories?"

"Is that a fact?" he said, unimpressed. "Let's see her try and figure

184

this out."

"Why? What are you going to do?"

"*We* are going to split up."

"Split up?" Gina said, confused.

"Trust me," he said. He nodded toward the far end of Emerald Street. "You go that way. We'll meet at the back door of the library." Before she could object, he took off down Lake Street.

"Wait! How do I get there?" she yelled.

"Take the back way," he shouted over his shoulder.

Catharine Chase was running now. "Young lady," she called out. "Wait right there. I want to ask you some questions." Behind her, the news van had followed the blue pickup truck around the yellow sports car and was circling back.

Gina turned down Emerald Street and pumped the pedals as hard as she could. As she picked up speed, she heard a vehicle come to a screeching stop back at the corner.

Nathan heard it too, and looked back over his shoulder. The van was sitting in the road across from Emerald Street. The driver shouted something at Catharine Chase.

She shouted something back.

He pointed at Nathan.

She pointed at Gina.

This went on for several seconds.

"Are you serious?" Nathan groaned. He stopped pedaling and twisted around in the seat, waving his arms in the air. "Hey! I'm right here. Come and get me."

Gina heard the shouting and pedaled faster. She flew past homes with well-manicured lawns, brightly painted mailboxes, and giant flower pots overflowing with color. Soon she came to an old stone bridge, cradled on both sides of the road by a thick forest of trees. As she rode over the bridge, she could hear the gurgle of water passing below.

After that, the road went straight for a short distance and then forked to the left and right. Without thinking she went to the left, keeping her eyes peeled for the back way to the library. "Take the back way," she crabbed, repeating Nathan's cryptic instruction. *And which back way would that be?*

She checked over her shoulder and saw no one chasing her. Still, she kept up her speed, following the road as it made a long sweeping turn to the right. Up ahead she saw the stone bridge again. "Oh, this is just great, Nathan!" she yelled. "I'm going in a circle!"

Catharine Chase finally gave in and ran across the street. Nathan's heart began to pound as he watched her climb into the van.

"Yeah, that's it," he said, watching to see if they'd take the bait. Which he assumed they would. After all, he was just a kid on a bike. They had a gas-powered automobile. It was no contest.

He was right there, in full view.

Three hundred feet away.

Maybe less.

Catharine slammed the door and said something to the driver. He immediately yanked on the steering wheel and hit the gas. But he didn't take the bait—he ignored Nathan completely and sped down Emerald Street.

In the blink of an eye, the van was gone from sight. Nathan

balled his fist and pounded on the handlebars. "No," he shouted, "you were supposed to follow *me*."

Suddenly, he feared the worst.

Why did they choose to follow Gina?

Did she fall down?

Is she lying in the middle of the road? Hurt and bleeding?

He had to go find her. Reporters or no reporters, he had to make sure she was all right.

Gina started back up the street when she saw the news van coming straight at her. At the same time, the driver saw her and pointed. Catharine Chase sat forward, grinning, and yelled at him to speed up.

With the van bearing down on her, Gina frantically scanned both sides of the street. All she saw were the same driveways, the same mailboxes, and the same flower pots she'd already passed. She was almost to the stone bridge when she spotted two steel posts on the right. They were painted bright yellow, and set just far enough apart to allow a pedestrian to pass through.

Or someone riding a bike.

Thinking quickly, she cut across the road and jumped the curb. The bike shot into the air and flew between the posts as the van came to a screeching stop on the bridge.

Nathan rode back to the corner of Emerald Street, but Gina was nowhere in sight. Halfway down the street he saw the news van stopped next to the old stone bridge. Catharine Chase and the driver had gotten out and were leaning over the side, staring down at the brook. Suddenly, they both turned and rushed back to the van. When Nathan saw that, he turned the bike around and began pedaling again.

Seconds later, the van came to a stop at the corner of Emerald Street. The driver was about to turn right when Catharine Chase looked left and saw Nathan speeding toward the sharp corner at the far end of the street. She barked something at the driver, who cranked the wheel to the left and stepped on the gas just as Nathan rounded the corner and disappeared from sight.

Gina held her breath, gripping the handlebars with all her strength, as the bike slammed down on a narrow path of hard clay. The ground fell away down a gentle hill and she followed it for a short distance before stopping to catch her breath. She was in a sparsely wooded forest. To her left was the brook. The water gushed and bubbled through a maze of moss-covered rocks, and the banks on both sides were lined with skunk cabbage and ostrich ferns. To her right, through the trees, she saw the backyard of a house where two kids were playing on a swing set, their shrieks of laughter echoing into the forest.

She looked at the path up ahead. It wound through the woods and followed the twists and turns of the brook. "This is some great plan you cooked up, Nathan," she called out. "A real beauty." *Just wait 'til I see you again.*

The kids on the swing set stopped playing and looked over.

"What did you say?" one of them yelled.

Gina was about to yell back when she heard a scuffling sound off to her left. She turned and looked down at the brook, and saw a small patch of ferns swaying back and forth. Something was scurrying between them—something big—and it was coming straight toward her. "Now what?" she said.

In a panic, she fumbled with the pedal, her foot slipping off it once, twice, and then a third time. Five feet away, the ferns bent and swayed, punctuated by a sharp chattering sound. As it grew closer, she finally managed to stand on the pedal and launch the bike down the path.

Nathan heard the roar of an engine. He was pedaling as fast as he could and didn't turn to see who it was. He didn't have to. It was the news van, he was sure of it. They were coming after *him* now. "Took you long enough," he shouted as he came out of the turn. The road began a long straight descent down to the lake, and he had just started down the hill when the news van came screaming around the corner. The whine of the engine grew louder as it closed in on him, and he knew it was only a matter of seconds before they caught up with him.

He shifted gears and the bike shot forward.

"Getting closer," he muttered.

He scanned the sidewalk up ahead.

"Any second now."

Then he saw the sign post.

"Almost there."

Next to the sign was the opening of a narrow path.

"Bingo."

The final part of his plan.

The van had just pulled even with him when he squeezed the

rear brake lever as hard as he could. The back tire chirped as it bit into the tar and the news van shot past him. He saw the brake lights flare as he turned down the West Shore Bike Trail, a long winding path that skirted the southern shore of the lake.

"YES!" he shouted as he coasted down the path. It stretched along a high ridge that looked down at the water. A lone speed boat was racing up the channel, its hull slamming against the chop, the sound like a fist pounding on a hollow metal door. Somewhere nearby a dog was barking. Music was playing.

He ignored all of it and pedaled faster.

Gradually, the trail turned away from the lake and crossed the lower end of Bow Street. He stopped where the trail met the edge of the paved road and eyed the far end of the street. He could see the library building and a steady stream of cars passing by on Main Street. Other than that, the street was clear. No Gina.

He rode up Bow Street, keeping a sharp eye out for any unwanted surprises—like the news van. If it suddenly appeared, his only option would be to turn quickly and ride across one of the front yards on his left. From there he could hide behind one of the houses or double back. Luckily, he made it all the way up the street without seeing anyone, or anyone seeing him. He had just turned into the library parking lot when shouted out, "YES!"

His old bike was parked in the metal rack next to the building.

Ernie Bell had the day off. As he walked out of the grocery store, a bag of groceries in each hand, he stopped and studied the sky overhead. Bright blue and not a cloud in sight. A perfect day for fishing. He walked to his Jeep and loaded the groceries in the back. Then, as he pulled out of the parking spot, he worked out his plan for the day. "Go back home, drop off the groceries..." He paused at the exit and checked the oncoming traffic. "Grab my fishing gear, maybe head up to..."

His words fell off when he looked to his right and saw a battered old station wagon sitting at the corner of Bow Street. Wynn Barrett had just climbed out and was saying something to the driver through the open window.

"Well, well, what do you know," Bell muttered. "Wynn Barrett, in the flesh." He double checked the traffic and then jammed his foot on the gas, the jeep's engine emitting a loud roar as Bell sped out of the exit onto Main Street. As he approached the library, the station wagon chugged past him, trailing a cloud of exhaust. The driver waved but Bell didn't notice; his eyes were surveying the sidewalk up ahead.

When he reached Bow Street, he turned in and quickly pulled to the curb. "You've got to be kidding me," he shouted, scanning the area. Wynn Barrett was nowhere to be seen. He exhaled loudly and then chirped the tires on the pavement as he sped down the street.

Nathan stashed his uncle's bike in the rack and did a quick scan of the area. "Gina?" he called out, keeping his voice low. She had to be hiding in the bushes nearby, waiting for him. At least, that was the plan.

When there was no reply, he called out again, a little louder. "GINA!"

Still no answer.

He went to the corner of the building and peeked around the

side. Nothing. "Where are you?" he grumbled, turning back to the bike rack. He stood there for a moment, trying to sort it out, and that's when his eyes locked on the back door.

No way.

He walked over to the door and paused.

She wouldn't.

He took a deep breath and let it out.

There's only one way to find out.

He pulled the door open and slipped inside.

Wynn Barrett was hiding in the bushes next to the library. When he'd seen Bell earlier, thundering out of the grocery store parking lot, he made a beeline for the bushes. Bell was looking for him, that much was obvious. Why else would be turn onto Bow Street and stop at the curb?

He waited and watched as Bell sat there momentarily, surveying the street, then raced away. Only then did he ease out of the bushes. To his left, he saw Bell continue down Bow Street and turn left on Pleasant Street, which ran parallel to Main Street. But seconds later, when Bell's jeep reappeared, he quickly ducked back into the bushes.

Nathan stepped through the back door and paused. The small room with the coat rack was empty. *So far so good.* He hurried over to the stairs and eased his way up to the first floor, all the while watching for any sign of Jeffrey. When he reached the top step, he stopped and peeked around the corner. *All clear.*

The library was eerily quiet as he made his way along the back wall, stopping at the end of each bookcase.

Listening.

Watching.

As he came to the last bookcase, he heard a voice.

"Oh, there you are."

A jolt of fear shot through his body and he spun around to find the librarian standing directly behind him. Cradled in her left arm was a short stack of books.

"Your friend is in the Reference Room," she said.

"Excuse me?" he asked.

"She said you'd be along shortly."

"She did?" *Why in the world would she do that?*

The librarian nodded and went on with her business. Nathan's heart was still racing as he hurried to the Reference Room. When he got there, he found Gina sitting at the table in the back corner. Her eyes were glued to the microfilm machine.

"What are you doing?" he demanded, as he walked toward her.

"I'm working. What does it look like?"

On the screen he saw a page from *The Lakes Region Gazette.*

"I thought we were going to meet at the back of the building."

"So did I, but when I got here you were nowhere to be found. What took you so long?"

"Well, let's see," he said, "I had someone chasing me…"

"So did I," she shot back. "And by the way, thanks for telling me about the path by the river."

"You mean the brook."

She threw him a nasty look. *DO NOT start with me!*

"What's that face?" he said. "You found the path. It's a shortcut to Bow Street. You got here without being followed. What's the problem?"

She sighed and shook her head in frustration. *Unbelievable.*

"Did you see Jeffrey anywhere?" he asked, changing the subject.

"He's off today," she said, her eyes returning to the screen. She couldn't find what she was looking for and it was starting to annoy her, so she stopped advancing the reel and rewound it.

"Off today? How do you know that?"

"The librarian told me," she said. "Now, if you don't mind, I'm kind of busy."

"With what?"

"This," she replied, picking up a sheet of paper off the table.

"What is it?"

"The rest of the story about the storm."

"Ah," he said, in a cryptic voice. "The mysterious Page 10."

She gave him a look. *Not funny.*

He took the paper from her and read it aloud.

CRAWFORD

(CONT. FROM PREV. PAGE)

our progress in the case will be severely affected. We will continue, despite the physical challenges, to see this matter to it's swift conclusion. Our intent is to find those responsible and bring them to justice. Local authorities have assured us that the help we need will be forthcoming in the next few days."

When he was finished reading, he continued to look at it without speaking.

"What are you doing?" Gina asked.

"Looking for the part that was so important," he replied.

"It's right there," she said. "The top line."

"Our progress in the case will be severely affected?" he said, reading directly from the page. "Why is that important?"

"They needed more manpower, but everyone was busy helping victims of the tornado," she explained. "There was no one to help with the investigation."

"Yeah? So?"

"So, whoever took the boxcar had more time than we first thought. Maybe they really did take it apart."

He looked at her and frowned. *Really? This again?*

"Hey, I'm just saying…"

"I told you," he said. "It didn't happen. Besides, it says right here that help was on the way."

"That's right," she countered. "That's what it says… but…"

"But what?"

"But nothing," she said, flinging her hands in the air.

"Huh?"

"There's nothing here," she exclaimed, gesturing toward the screen.

"What are you talking about?"

"There's not another word about the missing boxcar, or about the investigation, or the search that followed."

"Are you sure you have the right reel?"

She turned and stared at him. *What am I, an idiot?*

"All right, relax," he told her. "I'll tell you where to look."

He walked over to the bookcase beneath the window and got the index for 1870. He did a quick check of the listings under Railroad

Stories, then slowly looked up at her, baffled.

"What?" she asked.

"There aren't any more listings for *The Lakes Region Gazette* after July 7th."

"Yeah, I know. I *told you* that."

"Yes, you did," he replied. "But what I'm saying is, there are no more listings for the paper at all."

"I don't understand," she said.

"Neither do I."

He stood there for a moment, thinking. Then he said, "Follow me."

They walked out to the front desk, where the librarian was busy inspecting a small pile of books. She looked up as they approached the counter. "Did you have a question?" she asked.

"Yes," Nathan said. "We can't find any newspaper stories from *The Lakes Region Gazette* after July, 1870."

She looked past him, thinking. "That sounds right," she said. "The building that housed the newspaper was destroyed by a terrible fire that year. They never rebuilt it."

"Oh," Nathan said. Then, with a curious look, "Why didn't they rebuild it?"

"Because the owner of the paper was killed in the fire."

"So, no more *Lakes Region Gazette*," Gina said.

"That's right," the librarian replied.

Gina's body sagged. *Great.*

"But," the librarian said, "another paper began printing the very next year."

Gina perked up. "Another paper?"

"Yes, it was called *The Lakes Courier*."

They thanked the librarian and hurried back to the Reference Room. Nathan searched the shelf and found indexes for *The Lakes Courier* bunched together at the very end of the shelf. He chose the one with the earliest date: 1871.

"Okay," he said, as he checked the stories and their issue dates. "It looks like the paper didn't start printing until the late spring."

"Do you see anything about the investigation?"

"Hold on," he said. He quickly read each listing and then flipped to the next page. A few seconds later, he flipped back to the first page and checked it again. Then he closed the index and stood there staring at it in his hands.

"What's the matter?" Gina asked.

"There's nothing here," he said.

She snapped her fingers and then waved him closer. "Come here, let me see it."

He walked over and handed it to her, then waited patiently as she scoured the listings on the first page.

Then the second.

Then the third.

"I don't believe it," she said. "There's not a word about the boxcar or the investigation." She closed the index and tossed it on the table, shaking her head in disbelief. "Some newspaper," she said.

"What's not to believe?" he said. "The *Courier* didn't start printing until almost a year after the boxcar vanished. That's a long time."

"What are you saying?"

"They searched the whole area. They found nothing. They stopped."

He picked up the index and stared at it for several seconds, then shook his head.

"End of story."

16

Ohio

Ernie Bell drove back up Bow Street, scanning both sides of the street. When he reached the corner, he turned onto Main Street and cruised past the library. There was no one on the sidewalk. There was no one anywhere. "This isn't happening again," he muttered, tightening his grip on the steering wheel.

Just past the library, he turned right onto Arch Street and circled the block.

Four streets.

One giant rectangle.

And no sign of Wynn Barrett.

Wynn watched through the bushes as Bell's Jeep turned onto Main Street. When it was gone from sight, he climbed out of the bushes and hurried down the sidewalk. He eyed the two bikes in the rack as he approached the back door, then quickly ducked inside.

Walking directly and with purpose, he made his way up the stairs. When he reached the first floor, he eased along the back wall a short way and then stopped. He could hear voices coming from the far end of the building. Very faint, but definitely kid voices. He continued to the corner and stopped again, this time hiding behind a tall bookcase. Ten feet away was the arched entrance to the Reference Room. The voices he heard belonged to Nathan and Gina.

He was sure of it.

The Reference Room, he thought. *Of course.*

Gina was still stewing as she rewound the microfilm. "The boxcar vanishes, there's this big investigation, a massive storm hits and tears the town apart." She removed the reel and tucked it back in the metal canister. "And then what?"

She returned the canister to its drawer and pushed the metal cabinet door shut. "Did more help show up?" she asked on her way back to the table. "Did they find any new clues?"

"Who knows?" Nathan said as he walked over to the bookcase beneath the window.

"I want to know," she exclaimed, pounding her fist on the table. "We need to know what happened."

Nathan slid the index back onto the shelf and paused. He couldn't remember the last time he'd seen her so worked up. It might have been the time he glued her puzzle book shut. Or maybe the time he put the dead fly in her—

"Nathan!" she snapped.

"Huh?"

"I asked you a question."

"I'm sorry, what was it?"

She let out an exasperated breath. "I said... What. Do. We. Do. Now?"

He walked back over to the table and pulled the old book out of his backpack. "We find out about this," he said, showing her the small newspaper clipping.

"Oh joy, the bookmark," she huffed.

"It's not a bookmark. You said it yourself, it's an obituary."

"Fine. The obituary bookmark." *Whatever.*

He tucked it back in the book and said, "Come on, let's go check it out."

"Check it out? Where?"

He shoved the book back in his pack and left it on the table. He was halfway across the room, headed for the entryway, when she jumped up out of the chair.

"Hey, slow down."

The librarian was talking on the phone when Nathan got to the front counter. Gina came up behind him just as she was finishing the call. "Quit ditching me," she whispered.

"I didn't ditch you," he said. "You walk slow."

Before she could respond, the librarian came over to the counter. "Yes?"

"I have a question," Nathan said. "Let's say you want to find out about someone who died."

"Did this person live around here?" the librarian asked.

"Uh, we're not sure, but we know where he died, sort of."

"*Where* he died?" the librarian asked, looking confused.

"Let me handle this," Gina said, then stepped around him.

He fought back a smile. *She's back.*

"It was a hospital called St. Clara's Infirmary," Gina explained.

"St. Clara's," the librarian repeated. "I've never heard of it." She went to the computer and typed in St. Clara's Infirmary. Seconds later, a list appeared on the screen. "Okay," she said, scanning the names. "There's a St. Clara's in Gainesville, Florida, one in San Francisco, another in Cleveland Heights—"

"That's it," Gina blurted out.

The librarian reached for a piece of scrap paper and jotted down the name and address.

Nathan gave Gina a nudge. *Nice going.*

She looked back and frowned. *Please…that was easy.*

"Now," the librarian said, "do you know when this person died?"

"Uh," Nathan said, looking over at Gina, "not exactly."

"We know it was in the 1800s," Gina said.

"Very good," the librarian said. "Do you have a name?"

"Yes, we do."

When Ernie turned onto Bow Street, he pulled over to the curb. He thought back to when he saw Barrett climbing out of the station wagon on the corner. He took his eyes off him for no more than ten seconds. Where could the old man possibly go in that short amount of time? He wasn't that fast.

He eyed the far corner of Main Street and Bow, where the station wagon had stopped. Then he shifted his gaze to the bushes along the side of the library, up ahead on the right. "The bushes," he muttered.

Why didn't I think of that before?

He pulled his Jeep up to the side of the library and got out. After a quick visual inspection of the area in front of the bushes, he pushed his way through a knot of branches and studied the ground next to the building. The dirt was a mishmash of footprints. Mostly he saw small, kid- sized prints. He moved along the base of the building, and that's when he found another set.

Larger.

Not made by a kid.

"Brooten. B–r–o–o–t–e–n?" the librarian said.

"Yes," Nathan replied.

"First name?"

"William."

"Thank you," the librarian said, quickly typing it in.

Curious, Nathan leaned across the counter, straining to see what she was doing. "What is that?" he asked.

"I'm doing what they call an inter-library loan."

"A what?"

"An inter-library loan. I send an email to the library in Cleveland, Ohio, asking for a copy of the original obituary for William Brooten. The library tracks it down and sends me back either a fax or an email."

"How long does it take?"

"Not that long," the librarian replied. "We should hear something within an hour or two. If you're still here, I'll come find you. Or, you can come back another time. I'll have it here at the counter."

Nathan looked up at the wall clock. It was just after 11 o'clock.

By his calculation, their parents were somewhere at the far end of the lake. "We'll wait," he said.

They went back to Reference Room and sat down at the table.

"So we're just going to sit here?" Gina asked.

"Uh… *yeah*," Nathan said. *Duh.*

"You can't be serious," she moaned.

"Relax, will you? The librarian said it wouldn't be long."

"It better not be," she warned. "You know what's going to happen if our parents get back before we do. Or did you forget what your mom said?"

"Don't worry," he said calmly. "They're at the opposite end of the lake right now. Knowing my parents, they'll stop somewhere to eat lunch."

Gina gave him a look, eyebrows raised. *You'd better be right.*

"Do you want to check out some more papers? You know, see if there's anything we missed?"

"No thanks, I've seen all there is. Besides, what we really need to see doesn't exist because the stories were never written." She shook her head in disgust. *There had to be a fire, right?*

A minute passed and neither of them spoke. Nathan began tapping his foot on the floor. Another minute passed. He looked around the room. That's when his eyes locked on an odd-looking cabinet in the corner. It was drab green and very short, no more than three feet tall and at least four feet wide. There were a series of drawers on the front, each one only a few inches high. Hardly deep enough to hold anything of interest. Or so he thought. "Look at that," he said.

"Look at what?" Gina asked.

"That cabinet over there," he said, pointing.

She made a face, then turned and looked. "What about it?"

"It's funny looking, don't you think?"

"Not really."

"I wonder what they use it for?"

"Well, here's an idea. Why don't you go over and see?"

"You're no fun," he said as he got up from the chair.

She ignored his comment and eyed the low bookcases spread throughout the room. "I might as well read something, since we're *stuck* here waiting." She got up and walked over to the nearest bookcase. *I wonder if they have any puzzle books.*

Nathan stood in front of the cabinet and eyed it from top to bottom. There were five drawers in all, each labeled with a small, handwritten sticker. The top one read State, followed by County, Town, Building, and Flood. He moved closer and pulled open the top drawer. "Whoa," he exclaimed.

The drawer was filled with state maps in various sizes, new and old, printed on different colors of paper. He looked through the stack, examining each map briefly, and then slid the drawer shut. There was nothing there he hadn't seen before.

In the second drawer, he found New Hampshire maps broken down by county. The edges on some were torn and uneven, patched with clear tape that had yellowed over time. He closed the drawer and eyed each of the handwritten stickers. "I get it," he said, "State is for state maps, county is for county maps." His heart began to race as he opened the third drawer—the one labeled Town. In it, he found maps of Crawford, printed in color and in black and white.

Many were old and wrinkled, and most had long creases in the paper where they had been folded and unfolded repeatedly over the years. He examined the print date of each one, but the oldest one he found was from 1960.

He moved on to the fourth drawer, where he found a collection of detailed plans for various old buildings in town. The moment he saw them, his mind flashed back to the first book from his grandfather's bookcase. The things it did, where it led him, and what he and Gina found. They were images that would reside in his memory forever.

He opened the last drawer and found a handful of aerial maps showing different flood zones. He looked at them briefly and then pushed the drawer shut when it jammed. He pushed harder but it wouldn't budge. "Are you kidding me?" he groaned, pulling and pushing to try and free it up.

He was still wrestling with it when it suddenly broke free, sending him tumbling backwards. In the process, the drawer flew out of his hands and crashed to the floor.

"Hey, take it easy," Gina said. "Are you trying to break it?"

"Too late," he mumbled as he climbed to his feet. He collected the maps that were scattered across the floor and put them back in the drawer, then picked up the whole thing and lined it up with the drawer slides. That's when he saw something inside the cabinet. It was on the very bottom, only visible by the thin stream of light that broke through the narrow opening.

He set the drawer aside and reached in to get it. When he first took hold of it, it felt like a pile of papers or a stuffed envelope. But when he pulled it out into the light, he saw that it was a large document that had been folded into a neat square. The paper was stiff and made a faint creaking sound as he carefully opened it to its full size. What he saw made him stop and stare.

It was a detailed map of the entire area, from Concord to the Lakes Region. The ink was faded but still readable, and his eyes were drawn to the area surrounding the town of Crawford.

Something was different.

Wynn peeked around the bookcase, straining to hear. But there was nothing. No talking. No hum of the microfilm machine. Just silence. Very slowly, he stepped around the end of the bookcase and inched his way forward until he was a foot away from the entrance. From there, he could see Gina kneeling in front of a bookcase, examining the books on the middle shelf. Nathan was over in the far corner, rummaging through the map cabinet. *What are they looking for?*

"Well, what do you know," Gina grumbled, when she came to the end of the shelf. "These books are just as boring as the ones on the first shelf. Would it kill them to keep a few puzzle books around?" She moved to the third shelf when she noticed that the room had gone completely silent. The only sound to be heard was the passing of cars outside on Main Street.

"Nathan?" she called out softly.

There was no answer.

She pushed herself up off the floor and looked around the room.

Nathan was over in the corner, staring at something on top of the metal cabinet. "Hey," she called out.

He didn't move.

"Nathan," she called out, a little louder.

Again, no response.

Then, without turning around, he raised his hand in the air and motioned to her. His gesture was frantic, his meaning clear.

Come over here.

Hurry.

17

Ernie Bell

Ernie Bell climbed out of the bushes and walked back to his Jeep. He hated being fooled. Once was bad enough. Twice was simply unacceptable. Day off or no day off, he had to figure this out or it would just keep eating at him.

He tapped his finger impatiently on the gear shift as he peered through the windshield. Main Street was dead ahead. To the left was a row of hedges that lined the corner lot. To the right was the library. "Wait a minute," he muttered.

He backed down the street and into the library parking lot. With the nose of his Jeep facing the building, he scanned the tall windows that lined the first floor, then the basement level. That's when he noticed the bikes in the rack next to the door.

Nathan was still hunched over the map when Gina walked up

behind him. "You know, you've been ignoring me a lot lately," she said.

"Look at this," he said, moving aside so she could see the map.

"See? You just did it again."

He pointed to the map. "Look."

She stared at him for another few seconds and then glanced down at the map. She saw the town name and the outline of the lake, but that was not what held her attention. The whole area surrounding Crawford was dotted with clusters of black dots and small X's.

"What are all those markings?" she asked.

"I'm not sure," he said slowly.

His voice was different, and when she looked up, she saw a vacant expression on his face.

"What's wrong with you?" she asked.

He stood there for several seconds without speaking, sorting through the images that were streaming through his memory. "There," he said, tapping his finger on the map.

"Yeah? What about it?"

"That's where we were."

"What are you talking about?"

"Yesterday," he said.

"You mean the state park?"

He nodded his head.

"What about it?" she asked.

His eyes remained fixed on the map as he spoke. "When we explored the shoreline, we came to a bridge." He remembered the sound of his footsteps on the wooden planking, and how it echoed across the water.

"Yeah, so what?" she said.

"I stopped halfway across."

The cryptic tone in his voice was starting to creep her out.

"I was looking at the lake," he said softly, "and then I went to the other side and looked down at the river." He paused, seeing it all over again in his mind.

'Yeah?"

"I saw something," he said.

Gina made a face. "What are you mumbling about?"

He explained it all: the slow-moving stream that emerged from the forest, its water the color of tea; the feathery plants swaying gently beneath the surface, as if dancing to a melody only they could hear; the age-old trees that lined both banks, their tired branches sagging over the surface of the water, and the remains of an old wooden structure that hid among their murky shadows.

"I only looked at it for a split second," he told her.

"It could have been anything," she replied.

"That's what I thought, until I saw this map."

"So what do you think it was?"

"The remains of an old railroad trestle."

"A railroad trestle? Why would you think that?"

"Because a set of railroad tracks crossed that river," he said. "Here, see for yourself."

Wynn leaned forward, watching Nathan and Gina huddled over the map cabinet. They were having a serious discussion, but with their backs turned to him he couldn't hear a word they were saying. Whatever it was, it had their full attention. He stepped back from the entryway and rubbed his lower back. After being hunched over for so long, it was starting to ache. Just then, out of the corner of his eye, he saw the librarian at the far end of the building. She had stepped out from behind the front counter and was walking down the main aisle directly toward him.

Gina bent down closer to the map and examined the area that was now the state park. She saw a wide black line that marked the river they crossed, winding its way across the crinkled paper, twisting and turning like the root of a tree. The further it went, the smaller it got, until it was no wider than a human hair. But then she saw another line. It was just a series of dots, so small and so faded that she had to lean even closer to see them. They crossed the river, not far from the edge of the lake. "You think that's a railroad line?"

"Follow it back," he said.

Using the tip of her finger, she traced the dots away from the river. They angled downward and then looped up to the left, where they joined another line. Not dots. These were dashes, in heavy black ink. "Is this what I think it is?"

"The Lakes Region Line," Nathan said.

She considered the dotted line again. "We haven't seen this before, on any map."

"That's right," he replied. "Now follow it the other way."

She traced the dots away from the main line and back across the river. From there they turned away from Jewel Lake and continued for a distance before coming to an end at a small black X. She looked closer and saw something written next to it. "What are these letters?

"That's what I was trying to figure out when you called my name."

"W—M—C?"

"That's what it looks like," he said.

"What does it mean?"

"Who knows?"

"Well," she said, standing up, "it's not important."

"Why do you say that?"

"Look at it. It's nothing. Just a bunch of dots. And this is the first time we've seen it. If it was important, don't you think it would've been on the other maps we looked at?"

"I…guess," he said, not having considered it.

"Besides," she said, tapping her finger on the map, "look where it is." She moved her finger across the map, stopping at a point between Crawford and West Branch. "The boxcar vanished somewhere over here."

"Yeah, you're right," he said.

She gave him a look. *Of course I'm right.*

"Oh well," he said, folding up the map.

Just then the librarian came walking into the room. "It must've been a slow day at the library in Ohio," she said, waving a sheet of paper in the air. "This just came in over the fax."

"Finally," Gina said, hurrying over to the doorway. She took the paper from the librarian, waited until she left the room, then took it over to the table in the corner and sat down.

"What does it say?" Nathan called out, as he went over to join her.

She scanned it briefly, then read it out loud. "William F. Brooten, age 38, died of liver disease at St. Clara's Infirmary in Cleveland, January 11, 1871, surrounded by his family."

"You were right," Nathan said.

"Shhh…let me finish. He was born in Cleveland, May 10, 1832, and is survived by his children, Noah and Victoria Brooten. An avid lover of trains, he worked for several railroad companies throughout his life, starting at the age of fifteen."

She looked over at him briefly, a curious look on her face, then kept reading. "His last job was in New Hampshire, working as a rear brakeman for the New England Central Railroad Company during the famed tornado of 1870."

"Whoa!" Nathan exclaimed.

"Wait," she said, gesturing with her hand for him to be quiet. "His friends and family will lovingly remember him by his nickname, Little Bill."

Nathan leaned on the edge of the table as he sat down next to her. Everything was happening too fast. First the map inside the cabinet, then the faded line of dots that led to something called W.M.C., and now the obituary. "That was no bookmark," he said in a stunned voice. "It was put in the book for a reason."

"Well, it's definitely connected," Gina said. "I mean, it pretty much says here that the guy was around when the boxcar vanished."

"Let me see that," he said, reaching out his hand. "There's something here my grandfather wants me to find. I know there is."

She handed him the paper, and he considered each sentence one by one, reading the key words aloud. "He was 38 when he died. We know St. Clara's Infirmary was in Ohio." He paused for a second. "What's liver disease?"

"It's something you get from drinking too much."

"Oh," he said slowly, then he continued. "His family was there with him. He was born in Cleveland, had two children." He stopped and looked at Gina. "Does any of that sound important?"

She shook her head. "Not really."

He looked down at the paper again, determined. *It's here,* he told himself. *I just have to find it.* "It says he loved trains, worked on several, started when he was fifteen, and his last job was here in New Hampshire, working as a rear brakeman." He stopped again. "What's a rear brakeman?"

"You're asking me?" she said.

"Of course," he replied, like she shouldn't be surprised.

"Why?"

"Because I can never tell what you might know," he said.

She smiled the tiniest of smiles. *Well, yes, of course… I do know a great many things.*

"And it sounds like it might be important," he added.

She looked around the room, eyeing the various bookcases. "There must be a book in here that can tell us what it is."

He checked the clock on the wall and bit the edge of his lip. "That'll take too long," he said. He set the obituary down on the table and stood up. "I have another idea."

She got up and followed him as he walked toward the entryway. "Why don't we just check the indexes?"

"For what?" he said.

"The name Brooten, or Little Bill."

"We could," he said as they walked out of the room, "but let's try this first."

Wynn Barrett couldn't believe his ears. When he heard Gina

utter Little Bill's name, his jaw fell open. *How could they possibly know that name?* He hurried after them, moving along the back wall of the building, hoping to hear more. Through the shelves of the tall bookcases to his right, he saw them turn and walk to the front counter. After that, their voices faded away, and all he could do was watch, and wonder.

"Back again?" the librarian asked, smiling, when they reached the front counter.

"Could you look something up for us on the computer?" Nathan asked. Time was growing short, and they didn't have time for idle chit chat.

"Why certainly," the librarian replied. "What is it you're looking for?"

Nathan gave her the basics: rear brakeman and 1800s train, then watched as she went over to the computer and keyed in a search. Thirty seconds later, she had the information.

"Okay, here we go," she said. "A rear brakeman is part of the train crew and rides on the caboose. He has a wide range of jobs, which includes braking, to help slow down the train, inspecting different parts of the train, like the couplings between cars."

Nathan and Gina exchanged a look of shock.

"He operates the railroad track switches, and sends signals to the conductor by hand or by flag."

They looked at each other again.

"He also watches the train as it moves along."

"Wait," Gina said. "He watches the train?"

"Yes," the librarian said, reading further. "Sometimes from the sides of the caboose, other times from the cupola." Before they could ask, she said, "That's the structure on top of the caboose."

Nathan looked down at the counter, too stunned to speak. Now he knew why the obituary was in the book, and why his grandfather wanted him to find it. One tiny little scrap of paper. At first glance forgettable, but possibly the most important clue of all.

"Is there anything else you'd like to know?" the librarian asked.

When Nathan didn't answer, Gina said, "Uh, no, that's exactly what we were looking for. Thank you."

She eased Nathan away from the counter and they went back to the Reference Room. The whole way back, Nathan didn't utter a word. Thoughts of Bill Brooten and his obituary were racing through his mind, stirring up a whole new slate of questions.

As Wynn watched them talking at the front counter, he was overcome with questions of his own. Where did they get Bill Brooten's name? How much did they know about him? Did they know what he did? He shook his head in amazement. The news stories he'd seen on TV were right. These two kids were uncanny. He watched them leave the front counter and go back to the Reference Room. After they passed by, he retraced his steps along the back wall, passing through the wide beams of sunlight that streamed in through the full-length windows, angling downward onto the carpet like giant trusses holding up the wall.

Ernie Bell sat in his Jeep, eyeing the two bikes. One was clearly an adult bike and the other was for a kid. But what parent would be at the library with their child when school was in session? *Unless.*

His thought process was interrupted when he saw someone walk past one of the long windows on the first floor. It happened so fast that he couldn't tell who it was, but when the same person passed the next window, he got a better look. At the third window, he saw all he needed to see.

Wynn Barrett wasn't outside the library.

He was inside.

And so were the kids.

"You know what this means?" Gina said, when they got back to the Reference Room.

Nathan plopped down in the chair next to the microfilm reader. He still hadn't spoken.

"HEY," she said, taking hold of his shoulders and shaking him. "Wake up."

He snapped to and looked up at her. "Sorry," he said. "This whole thing is just—"

"Insane, right?" she blurted out, sitting down in the chair next to him. "Brooten saw something. He had to. He was at the back of the train. He was watching."

Nathan was thinking the exact same thing, but something about it wasn't right.

When she saw the uneasy look on his face, she asked, "What is it?"

This is all wrong," he said.

"What are you talking about?"

"He died six months after the boxcar vanished."

"Yeah?"

"In *Cleveland*," he said.

"That's right," she replied.

"So why did he leave the area?"

Gina thought for a moment. "Maybe he got fired."

"Fired? Why? Because he was involved in the disappearance of the boxcar?"

"It's possible," she replied.

"No. If that was the case, they would've solved the mystery and he never would've gone to Cleveland. He would've died. Here. In jail."

"Oh, right," she said. *Why didn't I think of that?*

He sat up in the chair and looked at the obituary again. For several long seconds, his eyes were glued to one sentence. Then he looked over at Gina with a knowing smile.

"What is it?" she asked.

"I know exactly what happened."

18

W.M.C

Gina raised both eyebrows. "Excuse me?"

"Think of what we know so far," Nathan said. "Brooten was on the train. He worked at the back, where he could see everything. He didn't report anything unusual during the investigation, or we would have read about it. Right?"

"Right," she said slowly, anxious to see where he was taking this.

"Then, after the boxcar vanishes, he leaves town and dies six months later of liver disease."

She suddenly realized what he was driving at. "You're saying he *didn't* see anything."

Nathan nodded his head. *Correct.*

"Because he was what? Drunk?"

"Maybe even passed out," he suggested.

She flopped back in the chair and threw her hands in the air.

"Well, that's just great. Whatever happened took place right in front of his eyes. The answer to this whole mystery, and he never saw it."

Nathan looked away momentarily, letting her words hang in the air. A thought flickered in the back of his mind and he quickly pushed it away. It was too farfetched. But then it came back again, and the more he thought about it, the more he couldn't shake it loose. "He didn't see it," he whispered.

"What did you say?"

He turned and looked at her as the thought took hold. "He didn't see it."

"Yes, I know, I just said that."

He jumped up from the chair.

"What is it?" she asked.

"We need the map."

"What map?"

He sprinted over to the corner and grabbed the map from the top of the cabinet. On his way back, he stopped at the bookcase beneath the window.

"What are you doing?" she demanded.

"You'll see." He pulled out the *Lakes Region Gazette* index for 1870 and did a quick check of the listings. "There's nothing here," he mumbled. He closed the index and thought for a moment. "We need to go back earlier."

"Go back? Go back where?" she asked.

"Hold on." He chose an index from 1868 and skimmed the first page. Nothing. He turned the page and there it was: second listing. "Bingo!"

"You're doing it again," she said.

He climbed to his feet and went over to the microfilm cabinet in the corner. When he came back to the table, he handed her a small metal canister.

"Load this," he said.

"What is it?"

"You'll see," he told her, then spread the map out on the table.

Ernie Bell jumped out of his jeep and sprinted across the pavement. When he got to the back door, he looked over at the two bikes, then up at the windows. "I've got you now," he mumbled, then yanked the door open. Once inside, he ran to the stairs and sprinted up them two at a time. At the top step, he paused and peeked around the corner to the left and then to the right. The first floor looked deserted, but he knew Barrett was in the building.

Somewhere.

Gina turned on the microfilm reader. When she had the film loaded, she scrolled forward and said, "Okay, what am I looking for?"

Nathan stood next to her with the open index. "Go to the issue of..." he began, reading down the list of stories. "February third."

She advanced the reel a short way and centered the front page on the screen.

"There!" he said, pointing to the top of the page.

She bent forward and read it aloud.

WHITNEY MINING COMPANY FACING SAFETY VIOLATIONS

"Whitney Mining Company," she said. "W.M.C.?"

"Uh-huh."

She read the first few sentences of the story. "It says two men were injured in a mining accident. Is that important?"

"Hold on," he said, checking the index again. "Go to the issue of March 27th."

"Whatever you say," she mumbled, advancing the reel again. When she reached the March 27th issue, the top headline caught her attention right away.

WHITNEY MINING COMPANY FINES CONTINUE TO MOUNT

She read the first few sentences and then shrugged her shoulders. "Three men died when a tunnel collapsed. What does this have to do with the missing boxcar?"

Nathan considered the story on the screen for a moment and then glanced down at the map on the table. Something was missing. He went back to the index, searching the listings.

"Uh…hello?" she said, rapping her knuckles on the table. "Anybody home?"

"Wait," he said. "Just one more."

She let out a long breath in defeat. "All right, tell me the date."

"May 12th."

She mumbled something under her breath and then pressed the film advance button. The reel jumped forward again, and when she stopped at the issue of May 12th, the headline was impossible to miss. It was set in letters so large they took up the full width of the page.

WHITNEY MINE CLOSED

"Gee, what a surprise," she snorted.

"What does it say?" he asked.

She leaned closer and quickly read through the story. "Well, according to this, after months of safety violations, which had taken the lives of six men, the Whitney Mine was shut down." She turned from the screen and raised both eyebrows. "Gee, you think?"

"Keep going," he said.

"Are you going to tell me—?"

"Please," he said, cutting her off. He checked the clock on the wall again.

They were out of time.

"All *right*," she sighed, turning back to the screen. "The owner of the property, The Whitney Mining Company, paid thousands of dollars in fines and lost valuable employees." She paused for a moment to skim the next paragraph.

"What is it?" he asked.

"Nothing," she replied. "It just says the track leading up to the mine will be taken out of use."

"Taken out of use?"

"Yup," she said.

"Can't be," he said.

"See for yourself," she said, getting up from the chair.

He closed the index and sat down in front of the screen. It was just as Gina had described it. He read it twice, plus another few paragraphs on the next page. When he was done, he sat back in the chair, thinking it through.

Gina let out a heavy breath. "Why are we still talking about this?" she said. "It's a dead end. Excuse, me, *another* dead end."

"What are you talking about?"

"This whole thing. It's been one dead end after another. First it was the investigation. The newspaper building burns and the stories stop. Dead end. Next was the obituary of William Brooten, the man who wasn't watching. Dead end again. And now this. The tracks to nowhere. Another dead end. In baseball, they call that strike three."

Wynn Barrett had his back pressed up against the wall, inches from the entryway. The kids were back at the microfilm reader. He couldn't see them, but he could hear bits and pieces of conversation as they talked about Little Bill. Then something changed. There was a new energy in the room. More talking. Movement. Agreement. Disagreement. *What did they find?* he asked himself. Then, amidst the banter, one phrase jumped out at him: Whitney Mining Company.

He stepped back from the entryway searching his memory from years ago. *Why are they talking about that?* Further up the aisle, he noticed the librarian talking to Ernie Bell, gesturing toward the front counter and then the Reference Room. Wynn ducked out of sight just as the conversation ended and Ernie Bell started walking toward him.

Gina continued to rant as Nathan stared at the newspaper story on the screen. In his mind, he was piecing together the fate of boxcar #5401, but not the way the book told it. If his version was correct, then he and Gina had it wrong from the start. Everyone did. There was just one more piece of the puzzle he had to work out.

"Are we done here?" she asked impatiently.

"We have to go back," he whispered.

"Excuse me?"

He looked up at her and said, "We have to go back."

"Back where?"

He looked over at the clock on the wall. "Oh, crap."

"What's wrong?"

"We have to go," he said, jumping up from the chair. He took the index back to the bookcase under the window, and when he turned around he saw Ernie Bell standing in the entryway.

"Hey guys," Ernie said, leaning into the room. He looked from corner to corner and then turned and looked back down the center aisle. When he turned around again, he had a strange look on his face, one Nathan had seen before. It was the same look his father made when he couldn't find his car keys.

"Are you looking for something?" Nathan asked.

"Not exactly," Ernie said. He gave one more look over his shoulder then walked over to the table. "You guys all right?"

Nathan made a face. "Uh, yeah, why wouldn't we be?"

"No reason," Ernie replied. He glanced at the computer screen and then down at the map on the table. "Don't tell me you guys are still doing homework. I thought you were going to take some time off."

"Actually, we were just leaving," Nathan said. He glared at Gina and nodded at the microfilm reader. *Let's go.*

While she rewound the reel, he folded the map and raced over to the map cabinet in the corner.

Ernie watched them both, overcome with curiosity. *What's happening here?* he asked himself. *Why the big hurry?*

Gina said nothing as she finished rewinding the microfilm and packed it in the canister.

"Okay then," Ernie said at last, as he backed away from the table. "You two be careful."

He left the room, checking to his left and right the whole way.

"What was that all about?" Nathan asked as he came back to the table.

"Beats me," Gina replied. She closed the canister and took it over to the metal cabinet.

Nathan eyed the time again. By now his parents were on their way back from Little Bear. If they made it back first, he'd need a good reason for not being there, something that didn't include being seen by another human being, especially news reporters. He could tell them they took a break from their project and took a bike ride. But where to? The state park? Down one of the old rail trails?

Gina tugged on his shirt. "Hey, are we going or not?"

"Yeah," he mumbled, snapping out of his funk. "We need to hurry."

Wynn Barrett was already long gone. He hid behind the bookcase until he heard Ernie talking to the kids in the Reference Room, then he darted along the back wall and took the back stairs to the lower level. With every step, he tried to sort out what he overheard from the kids.

He pushed through the back door, into the warm afternoon sunlight and stopped. He looked over at Bow Street, trying to decide his next move. Bell was seconds behind him, minutes at the most, but he couldn't leave. Not now. He had to stay close to the kids because they were clearly on to something. But what?

After Ernie left the Reference Room, he did a sweep of the entire main floor from end to end. Barrett had vanished once again. As he walked down the back stairway he realized his error. He had stormed into the library, making himself visible to Barrett, who must have seen him and slipped out. It was a mistake he wouldn't make again, and by the time he got back to his Jeep, he had already planned his next move.

It was time to disappear.

Time to make Barrett believe he'd given up the chase.

He climbed into his Jeep and pulled out of the parking lot. But instead of turning right toward Main Street, he took a left, circled the block, and was gone.

The antique clock in the front foyer was chiming one o'clock when Nathan and Gina left the Reference Room, a grim reminder that time was suddenly working against them.

"We should've left an hour ago," he groaned as they hurried along the back wall of the building.

Gina didn't respond. If she had her way, they never would've come downtown in the first place. But once Nathan had something in his mind, no matter how crazy, there was no stopping him.

"We need to be careful going back," he warned her. "We don't want a repeat of what happened earlier."

Again, she said nothing.

He was almost to the stairs when he heard her call out. "Nathan, STOP!"

He turned around and saw her halfway back down the aisle. She had stopped beside one of the windows and was peeking around the edge of the frame.

"What's wrong?" he asked.

"We're not going anywhere."

19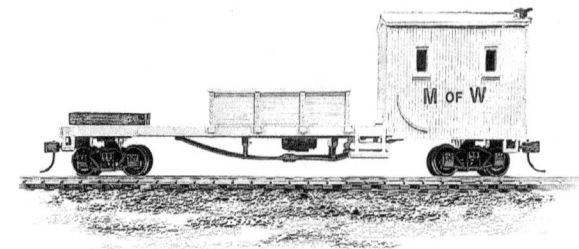

The Park

Nathan rushed back down the aisle and stopped at the first window he came to. "You've *got* to be kidding me," he groaned. The Channel 5 news van was sitting in the parking lot. Catherine Chase and the driver had gotten out and were standing in front of the bike rack.

"Nathan?" Gina called out. There was alarm in her voice. "Any ideas?"

He backed away from the window and looked over at the stairs, seeing the next 60 seconds play out like a slow-motion movie.

They'll come in the back door...

His head swiveled toward the front desk.

And go talk to the librarian...

Then, he looked at the far end of the building.

She'll point them to the Reference Room..

That gave them all the time they needed.

He turned to go just as Catharine Chase and the driver started for the back door.

"Follow me," he told Gina, pointing toward the front desk.

Gina saw him disappear down one of the short aisles and took off after him. When she got to the front counter, he was standing there waiting for her. The librarian was in the far corner, in the kids' section, showing a book to a mother and her young daughter.

"What's the plan?" she asked.

Behind them, the frantic echo of footsteps on the metal stairs leading up from the ground floor.

"This way," he said, turning toward the front foyer.

"Wait," she blurted out. "Where are you going?"

"No time to explain."

Across the street, Ernie Bell watched and waited. Parked in the side lot of the Municipal Building, he had a clear view of the library, the lot next door, and the corner of Bow Street. He had just taken the binoculars out of his personal duty bag when the front door of the library flew open. Nathan came running out and raced down the front steps two at a time. Gina following close behind, trying her best to keep up. When Nathan reached the street, he took an abrupt left, sprinted up the sidewalk a short distance, then ducked into the lilac bushes that lined the front of the building.

"What are they doing?" Ernie mumbled, focusing the binoculars. He checked the front door of the library, the front windows, and the opposite corner of the building.

Still no Wynn Barrett.

"This is nuts!" Gina griped, as she fought through the wall of lilacs. The branches tore at her clothing and scratched her hands and face. Once through, Nathan turned and made his way along the narrow strip of packed gravel between the bushes and the cinderblock foundation.

"WILL YOU *WAIT?*" she yelled.

He turned and motioned with finger to his lips…*quiet!*…then continued on.

When she caught up with him seconds later, she grabbed his arm, stopping him, then bent over and put her hands on her knees. She was out of breath and her hair was tossed about like an old string mop. "Give me a minute," she said between breaths.

"There's no time," he said. "Come on, we have to keep moving."

"Keep moving?" she huffed. "Where are we going?"

"This way," he said, then continued along the front of the building.

She took a deep breath and stood up, just as he disappeared around the corner. "Why did I agree to this?" she muttered.

The side of the building was only slightly better than the front. Instead of dirt, they were now running on dead grass and weeds. Another long hedge of lilacs ran the whole length of the building, but it was set back far enough that Gina didn't have to dodge any branches.

As they neared the back corner of the building, Nathan paused. Several feet away he saw the news van. The engine was cooling in the shade, making a soft ticking sound like a click beetle in the tall grass. He eased up to the corner and peeked around the side. "Okay, let's go," he said.

He started to move when Gina grabbed his arm for the second

time. "Wait," she said. "What's the plan?"

"Just follow me," he replied, "and don't fall behind."

Before she could object, he dashed around the corner and pulled his uncle's bike from the rack.

Wynn Barrett was crouched down behind the neatly trimmed hedgerow that lined the parking lot. The last few minutes had been a whirlwind of activity. First Ernie Bell, then the news van with the woman he remembered from one of the Boston news stations, then the kids, sneaking around the side of the building.

He waited until they rode out of the lot and then climbed to his feet. By the time he reached Bow Street they were gone from sight. He quickly made his way up to Main Street and checked the street in both directions. *Now what?* he asked himself.

From where Ernie Bell was parked, the front of the library was quiet. Nothing happening to the left. Nothing happening to the right. The Bow Street intersection, deserted. He pulled the binoculars away from his face and let out a long breath. It had been several minutes since he saw Nathan and Gina slip into the bushes. Since then, nothing.

"Where did they go?" he asked out loud. Just then he saw them appear at the corner of Bow Street. They rode to the edge of the sidewalk and paused to check the traffic. He lost sight of them when they crossed the street and rode into the park. Not long after that, he saw Wynn Barrett come up Bow Street and stop at the corner. "There you are," he muttered, as he started the Jeep.

Barrett eyed the passing traffic for a moment and then flagged down a ratty old Toyota pickup truck. The red paint was faded and peeling and spotted with patches of rust. The bed was overflowing with an unruly collection of scrap metal. Seconds later, the truck took off down the street, billowing a cloud of steel-gray exhaust.

Bell pulled onto Main Street and saw the pickup in the distance. When it reached the intersection, it turned onto Jewel Lake Road, just as he expected. He slowed and followed the same route, in no particular hurry.

There was plenty of time.

He knew exactly what to do next.

"Will you SLOW DOWN?" Gina shouted. They were racing down the wide path that cut through the middle of the park. Both sides were lined with colorful gardens, each filled with tall flowering bushes and ornamental grasses. When Nathan heard her shout, he pulled up to a park bench and waited for her to catch up.

Beyond the gardens that lined the path, he could hear the sound of traffic on Main Street. The tall bushes blocked the cars from view, and for the moment, he and Gina were as good as invisible. But that was about to change. There was only one way back home—a long stretch of open road where they would be completely out in the open and easy to spot. Especially for someone who was trying to find them. Like a nosy reporter.

As he stood there listening to the passing traffic, he wondered about Catharine Chase. Where was she now? After coming up empty-handed in the library, did she go toward the Marina downtown? Did she drive past the grocery store on Main Street? Or was she sitting just beyond the bushes at the traffic light?

He heard the rattle of his old bike, and seconds later, Gina came to a stop beside him. "That was some plan," she grumbled. She began pulling twigs and leaves from her hair, letting them fall to the ground. "What's next, climbing a tree? No wait, let me guess, we're going to swim across the lake."

He ignored the comment and eyed the path up ahead, trying to remember the layout of the park from years ago. They were almost to the large stone fountain. From there, the main path split in three directions. One path went left. One path went right. One path continued straight.

Gina saw the look of determination on his face. "What are you planning?" she asked, afraid of what crazy stunt he might be cooking up this time.

He ignored the question and climbed back on his uncle's bike, then pushed his hair back behind his ear. "Come on, let's go," he said, then he rode away from the bench.

Gina threw her hands into the air. *I don't believe it! He ditched me again.*

When Nathan reached the fountain, he made quick turn and disappeared down the path to the right, picking up speed as the path unfolded before him. He flew past the play area with the massive climbing structure, the duck pond, and the picnic tables painted the color of lima beans. But it was the images from the library that occupied his thoughts: the Brooten obituary, the outdated map hidden in the base of the map cabinet, and the story from *The Lakes Region Gazette* that set his mind in motion. Together they told a completely different story than the one in the book. But one question remained—a giant piece of the puzzle that could either tie everything together or tear it all completely apart.

In the path up ahead, he saw a set of bright orange cones where the grounds crew had started installing a new raised flower bed. A truckload of dirt had been dumped on the side of the walkway, and right beside it was a pile of railroad ties. The steel bands had been removed, and the ties were strewn about on the ground. He came to an abrupt stop between the orange cones, staring at the mound of dirt, then the railroad ties.

And that's when he figured out the last piece of the puzzle.

Gina sped toward the stone fountain and took a hard right turn. Unlike Nathan, she cut it too close and had to dodge the branches of a flowering crabapple tree that nearly pulled her off the seat. "Don't fall behind," she grumbled, mocking his earlier warning. "How about you let me go first? Then we'll see who falls behind."

Nathan was still waiting next to the orange cones when she came skidding to a stop beside him. "Gee, nice of you to wait for me," she said, out of breath.

He didn't respond. His eyes were locked on the mound of dirt, but his mind was seeing something entirely different. Something from long ago.

"What are you doing?" she asked, pulling wayward strands of hair out of her face.

"Huh?" he said.

"I asked you what you're doing, but don't worry, I figured it out. You're standing here staring at a pile of dirt."

He turned and looked at her, trying to decide if he should tell her now or wait until later. If he told her now, she'd dismiss it before the last word left his lips. Better to wait. Sometimes she needed to see things for herself. He'd learned that lesson the hard way, on several different occasions.

"Well?" she asked impatiently. "Are we just going to stand here?"

He looked down the path, at the thick hedge of forsythia bushes that bordered the east end of the park. Just beyond that was Jewel Lake Road. *Too risky,* he thought. The reporter was out there somewhere, trying to find them. They needed to find another way back to the cottage.

He spotted a utility road up ahead on the right. It was nothing more than tire tracks, sunken in the grass and worn from repeated use. They cut between two rose beds and led to the southeast corner of the park, and the woods beyond. "This way," he said, then stood on the pedal and rode away from her.

Gina watched as he cut across the grass and followed the tire tracks toward the woods. "Wait," she called out. "Why are you going *that* way?"

"It's safer," he yelled back. "Trust me."

She made a face...*yeah, right*...then started after him. *Where have I heard that before?*

They followed the utility road past a large tool shed painted the same pale green as the picnic tables. Across from it were piles of dirt, gravel, and bark mulch. The road continued on for a short distance beyond that and then snaked into the woods.

Nathan rode into the forest and stopped next to a giant pile of composted leaves. He was surveying the woods to his left and right when Gina came to a stop behind him.

"You're not serious," she said.

237

"We need to stay out of sight," he replied.

"In the woods?" she said. "Really?"

"Have you forgotten about the reporters?" he asked. "The ones that chased us earlier?"

"Of course not," she said. "But why don't we just ride down the road like we did before? If we see them, we'll pull off into the woods and hide. That *was* the original plan, if memory serves me right."

"Yes, it was," he said. "But that was before they saw us. Now they know we're here. They're looking for us, and we have no idea where they are. For all we know they could be sitting at the traffic light, watching for us."

She looked away without responding. *I hate it when he's right.*

"Besides," he said, "these are mountain bikes. They're made for the woods."

"Yeah, yeah, yeah," she mumbled. *He did it again.*

"Don't worry," he said. "We'll ride through the woods a little ways and then cut back to the road."

"That's your plan?"

"That's my plan."

She let out a long breath and gestured with both hands. "After you." *Smarty pants.*

"Thank you," he replied. *Chicken.*

The woods held an eerie calm as they rode away from the leaf pile. The air grew cooler and the bright colors of the park were replaced by earthen tones of brown and gray. Nathan went slowly, winding his way around fallen branches, large rocks, and the numerous dips and mounds in the forest floor. Gina stayed close behind with her eyes glued to the ground in front of her.

"This isn't so bad," he called out.

"Yeah, we should do this more often," she replied. The words were barely out of her mouth when he came to a sudden stop.

"Hey, watch out!" she yelled, as their bikes collided.

He dumped the bike on the ground and ducked behind the thick trunk of a nearby pine tree.

"What are you doing?" she asked.

"Leave the bike and get over here," he said, motioning frantically with his hand.

She set the bike on the ground and walked over to where he was standing.

"Look," he said, pointing through the trees. Jewel Lake Road was 300 feet away. Parked in the middle of it was the Channel 5 news van.

Her eyes lit up. "Did they see us?" she said, moving back behind the tree.

"I don't think so."

"Then why are they just sitting there?"

"I have no idea."

She peeked around the tree, following the line of the road. "Oh look," she said. "That's why they stopped."

"What is it?" he asked

She stepped out from behind the tree. "Over there," she said, pointing to a spot further down the road.

He moved to his left for a better view, and that's when he saw it.

"It's a horse," she said. "But what's it doing in the road?"

He grabbed hold of her and pulled her back behind the tree.

"Hey," she snapped, pulling her arm free. "What's the matter with you?"

When he spoke, there was worry in his voice.

"That's not a horse.

20

The Whitney Spur

It was standing perfectly still in the road. Through the maze of trees that blocked their view, they could only make out its rough size and the color of its fur.

But then it moved.

It ambled slowly across the road and loped down the embankment. When it reached the tree line, it charged into the woods, its massive antlers snapping off pine branches with ease. The resulting sound echoed through the woods like the crack of gunfire.

Gina's eyes went wide. "Is that a—?"

"YES," Nathan yelled, "RUN!"

Gina spun around and bolted into the forest, pushing tree branches out of her way as she ran. Nathan followed behind her for a short distance, then grabbed her arm and pulled her down behind a boulder the size of a small car.

"Hey," she barked as they tumbled to the ground. "What are you doing?"

"Quiet," he said. "And stay perfectly still."

Behind them, the sound of breaking branches grew louder.

Forty feet away.

Thirty feet.

Then twenty, and closing fast.

Now they could hear its hooves pounding the forest floor. Gina closed her eyes and pushed her body against the rock, as if she might break through to a secret hiding place deep inside.

The moose was 10 feet away when it stopped. The forest turned quiet, except for the sound of heavy breathing—throaty and deep.

Nathan and Gina remained motionless, hearts pounding, for most of a minute, until the moose snorted and slowly moved away. Nathan turned and watched as the huge beast cut back into the woods. It was more than six feet tall at the shoulder and maybe ten feet long. When it was a good distance away, he gave Gina a gentle shake. "It's gone," he said.

Her eyes opened and darted from side to side, peering nevously through the loose strands of hair that hung across her face.

"Are you okay?" he asked.

"No, I'm *not* okay," she snapped. She climbed to her feet and checked over her shoulder to make sure the moose was really gone, then brushed the dirt and pine needles off her pants.

Nathan scrambled to his feet and checked the road. The van was still there. "Get down," he said. "They'll see you."

"Good. I hope they do," she shouted, as she marched back to get her bike. "I'll take a nosy reporter over a moose any time."

"Gina, stop!" he yelled. He checked the road again and saw the news van turn and head back into town. "Will you wait?" he called out.

She ignored him and picked the bike up off the ground, then made a beeline for the road. When she reached the edge of the woods, she wheeled the bike up the embankment, climbed on, and pedaled as fast as she could.

Away from the woods.

Away from the moose.

Away from Nathan.

He emerged from the woods moments later and saw her racing away from him. He knew that yelling for her to stop would be a waste of time. She was too far away and she wouldn't listen anyway. But he needed her to listen, now more than ever. He raced down the street after her and caught up with her at his uncle's mailbox. "Will you *stop?*" he said, as she turned in the driveway.

She rode another ten feet and then jammed on the brakes, leaving a long skid mark in the dirt.

"What is your problem?" he asked, stopping beside her.

"My problem?" Her face boiled red as the tension of the morning erupted. "This whole thing is crazy."

"What are you talking about?"

"We got chased on our way to the library. We got chased coming out of the library. We got chased in the woods by a giant moose." She threw her hands in the air and shouted, "EVERYONE IS CHASING US!"

"Hey!" he yelled, then clapped his hands together. "STOP!"

The loud *SMACK!* gave her a start and she broke out of her rant.

"Do you want to solve this thing or not?" he barked.

She let out a long breath as her anger receded. "Yes," she said softly

"DO YOU?"

"YES," she shouted.

"Then there's something we need to check out."

She looked at him for several seconds without speaking, studying the look on his face. It was Nathan The Serious. Very rare. She was much more accustomed to Nathan The Clown.

"What is it?" she asked, cautiously.

"Not here," he said, as he climbed back on his bike. "I'll explain on the way."

When they got back to the house, he set his bike against the screen porch and looked down at the dock, then out across the lake. His parents were nowhere in sight. The whole way back from town, he'd been preparing for what he'd say to them. How he and Gina would get back out of the house without arousing suspicion. But that was no longer a problem, and a surge of anticipation rippled through his body as he hurried into the house and straight to his room.

He checked each pocket of his backpack to make sure he had everything he needed. Then he stashed the book under his pillow for safekeeping and raced back out to the kitchen.

Gina was leaning against the counter, chewing on a celery stick. "So where are we going?" she asked between bites.

"Not far," he replied, as he went over to the back window. The cove was clear and there was still no sign of his parents. When he turned around, he noticed the celery stick in her hand. "Where did you get that?"

She held up a small plastic bag stuffed with celery sticks and carrots. "Refrigerator," she said, out of the side of her mouth.

"Bring it," he said, moving quickly toward the door. "We don't have much time."

Then he stopped.

"What's wrong?" she asked.

"We should leave a note."

"Let me do it," she said, reaching for the notepad and pencil next to the cookie jar. She'd seen his notes. They were hard to read and even harder to believe. With pencil in hand she asked, "Are we walking or riding?"

"Riding," he replied.

"Destination?"

"Be creative," he said.

"Timeframe?"

"Unknown."

"Got it," she said.

Nathan was outside watching the boat traffic across the lake when Gina came down the porch steps. So far, he'd seen nothing that resembled his uncle's boat, and no boat of any kind coming into the cove toward the house. "All set?" he asked.

"I guess," she said, "but it would be nice to know where we're going."

"You'll see," he told her as he climbed on his uncle's bike.

They pedaled to the end of the driveway and paused to check

for traffic, then Nathan turned right and headed away from town. At first, they rode without speaking, and then Gina couldn't stand it anymore.

"Where are you taking me?" she called out.

"Not much farther," he replied.

"That's all you're going to say?"

"For now."

Ten minutes later, they arrived.

"The state park?" she groaned, as they turned down the gravel road. "We've already been here."

"I know," Nathan said without stopping. He rode straight across the gravel parking lot to the ranger's station. It was the color of dark chocolate, with a deck that stretched along the front of the building. On either side of the front door sat a crude bench fashioned from pine logs.

Gina pulled up behind him as he was leaning his uncle's bike against the side of the building. "This is what you wanted to show me?"

"Nope," he answered, walking away from the building.

She climbed off the bike and ran after him. "So what is it?"

"You'll see," he said. "Follow me."

They walked across the parking lot, to the stepped path that led to the picnic area. When they came to the edge of the lake, Nathan turned left and followed the path they'd explored the day before. No words were spoken as they walked deeper into the woods, and he didn't stop until they reached the wooden bridge. He walked halfway across and stopped. "Over there," he said, pointing to a spot up the river.

She leaned on the railing and fixed her eyes on the water, following it back into the woods. Halfway up the long expanse, she saw four wooden posts jutting out of the water, blanketed by the shade of the overhanging limbs. The posts were made from heavy timbers that had faded and cracked over time. Directly across from them, on the opposite side of the river, was another set, equally crooked and broken.

"That's what you were telling me about in the library?" she asked.

"Yes."

"And you think that's an old railroad trestle?"

"I'm sure of it."

"Great," she said, as she stepped back from the railing. "Can we go now?"

"Not yet. There's something else you need to see."

He crossed the bridge and continued up the trail. Soon they came to the narrow side path that snaked up the hill to the left. "This way," he said.

They followed the rocky trail to the top of the rise, past the lean-to and straight into the woods beyond. They hadn't gone far when Gina stopped short. "Did you hear that?" she said, looking around nervously.

"Hear what?" Nathan replied.

"I thought I heard something."

He stopped and surveyed the woods in every direction. "Probably just a deer or something. Come on, let's keep moving."

She looked around nervously and then stepped in front of him. "Me first."

They walked to the far side of the plateau and stopped where the trail descended into a deep ravine. Directly across from them was another hill, slightly bigger than the one they were on.

"Please tell me this is it," she groaned.

"It is," he said.

"This is what you wanted to show me?"

"Yes."

She glanced down the hill briefly. "It's very nice. *Now* can we go?"

"Not so fast," he replied. It was time to tell her. Time to lay out the pieces of the puzzle that told a very different story than the one in the book. "Look down there," he said, pointing into the ravine.

"What about it?" she asked.

"See the narrow corridor? See how it winds between these two hills?"

"Yeah?"

"This was the Whitney Spur."

"The what?"

"The Whitney Spur. It's the dotted line you saw on the map this morning. The sidetrack that crossed the river."

She shook her head and sighed. *He's still hung up on that crusty old map.* "And how do you know all this?" she asked.

"It was in *The Lakes Region Gazette*, at the end of the Whitney Mine story."

"Okay, fine, whatever," she said. "We came. I saw. Now let's go."

"Not yet," he said.

She exhaled loudly, and then said, "Why are we wasting our time here? You saw the story in the *Gazette*. They shut the Whitney Mine down and tore up the tracks two years before the boxcar disappeared." She waved two fingers in his face. "Two years."

"You're absolutely right," he said calmly. "The Whitney Spur was long since shut down when the boxcar vanished."

Her eyes flared. *That's what I just said.*

"Which means they probably didn't check it."

"Why would they?" she fired back. "The boxcar vanished somewhere between Stone Point and West Branch. You've been telling me that from the very start."

"What if it didn't?" he said.

"Whoa, stop right there. Now you're saying the boxcar vanished *before* Stone Point?" She shook her head back and forth. "No, that's impossible."

"Why?"

"Because you told me when they got to Stone Point the boxcar was still there. They talked to everyone, remember? It said so in the book." *Hello.*

"That's right," he said. "They did question everyone. They even did background checks on some of them. But I was wrong."

"Say that again?"

"I was wrong."

"One more time?"

"I was…" He stopped and gave her a look. *Very funny.* "As I was saying, they talked to everyone, but here's the thing—the passengers wouldn't know if one of the cars was missing. But they *would* know if something unusual had happened. Like an unscheduled stop. A breakdown. A robbery."

She tried to think of a comeback, but what he said made sense. For a change.

"And yes, they also talked to the train crew, but it was Brooten's job to check the cars. Like I already said, I don't think he was in any condition to do it."

She thought for a moment. "So he just *told* them he checked the cars?"

"That's right."

"Which means they searched the wrong area," she said, putting it all together in her mind. Her eyes suddenly grew bright with the realization that they had it wrong. All this time.

Nathan eyed the ravine below and said, "This was the only sidetrack before Stone Point."

"You mean, it *used* to be the only sidetrack before Stone Point. The tracks were already gone when the boxcar vanished, remember? How do you explain that?"

It was the question that haunted him from the moment they left the library—the last piece of the puzzle. The answer came to him when they were cutting through the park, and it was so simple. It was right there in front of their eyes from the very start, and they had completely overlooked it. But he couldn't tell Gina. Not until he brought her here. If she was going to believe him, she had to see it with her own eyes.

"What if there *were* tracks there?" he asked.

"That's easy," she said. "If the tracks were there, they would've checked them." *Duh.*

"But what if they were gone?"

She flopped her head forward and started to laugh. "First you say there were tracks. Then you say there weren't tracks. Which is it?"

"Both," he said.

She waved both palms in the air. "Whoa, whoa, whoa. You need to choose. It's one or the other."

"You're forgetting the storm," he said.

"The storm? Which one?"

"The one that hit on June 24th."

"The day the boxcar disappeared," she confirmed.

"That's right."

"What about it?"

"It tore everything up, remember?"

"Yeah?" she said slowly.

He paused to let her connect the dots, which took all of three seconds.

"So, hold on," she said. She was talking faster now. "You're saying there *were* tracks there the day the boxcar vanished."

He nodded his head.

"How can that be?" she asked.

"Think," he said. "A month before it disappeared, who was in town?"

She thought for several seconds, then her eyes went wide. "You think they—?"

"Uh-huh."

"And then the storm hits," she said, "and they get wiped out."

"Totally erased," he said.

She began to pace back and forth. This changed everything. "So whoever took the boxcar used the Whitney Spur to divert it."

Nathan nodded again, letting her piece it together on her own.

"No wonder they never found it," she mumbled under her breath. She stopped pacing. "So wait, how did they divert the car?"

"Who knows?"

Very slowly, they both turned and looked down at the old rail bed, each thinking the same thing.

"We have to look," he said.

"You better believe it," she replied, starting down the hill ahead of him.

A minute later they were standing on the floor of the ravine.

"We're going *that* way, right?" she asked, pointing to the west.

"Yup," he said, studying the gap between the two hills. It stretched another quarter mile before bending to the left and out of sight.

She sized it up and then charged ahead. "It's hard to believe that trains came through here," she said, squeezing between two massive boulders. "I mean, look at it, it's a mess."

"It is now," he replied, following close behind her. "But 150 years ago, there weren't any boulders or fallen trees, or any of these new trees."

They walked to the turn in the ravine, and from there it got even worse. Over the years, landslides, unleashed by heavy spring rains, had sent tons of dirt, rock, and trees tumbling down from both sides. Some of it they ducked under, other parts they climbed over, and some sections were so bad they had to hike up the ravine wall and walk around.

They came out of the turn where the track straightened briefly, then snaked back to the right and out of sight again. As they emerged from the 'S' turn, Gina stopped walking. "Wow!" she exclaimed.

The steep hills that skirted both sides of the old rail bed were cut away, creating an open canyon with sheer rock walls that loomed high over their heads. Gone were the fallen trees and the massive boulders. The floor of the chasm was a packed surface of dirt and crushed stone, scorched by years of direct sunlight. They walked on, stopping to explore one of many giant holes blasted in the canyon wall. It was rich with deposits of quartz, amethyst and feldspar.

"Look," Gina said, pointing straight ahead.

At the far end of the canyon was a massive rock face, cut into the side of the mountain. Huge openings had been carved into it, some of which had crumbled, sending an avalanche of broken stone out onto the canyon floor.

"Is that it?" she asked, her voice cracking with excitement.

"It has to be," Nathan replied softly, eyeing the ragged remains of the mountain. "The Whitney Mining Company, or what's left of it." As he stood there staring, an eerie feeling washed over him. It was the same feeling he'd gotten in the attic, and in the basement of the courthouse—an equal mix of fear and curiosity.

"Well, what are we waiting for?" she asked. "Let's go check it out."

Before he could respond, she took off running. He watched her sprint toward the mine, then he pushed his fear aside and raced after her. When he caught up with her, she was standing 15 feet from the giant wall of rock.

"What are those?" she asked, pointing to the small openings that dotted the surface.

"Who knows?" he answered. "Tunnels, maybe?" Then his eyes shifted to a cavernous entrance off to the right. It was divided in half by a large stone column carved out of the base of the mountain.

Gina stepped up to the wall, feeling the rough stone surface. It sparkled in the early afternoon sun. "Did you see this?" she asked.

He didn't respond. He had walked beyond the column and

stopped several feet into the opening of the tunnel. The floor was mounded with massive chunks of stone. The rubble continued for another 20 feet, up to where the tunnel walls had caved in and sealed it shut. "Gina, check this out," he yelled, his voice bouncing off the rock walls. When there was no response, he turned and walked back outside.

Gina was gone.

21

Gina

"Where did she go?" Nathan mumbled, looking back and forth. He shouted her name and heard his voice echo across the length of the gravel pit. It was followed by silence. He turned back to the mine, looking left and right, up and down. "She was standing right here."

One by one, he checked each of the openings, moving from his right to his left. Many of them were filled with broken stone. Others were just shallow cavities, tunnels that had been started and never finished. With every opening, he was reminded of the old newspaper stories they'd read in the library. *Three Men Dead as Tunnel Collapses.*

He moved farther left, trying not to think of the morbid history that would forever follow this hollow rock. He was looking into one of the openings when he felt a pebble bounce off his shoulder, then another off the top of his head. When he jumped back and looked up, he saw Gina peering out of a small hole, fifteen feet up the rock face.

"Miss me?" she said.

"What are you doing?" he snapped.

"Exploring. What are you doing?" she replied

"Looking for you!"

He took off his backpack and brushed dirt off his arms and shoulders as his heartbeat slowly returned to normal.

She leaned forward and surveyed the outer face of the mine. "This place is so cool."

"How did you get up there?" he asked.

"Down there," she said, pointing to his left. "There's a narrow opening. It led to this passageway through kind of a ramp-thingy, all carved from stone."

"Well, come on. I think it's better if we stick together."

"Now who's no fun?" she said.

"I'm serious," he told her.

"Oh, all right."

She had just ducked back in the tunnel when he heard a dull rumbling sound from somewhere inside the mine. When he looked up, he saw a puff of stone dust drifting out of the hole where Gina had just been sitting. "Gina?" he called out.

There was no answer.

"GINA!"

Still nothing.

He stepped back and did a quick visual search of the front of the mine, his eyes darting from one opening to the next. When he didn't see her, he took a breath to calm himself. "She said something," he muttered. "What was it? Small opening?" He thought hard. *No, she said "narrow" opening.* Was there a difference?

He scanned the rock face again, looking for a narrow opening. Then he saw it. It wasn't a hole as much as a sliver—clearly not man-made like the other openings. This one was a product of nature. The top and bottom formed a point, and at its widest point it was no more than fourteen inches across. The shape reminded him of a bird's feather.

"Narrow opening," he said, as he ran over to it and dropped his backpack on the ground. He turned his body sideways and squeezed through the gap. Once inside, it widened to almost three feet, and he moved forward, feeling his way along the sheer stone wall. It curved to the right, and came to an end at a large square opening that had been cut in the stone. He ducked down and looked inside, and in the hazy light he could see the floor angle upwards.

The ramp-thingy.

"GINA!" he shouted, hearing his voice echo in the tight space. When there was no answer, he crawled into the opening and followed it upward, clawing for purchase on the floor and walls with his fingertips. "GINA?"

Again there was no reply.

He quickened his pace, crab walking on his hands and feet up the incline. At the far end, he saw the opening where Gina had been perched. Beyond it, clear blue sky. Several feet back, he saw a large gap in the floor. All that remained now was a four-foot shadow where the stone had given way. He inched closer and peered down into the void. "GINA?"

From somewhere down below he heard a noise, a soft tapping

sound: rock on rock. "GINA!" he shouted, his heart pounding. Once again, he heard the muffled sound, like someone signaling in Morse Code.

It's her. It has to be.

With his mind racing, he backed away from the hole. Then, he remembered his backpack sitting outside in the dirt. "My flashlight," he muttered, as he turned and scrambled back down the incline. When he got to the bottom, he hurried toward the feather-like opening. He was halfway through it when his foot caught on the rock and he fell headlong onto the crushed gravel outside.

He sat up slowly, rubbing his elbow, when a long black shadow appeared at his side. He turned and looked over his shoulder, squinting directly into the sunlight, and saw the outline of a person. Before he could utter a word, a hand grabbed his shoulder and pulled him up. When he saw who it was, he said, "What are *you* doing here?"

Wynn Barrett stared back at him with a look Nathan hadn't seen before. It wasn't his usual *how-ya-doing-there-neighbor* face. "I heard you shout," he said. "What happened?"

Nathan's world was spinning and his words came out in gushes. "Gina... she was up there... in a tunnel... it collapsed... she's in there... I don't know if she's..."

Wynn grabbed both of Nathan's shoulders. "Listen to me," he said. "Have you got a flashlight?"

His voice was different.

"Yeah, that's why I came back outside."

"Is it in your backpack?"

"Yes"

"Go get it."

258

Nathan scrambled over to his backpack and tore through the center pocket until he found the flashlight. As he handed it to Wynn he asked, "How did you get here?"

"I'll explain later," he said. "Right now we have to find Gina. Tell me again, where did you last see her?" His voice was crisp, his words precise.

"She was up there," Nathan said, pointing to the small round opening where Gina had first appeared. "But she went through there," he explained, pointing to the narrow opening below it. "There's a tunnel that wraps around and comes out—"

"Yes, I know," Wynn said, cutting him off. He stared at the stone face with a knowing look. *So many lives lost.* "Let's go," he said.

"In there?" Nathan asked, pointing to the opening. "The two of us won't fit."

"No, we're going in *there*," Wynn said, pointing to a small breach several feet to the right. The entire opening was no more than three feet high and two feet wide.

"In there?" Nathan said, "but how?"

"Follow me," Wynn replied.

Since they'd arrived in Crawford, Nathan had only seen Wynn Barrett hobbling up and down the street or out to the mailbox. But when he reached the small opening, the old man dropped to the ground and crawled in. Nathan followed him into the darkness, and it wasn't until Wynn turned on the flashlight that he saw what was really inside.

The tunnel was at least six feet wide, and twenty feet deep, maybe longer. The ceiling was high enough for both of them to stand, but Wynn wasn't looking upward. He had the flashlight pointed at a mound of stones piled high against the wall. "There," he said, rushing toward them. "Help me move these."

They climbed up the pile and Nathan pulled on one of the stones. It was the size of a football, and all he could do was roll it end over end.

"That's it," Wynn said. "Just let it roll off the pile."

Nathan let go of the stone and it bounced down onto the dirt floor. Then he grabbed another and did the same.

Minutes later, Wynn said, "Hold up." He leaned into the shallow hole they had made and yelled, "GINA, CAN YOU HEAR ME?" In the tight confines of the tunnel his voice thundered. The response that followed was just the opposite—muffled, like someone talking with their hand over their mouth.

"It's her!" Nathan exclaimed.

They pulled away more stones, and several minutes later Wynn pointed the flashlight into the opening. Nathan crawled up to the hole and yelled. "GINA!"

Her voice was weak. "I'm here."

"Ask her if she's hurt," Wynn said.

"ARE YOU HURT?"

"My back hurts," she replied. "And my arm—"

"HOLD ON," Nathan yelled. "WE'RE GOING TO GET YOU OUT."

They pulled away more of the rock, working quickly and without speaking. Ten minutes later, they'd made a space big enough to crawl through. They found Gina to the right of the opening, lying in the dark on her side atop a pile of rocks. She was covered with stone dust, and her right arm was twisted awkwardly under her body. "The floor collapsed," she said, her voice uneven.

"I know," Nathan said. "But don't worry. It's over now."

Wynn knelt down beside her and slowly eased her onto her left side. He was pulling her arm free when she cried out in pain.

"Oww!"

"Okay, easy does it," he said, gently laying her arm down on the side of her body. He looked at Nathan and said, "I think it's broken."

"What do we do?" Nathan asked.

"Help me get her up," Wynn said.

Working together, they slowly eased her up into a sitting position. Then Wynn took off his belt and made a sling to hold her arm against her chest. While he was doing that, Nathan eyed their surroundings. Overhead, he saw the hole where the floor had collapsed. The light coming through it was very faint. The rock pile they were standing on extended several feet to either side. Behind them was nothing but a wall of darkness.

"You're very lucky," Wynn told Gina. "When you were in that tunnel up there," he said, glancing upward, "nothing fell from overhead. The loose rock was below you. It actually cushioned your fall."

Gina grimaced as she looked up at the broken ceiling, all the while holding the sling in place with her left hand. Then, something clicked in her mind. "Wait a minute," she said. "How did you get here?"

"Let's talk about that later," Wynn replied. "Right now, we all need to get out of here before any more of this mountain collapses."

"Right," she said, eyeing him suspiciously. Something about his voice. It was different. But there was more. His overall manner. And his clothes. A camo shirt and blue jeans? *What did you do with Wynn*

Barrett? she wanted to say.

"Come on, let's go," he said. He took hold of her left elbow and pulled her to her feet. She was sore and bruised and the change in position made her wince. "Do you need to sit down again?" he asked.

"No, I just want to get out of here," she told him.

He stood on her left side, keeping a firm grip on her elbow, while Nathan stood below her, ready to catch her if she stumbled down the rocky incline. They were inching their way toward the opening when Nathan saw something down by his right foot. "Wait," he said, stopping short.

"What is it?" Gina said, looking cautiously toward the ceiling.

"There," he said, pointing his flashlight.

In the moment that followed, no one spoke. Lodged among the stones at the bottom of the pile was a human skull. A few feet away, jutting out from beneath the rocks, was an arm. The shirtsleeve was torn and tattered, and the wrist was turned downward. Its boney fingers were dull white and curled inward, grasping a steel rail.

22

Josiah

G ina saw the skull and screamed. With lightning speed, Wynn and Nathan caught her as she lost her footing and fell backwards. When she was upright again, Nathan ran the light along the floor of the chasm, beyond the rock heap, along an old set of tracks. They ran another fifteen feet to a small circle of stones between the rails.

"What's that?" he asked.

"A fire pit," Wynn said.

Nathan stepped down off the pile of rocks and onto the dirt floor. Wynn and Gina followed, and together they slowly moved forward. When they reached the fire pit, it was Nathan's turn to jump. Off to his right were two more skeletons, sprawled out on the ground. The clothes that hung on their bones were torn and ratty, and spotted with mold.

"Come on," Wynn said, turning back toward the opening in the wall, "let's get out of here."

Nathan swung the beam of the light back on the fire pit, then along the track that continued on into the darkness. "Wait," he said, inching slowly past the fire pit. In the dim light ahead, he saw a massive ghost-like structure that stood over twelve feet high. Its narrow wooden planking was splintered and broken, and beneath it was a steel undercarriage that had rusted over time.

Wynn looked back and did a double take, then moved closer. "Well, I'll be damned."

Gina's eyes went wide. "Is that what I think it is?"

"Hold on," Nathan said, as he rushed forward. When he got to the corner of the boxcar, he moved to his right and ran the light along the side. In the murky shadows he saw something stenciled on the side.

Not a name.

Not a logo.

Just a number.

5401.

A surge of adrenaline shot through his body. "THIS IS IT!" he shouted. Then he uttered the three words that generations had longed to say. "We found it."

"Yes, you did, and I applaud you."

The voice came out of the darkness, somewhere behind them.

They all turned and looked, but in the faint light, all they could see was the rough outline of a person. He'd snuck into the tunnel while they were standing by the fire pit, and in all the excitement, they never heard him enter.

Nathan raised his flashlight at the same time Ernie Bell raised his service revolver.

"I'll take that flashlight, thank you," Bell said. "Right now."

Nathan was confused, and for a moment he couldn't move.

"I SAID *NOW!*" Ernie bellowed, his voice echoing in the dark chamber.

"You'd better give it to him," Wynn said.

Nathan walked over and tossed the flashlight.

"Now, let's all move down here where I can see you better," Bell said. He picked up the flashlight and pointed the beam at them as they began moving forward. Once they were closer, he waved his gun toward the far rail. "All of you—SIT!"

"Why are you doing this?" Gina asked.

"Yeah," Nathan said. "I thought you were our friend."

"Well, I was your friend, wasn't I?" Bell said in a mocking tone. "I gave you a ride in the cruiser. That's pretty friendly, don't you think?"

Nathan and Gina said nothing.

"What's your game here, Bell?" Wynn asked.

"What's *my* game?" Bell replied. "Why don't you tell me what your game is? I've been watching you for the last three days. I saw you slip the kid something. I saw you outside the library. Then inside the library. How come you're always hanging around these two kids, huh? Why'd you follow them out here today? That's right, I was right behind you the whole way. Not that I needed your help. I knew where they were going. It was right there on the screen."

"What's he talking about?" Gina whispered.

"The Reference Room," Nathan said, remembering Bell's curious visit.

"I had my reasons," Wynn replied. "But you didn't answer my question."

"Oh yeah, what am I doing here. Well, it started a long time ago, a *very* long time ago. I believe the year was 1870. That year bring back any memories for you?"

"A few," Wynn replied. His tone was different again, clipped and moody.

"It should," Bell said sarcastically.

"What's this all about?" Nathan asked.

"You don't know?" Bell asked. "Oh, that's right, you're from out of town. Well, let me enlighten you. Your friend Wynn here? His great grandfather was a railroad man."

Wynn flinched, and Bell quickly raised his gun. "Uh-uh, you stay right there," he said. "You see, great granddaddy liked to ride the train. In fact, he liked it so much, they promoted him to conductor."

"Your great grandfather was a conductor?" Nathan whispered.

"Was," Bell snickered. Wynn flinched again, but this time Ernie raised his gun and kept it pointed at him. "Easy."

"You never told us that," Nathan said.

"He didn't tell you because it's kind of a family secret, a dark secret if you know what I mean. That's because his great granddaddy... Joseph?"

"Josiah," Wynn said.

"Right. Josiah. Well, that boy just plain blew it. He let this big ol' soft belly here slip away right under his nose. You can imagine how that went over with the railroad folks. Truth is, they didn't take too kindly to one of their own employees losing their valuable property." Nathan could hardly believe what he was hearing. "Your greatgrandfather was the conductor of *this* train?" he said.

Wynn gave a brief nod, the look on his face unable to hide the pain he felt inside.

"That he was," Bell said, his tone growing more sarcastic. "But not for long. When the investigation was finished, they cut ol' Josiah loose. Sayonara. Adios. Goodbye."

Wynn closed his eyes and sighed, as if some terrible pain had driven the very last breath from his body.

"The conductor didn't blow it," Nathan said sharply. "It was the rear brakeman."

"Very good," Bell said. "Looks like you've been doing your homework. But here's something you didn't know. When the flatfoots came around asking questions, Josiah covered for the brakeman—"

"His name was Bill Brooten," Gina interrupted.

"Well, well," Bell said. "We're *very* good, aren't we?

"If Josiah covered for Brooten, then why did he leave town after the boxcar disappeared?" Nathan asked.

"Oh, that's easy," Bell said. "Once Josiah Barrett got the axe, Brooten lost it. Rumor is, that old boomer drifted back to the rail yards in Ohio."

"And just how is it that you know all this?" Wynn asked. "You've been in town for what, ten years?"

"Well now, that takes us back to your first question, doesn't it? What's my interest in all this? I know all about your family. Who doesn't? I'm just not sure how much you know about my family. My guess is very little. You see, my folks weren't from these parts, as they say. So you never met my father or my mother, probably didn't

Alfred M. Struthers

know my grandfather, or his father, for that matter."

Wynn had no reply, he was still struggling to make a connection.

"Then there's my great, great grandfather, but there's *no way* you could have known him... or his wife Cora."

"Whittier?" Nathan blurted out.

"That's right," Bell said, surprised. "You know? I see why every news station in the country is raving about you two."

"Cora Whittier was your great, great grandmother," Nathan said, his mind sifting through the things he'd read.

Wynn knew *that* name. After that, things started coming together for him as Bell continued to rant.

"Correct," he said. "But let's just call her Cora."

"Carson," Nathan said. "You're related to Seth Carson."

"Unbelievable," Bell replied. "How do you do it?"

Wynn slowly shifted his position as Bell carried on in dramatic fashion. Nathan saw it out of the corner of his eye and sensed that he was getting ready to do something. "The flowers," he said, trying to keep Bell distracted, "Carson helped save the flowers."

"Yes, that was a very productive visit, wouldn't you say?" Bell said in a curious tone. There was clearly something he wasn't telling them.

"But he left a month before the boxcar disappeared," Nathan said, egging him on.

"That's just what he wanted you to think," Bell said, laughing. "You see? He was sharp. He came to town and scoped out the job, then left town and made sure he was seen back home in Cleveland. But no one ever knew what happened to him. Not until now, that is." He gestured with his gun toward the far end of the tunnel. "As you can see, he did it," Bell nodded proudly. "He actually pulled it off."

"Wait a minute," Gina interrupted, "If he was here, who led the authorities out west?"

"This is amazing." Bell mumbled, rolling his head back in mock disbelief. "What do they feed you kids?"

As he spoke, Wynn inched forward, shifting his weight ever so slightly.

"What most people didn't know," Bell explained, "was that Seth had a brother, Simon. He wasn't a twin brother, but they sure looked like twins. He wanted to join Seth in the train robbing business, but as my grandfather told me, Seth didn't want his younger brother ending up in jail, so he gave Simon a 'special' job. While they were out east making preparations, Simon would take the train west, dressing like Seth and using his name. The best part was, the cops fell for it hook, line and sinker. For years they chased Simon all over the hills of California."

Then, Bell stepped closer and waved his gun at Nathan and Gina. "Say, how is it you two know so much about my family?"

Nathan stared at Bell, anger in his eyes. What could he say? His dead grandfather helped him? "Just curious," he mumbled.

"Well, you know what they say about curious people?" Bell said with a snicker. "A certain newspaper publisher in this town learned *that* lesson a long time ago."

"The fire," Gina said.

"Girl, you are *killing* me," Bell exclaimed, shaking his head in disbelief.

Nathan and Gina looked at him without speaking.

"Wait a minute," Bell said slowly, putting it all together. "You lied. You weren't at the library doing homework. But since you asked, yeah, the fire put an end to that nosey publisher once and for all. Printing all that trash about Seth. My family didn't take too kindly to that, so they put a stop to it."

"That happened generations ago," Wynn said. "How is it that you know so much about it?"

"Well, let's just say I have a very close family," Bell said sharply. "And we don't forget."

He was beginning another rant about his outlaw family when Wynn glanced over at Nathan. Their eyes met for only a split second, just long enough for Wynn to nod toward the opening in the wall. After that, there was no more talking. He launched forward and knocked Bell sideways with a powerful cross body block. Bell never saw it coming and the impact threw him backwards onto the rock pile.

Gina's rock pile.

And that's when his gun fired

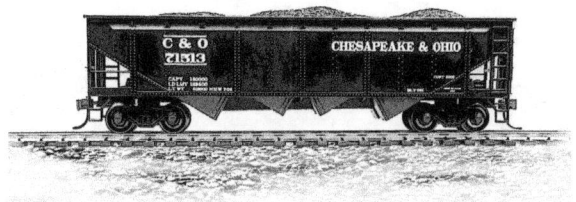

23

The Flying Switch

The sound was deafening. It boomed through the tunnel, releasing an avalanche of stone that fell in a blistering shower from the ceiling. Wynn rolled away as the first few jagged slabs landed on Bell's legs, pinning him to the ground. The pieces that followed got his arms and chest.

Nathan and Gina were halfway up the rock pile when the ceiling let go. With chunks of stone raining down behind them, they quickly crawled through the opening. When they reached the other side of the wall, Nathan pointed to the sunlit opening at the far end of the passageway and yelled, "GO!"

"WHAT ABOUT YOU?" Gina shouted back.

"I'VE GOT TO HELP WYNN, NOW GO!"

"BUT I WANT TO HELP YOU," she said.

"NO, YOU NEED TO—"

"LOOK," she screamed, pointing at the opening in the wall.

A cloud of dust and debris was billowing through the opening, and in the haze they saw a hand clutching desperately at the loose stones. Gina saw the camo pattern on the shirtsleeve and shouted, "IT'S WYNN!"

Nathan scrambled back up the rock pile and grabbed Wynn's hand, then pulled with all his strength. Wynn slowly emerged through the crawlspace, covered with dust and coughing. Nathan helped him down the rock pile and guided him through the narrow passageway to safety.

After that, things got really crazy.

Wynn found Ernie Bell's personal duty bag outside the opening of the passageway, next to Nathan's backpack. Inside was a cell phone, which he used to call 911. Thirty minutes later, they heard the *thwop-thwop-thwop* of distant rotors and watched as a police helicopter crested the treetops and landed in a torrent of dust and gravel. With it came the first of many state troopers and EMTs, who began working the scene both inside and outside the tunnel. While that was going on, the chopper lifted off and disappeared over the edge of the ravine.

"There's something you never explained," Nathan said to Wynn, as they sat on a pile of stones outside the mine. "How did you get out here today, to the mine?"

"Oww," Gina groaned as a woman in a black and yellow EMT jacket examined her swollen right arm. When she confirmed that it was broken, she wrapped it in an ACE bandage, followed by an air cast.

"Well, I have a confession to make," Wynn said. "I followed you to the library this morning. I overheard you in the Reference Room, talking about Little Bill and then the Whitney Mine. After you left, I put two and two together and came out here."

"You were *following* us?" Nathan said. "We never saw you."

"I heard you," Gina said, very matter-of-factly.

Nathan looked at Wynn and shook his head. *Don't believe her.*

"It's true," she said.

"By the way," Wynn said. "Riding into town? With those reporters sniffing around? That was pretty gutsy."

"Oh, you saw them?" Nathan asked.

"Yeah, outside the library…twice."

Overhead, the police helicopter was back again, circling the ravine and preparing to land.

"Well, thank you for watching out for us," Nathan said. "If you hadn't been in the tunnel with us, I'm not sure what would have happened."

"And thank you for saving my life," Gina said, looking at both of them. "If you guys hadn't found me, I don't think I would've gotten out of there." She shuddered at the thought of being trapped in the dark with the skeletons.

As they spoke, the chopper landed and their parents got out. They ran beneath the spinning rotor blades like most people do, bent down with one hand on their head.

"Uh-oh," Nathan groaned.

Gina took one look and said, "I am NOT looking forward to this."

Their parents were halfway to the mine when one of the state troopers stopped them and filled them in on what had happened.

The noise from the chopper forced him to gesture with his hands as he spoke. Several minutes later, they were all gathered in front of the mine. The helicopter pilot had turned off the engine, and the rotor blades hung motionless in the air.

All four parents were huddled together in a mild state of shock. Directly across from them, Nathan and Gina were still seated on the pile of rocks with Wynn Barrett between them. They were all listening as the officer in charge, state police Sergeant Pete Reynolds, reviewed the details.

"We've done a preliminary search of the tunnel and surrounding area and we found some interesting things," he told the group.

"Can you identify the bodies?" Nathan asked.

"Yes and no," Reynolds said. "We found some identification on two of them. The others will have to wait until we dig them out."

"There were more?" Gina said, a cold shiver running up her spine.

"The ones you identified," Nathan asked. "Was one of them Seth Carson?"

Reynolds checked his notes. "Carson? Yes. How did you know that?"

"It's a long story," Nathan said. He glanced at Wynn Barrett, who looked back and winked.

"We found a bottle of pills in his coat," Reynolds added. "The label was faded but we were able to make out a woman's name."

"Cora Whittier," Gina said without hesitation.

"Yes, that's right," Reynolds said, looking at her, astonished. "How could you possibly know that?"

It was what Ernie Bell wasn't telling them about Carson's visit with his aunt, even though he knew. He definitely knew.

"Bell said Carson came to town to scope out the job," Gina said. "If that's the case, then why was he visiting his aunt, when he was supposed to be preparing to steal the boxcar?"

Nathan nodded.

Wynn thought about it.

Reynolds just shrugged.

"And Bell said something about Carson's visit being productive," Gina added.

"What kind of pills were they?" Wynn asked.

"We won't really know until we get them to the lab," Reynolds replied. "It looks like a sedative, but that's just a guess."

"That might explain what happened to Little Bill," Nathan said.

"Little who?" his father asked, speaking for the first time.

"The rear brakeman," Nathan replied. "I'll explain it later, Dad."

"Carson could've drugged him so he wouldn't see what they were doing," Wynn said.

"And I bet that's why Josiah covered for him," Nathan added. "He wasn't drunk after all."

"I'm sure you're right," Wynn said sadly. "My grandfather told me when they got to Stone Point, Josiah found Little Bill in terrible shape. Everyone just assumed he was drunk, but it was worse than that. Josiah was so distracted trying to help Bill that he never noticed that the boxcar was already gone."

"I bet that was part of their plan all along," Gina suggested.

Gina's parents were speechless. A stolen boxcar? Their daughter trapped in a rock slide? And now pills? They'd been in town for less than four days and the kids had somehow gotten themselves smack dab in the middle of some age-old train robbery.

In addition to the life-threatening risk they'd taken, crawling around an abandoned mine, it meant they were about to be subjected to yet another media onslaught.

It was bad enough that they returned from their boat ride to find a state police cruiser parked in the driveway. From there they were quickly driven to the football field at the high school, where a police helicopter picked them up and whisked them over to the Whitney Mine. This was shaping up to be even worse than the courthouse.

Nathan's mother, Elizabeth, still hadn't uttered a word. She stood silently by, as the story unfolded, listening closely to the details and eyeing the crumbled mine several feet away. It was a very troubling situation, and clearly something needed to be done about it. First the courthouse? And now this?

"We found quite a few tools inside," Reynolds said.

"What kind of tools?" Wynn asked.

"Let's see," Reynolds said, reading directly from his notes. "Sledge hammers, steel bars, lanterns, and quite a few boxes of railroad spikes."

"They fixed the track," Wynn said.

Gina looked over at Nathan and said, "You were right."

He shrugged his shoulders. "It was the only possible explanation. I mean, how else would they have gotten the car down the spur?"

"And when did you figure that out?" she asked, pointedly.

"This morning, when we were riding through the park."

She thought back to their crazy bike ride home. "So that's why you were staring at that pile of dirt."

Wynn's face went blank as the truth was finally revealed. "After the mine closed," he said, "the railroad had no use for the track. It took them years to rip it up." He shook his head in disbelief. "To think, the whole time the authorities were out west looking for Carson, he was back here helping his gang fix the track. They had lanterns, so they must've worked at night so no one would see them. And they only had to repair it enough to handle a single car."

"All right," Gina asked, gesturing madly with her hands for them to stop. "I have to know. How did they do it?"

"Yeah," Nathan chimed in. "How did they separate the boxcar from the train?"

Reynolds was busy scribbling in his notepad, but when he heard the question he flipped to a blank page, pen at the ready.

"There was only one way they could've pulled it off," Wynn said. "It's called a flying switch."

"A flying switch?" Reynolds repeated, writing it down as he spoke.

"For it to work," Wynn explained, "the Carson gang would've boarded the train before it left Concord, hiding somewhere in the back. That way, when the train came out of the big turn in Glover, they'd already be in position. According to Bell, Seth Carson was pretty daring, so I'll bet he was on top of 5401."

"On top? As it moved?" Nathan asked.

"Exactly. When they came out of the turn, he uncoupled 5401 from the car directly ahead."

"Wait, he uncoupled it?" Gina asked. "You can do that on a moving train?"

"Oh sure," Wynn said. "He used the cut lever. It's on the corner of the car."

"Oh," she said softly. *I didn't know that.*

"So, once he uncoupled 5401, the front of the train pulled away, but his car and the ones behind it kept rolling."

"It didn't just stop?" Gina asked.

"Nope."

"How is that possible?"

"Momentum," Wynn answered. "They had just come out of a turn and were starting down a two percent grade."

"Momentum," Gina said, thinking out loud as she pictured it in her mind. "The rear section of the train kept rolling…"

"That's right," Wynn said. "Carson probably stayed on top of 5401. After all, he was the ringleader and I'm sure he didn't want to let it out of his sight. But another one of his gang would've been on top of the car directly *behind* him. And a third member of the gang was waiting at the Whitney Spur."

"The what?" Gina's father asked.

"The track that came through that ravine," Nathan said, pointing to the far end of the gravel pit.

"Once the front section of the train passed the Spur, Carson's accomplice switched the track," Wynn explained. "And here's where it gets tricky. The man riding on the car directly behind Carson had to uncouple his car from 5401. Then, using the handbrake, he had to slow *his* car and the cars behind it."

"Can one man do that?" Nathan asked.

"Sure," Wynn replied. "In those days, they used something called a brake club. It was a hickory stick, about three feet long. They used it to tighten the hand brake."

"So he slows the cars in the back—" Gina began.

"And 5401 pulls away," Wynn said.

"I get it," Nathan said. "5401 gets redirected down the Whitney Spur."

"That's correct," Wynn said. "Then the accomplice quickly switches the track back to its regular position. The rear section of the train, minus 5401, continues down the main line and eventually catches up with the front section."

"But wait," Nathan's father said. "Isn't the front section of the train traveling much faster than the rear section?"

Reynolds was scribbling furiously now.

"Yes," Wynn said. He paused for a moment, thinking about the track alignment leading up to Stone Point. Then he shook his head and grinned. "Oh, they were good," he said. "They were very good."

Nathan's father shrugged his shoulders. *Huh?*

"There's a flag stop just before Stone Point," Wynn explained.

"Flag stop?" Gina's father asked.

"A stop that's only required when a flag is present. In this case, at the junction of the Lakes Region Line and the Danbury Extension. The front of the train began to slow before the junction, until the engineer could see if there was a flag. That allowed the rear section to catch up."

"Wouldn't the passengers have noticed the cars reconnecting?" Nathan's father asked.

"Doubtful," Wynn said. "In those days the train was a pretty bumpy ride. Nothing like the smooth trains of today. A little nudge from behind as the coupler engaged probably wouldn't have been that noticeable."

"I have a question." It was Gina's father again. "If they repaired the track, this Whitney Spur, wouldn't someone have discovered it later?"

Gina spoke first. "There was a storm, Dad. A tornado that hit on the night of the robbery and wiped out half the town."

"Along with all the evidence," Nathan added.

"That's incredible," Wynn said, shaking his head. "I never even considered it."

"Is that why the investigation was so short?" Nathan asked.

"It has to be," Wynn answered. "I remember my grandfather talking about that. He was pretty steamed about the way it was handled."

Gina rolled her eyes. *Tell me about it.*

"So, this storm you mentioned," Nathan's father said. "Is that how the boxcar and the robbers got trapped in the tunnel?"

"Absolutely," Wynn said. "This old mine was really shaky to begin with. That's why they closed it down. Throw a twister at it and it didn't stand a chance."

After that, no one spoke. There was one question remaining, and it was Nathan's father who finally broke the silence. "So why did they do it?" he asked. "What was on that train that was work risking life and limb for?"

All eyes turned to Reynolds.

"We checked the boxcar," he said, "and we found four wooden crates."

"Crates?" Wynn asked. "Crates of what?"

Reynolds checked his notes. "Candles."

"Excuse me?" Wynn blurted out.

Once again, Reynolds read directly from his notes. "From the Richmond Refining Company in East Palestine, Ohio."

"They stole the boxcar for a shipment of candles?" Nathan's father asked.

"No, that's not right," Wynn mumbled, shaking his head as he spoke.

"What's not right?" Reynolds asked.

"The boxcar was empty," Wynn replied. "Everybody knows that."

Nathan and Gina exchanged a look of shock. *Empty?*

"Am I missing something here?" The sergeant asked.

"It was on the manifest," Wynn explained.

"The what?"

"The manifest. It's a list of the cars on the train, what's in them, and where they'll be dropped off."

"OK," Reynolds said. "So according to this manifest—"

"There was nothing in the car," Wynn cut in, "which is why it made no sense."

"What do you mean?" Reynolds asked.

"The car vanishing like it did? Who would steal it? It was empty."

Reynolds thought about it for a moment and then said, "So what you're telling me is that these crates weren't supposed to be in that car?"

"Correct," Wynn replied. "According to the paperwork, anyway."

"Okay," Gina said slowly. "That explains why there was nothing in the newspaper."

"Huh?" Reynolds muttered.

"In all the old newspapers we looked at, there wasn't a single mention of what was in the boxcar."

"Yeah, you're right," Nathan said slowly. "But now it makes perfect sense."

"What does?" Reynolds asked.

"Nothing was missing," Nathan said.

Reynolds shook his head, confused.

"If there was something in that boxcar," Nathan explained, "it never would've been delivered."

"Which would've come out in the investigation," Wynn said.

"And reported in all the newspapers," Gina added.

Reynolds looked at Nathan and Gina and shook his head. *Who are these kids?*

After a brief silence, Wynn asked, "Did you look in the boxes?"

Reynolds didn't answer. He turned to one of the other officers and mumbled something, gesturing toward the mine as he spoke. When he was done, the officer sprinted to the narrow opening in the stone and disappeared inside.

Reynolds turned back to Wynn. "Tell me about this manifest."

"It's standard procedure," Wynn said. "When the train arrives to pick up the cars, the station agent gives the conductor the manifest."

"The list of all the cars," Reynolds confirmed.

"That's right. The station agent is the one who actually checks the cars."

"So maybe he's the one who put those crates into the boxcar," Reynolds suggested.

"It's possible," Wynn replied. "But remember, the Carson gang was involved. They were train robbers. I'd bet anything they put the crates in the boxcar after it was checked. And since it was supposed to be empty, it probably wasn't sealed."

Reynolds was still writing when the officer emerged from the break in the stone. He hurried over to where Reynolds was standing, and the two men spoke in hushed tones for nearly a full minute. When they were done, Reynolds called out to the other officers. "SEAL IT UP!" he shouted. "FROM NOW ON, NOBODY GOES IN WITHOUT MY SAY-SO."

"What's going on?" Nathan's father asked.

"This just became an FBI matter," Reynolds said.

Nathan and Gina exchanged a look of shock. *FBI?*

Gina's father threw his hands in the air, "Well, that's just perfect."

In the clamor that followed, Wynn eyed the detective suspiciously. "What did you find?" he asked.

A hush fell over the group.

"The crates are filled with banknotes," Reynolds said, "along with several printing plates."

"They were printing *money?*" Wynn asked, a look of shock on his face.

"Somebody was," Reynolds replied. "And by the looks of it, they weren't finished."

As the chatter erupted again, Reynolds moved away, took out his cell phone, and began making calls. As he was doing that, the front of the mine was quickly sectioned off with yellow crime scene tape.

By days end, the story would go viral as news spread about the most famous train robbery in New Hampshire history.

Ernie Bell was flown aboard a Medevac helicopter to the hospital in Concord. His days as a member of the Crawford Police Department were over. Reynolds took statements from Nathan, Gina and Wynn, and told them to expect a visit from the FBI, as part of their investigation. Then it was time to go.

Gina's parents escorted her to the police helicopter and Wynn followed close behind. Just before he climbed into the chopper, he stopped to look back at the Whitney Mine for what would likely be his last time. There was no need to come out here again. Not now. He'd gotten the satisfaction he'd dreamt of for most of his life. Justice would finally be served.

Nathan's parents started walking toward the chopper when they noticed Nathan wasn't with them. They turned back and saw him talking to Sgt. Reynolds. The two spoke briefly and then shook hands.

On the way back to the chopper, Nathan's mother asked, "What was that all about?"

"Nothing," he replied, casually. "I was just asking Sgt. Reynolds something."

"Dare I ask?"

"Just a favor," Nathan said.

"What kind of favor?"

"You'll see."

His mother stopped walking and stared at him. *Now what?*

"Don't worry Mom," he said. "You'll like it. Really."

Several minutes later, the chopper's engine screamed and the giant bird lifted gently off the ground. As it rose in the air, the pilot banked to the right and the Whitney Mine gradually disappeared from view. They passed over Jewel Lake, glittering in the late afternoon sun like a precious diamond, on their way to the Lakes Region General Hospital in Laconia. But Nathan and Gina didn't see it. They had both fallen fast asleep.

That night, the house was very quiet. Nathan and Gina ate dinner and turned in early. They would feel the effects of their adventure for quite some time, but for now they were just thankful to be back at Pine Point again.

The meeting in the kitchen was another story altogether. It went on well into the night, as all four parents planned their next move. Something had to be done. The mystery of the stolen boxcar had been solved, but this ordeal wasn't over yet.

Not by a long shot.

24

The Phantom Vale

Nathan woke up early the next morning, before anyone else, and quickly got dressed. He slipped down the porch steps, where he found his bike leaning against the side of the house, right next to his uncle's bike. Sometime in the night, the state police had returned the bikes, as directed by Sgt. Reynolds.

The main road was quiet as he rode toward town. The trees stirred gently and a group of crows were squawking somewhere deep in the forest. When he reached Wynn's mailbox, he turned down the driveway. There were no lights on in the house, but he knocked on the side door anyway. Wynn appeared seconds later, dressed in his usual long-sleeved plaid shirt and baggy pants. He was holding an empty coffee pot in his hand.

"Well, good morning," he said with a smile. "Didn't expect I'd see you. Come on in."

Nathan stepped inside the front hallway and was immediately drawn to an old photograph hanging on the wall. It showed a giant locomotive, and standing in front of it was a man dressed in a cap and coat, holding a lantern in one hand. "Is that who I think it is?" he asked

"Yes," Wynn answered. "That's my great-grandfather, Josiah Barrett."

"He looks young there."

"He was, but follow me. There's something else I want you to see." He walked back in the kitchen and set the coffee pot on the counter, then went into the living room. He sat down at the huge roll-top desk in the corner and opened the drawer on the lower right. From it, he took out the old black notebook, along with a number of other relics, which he spread out across the top of the desk. "This desk has been in my family forever," he said. "It was passed down through the generations and found its way to me."

Nathan nodded his head, thinking about the old bookcase in the attic, the one passed down through *his* family for generations. Not that he could talk about it with anyone.

Wynn opened the notebook and Nathan saw pictures of the Barrett family that dated back to the early 1800s. "Here's a picture of Josiah when he started with the railroad," Wynn said. "Look how happy he is." Then he turned the next page. "This is Marcus Barrett, Josiah's son. He was my grandfather. He went to work for the lumber company. And this is his wife Hannah, my grandmother. She had a dress shop in town and sold curtains, tablecloths, napkins, and such to the railroad for the dining car."

He turned to the next page.

"And this is Josiah's grandson, Daniel Barrett."

"That's your dad?" Nathan said.

"Yes. Each of these lives, in one way or another, was touched by the events of June 24th, 1870. The way they lived, the way they worked, the way they died. Even the way they'll be remembered. But now, thanks to you and Gina, an important part of that story will soon change. Honor will be restored to my family."

He started putting the family artifacts back in the drawer when Nathan said, "Hold on." He took the magazine article about Cora Whittier out of his back pocket. "I brought this back," he said.

Wynn took it and smiled.

"What is it?" Nathan asked.

"Josiah got the last laugh."

"Huh?"

"He was the one who found this magazine article. After the boxcar disappeared, he spent years trying to clear his name, without success. He obviously had a suspicion about Seth Carson, but he couldn't prove it because everyone believed Carson was somewhere out west. This article is his redemption."

"You didn't really give it to me for my school project, did you?"

"Did you ever really *have* a school project?" Wynn asked, giving Nathan a knowing look.

"Well, actually…" Nathan started to say.

"I didn't think so," Wynn said.

"So why did you give it to me?"

"When I saw you and Gina on TV, and heard about what you did, I was amazed. Then when I met you, I wondered if the same thing could happen here."

"So why didn't you help us?" Nathan asked. "You know, tell us what you knew?"

"I thought about doing that, but I was afraid I'd only slow you down. The way I saw it, you could come at it with an open mind. I had my ideas of what happened, of course, but they never panned out. For example, none of us, myself included, ever imagined that the boxcar was already gone when the train stopped at Stone Point. You and Gina, on the other hand, didn't have any such notions. You were a fresh new pair of eyes, seeing the situation for the first time."

Nathan nodded his head.

"So I helped you in the way that seemed best, by sharing some of the clues from this old desk and letting you figure it out for yourself."

"There's something that I've been meaning to ask you," Nathan said. "A few things, actually."

"Shoot."

"Well, from the first time we met you, you were… I don't know… old."

"I *am* old," Wynn said, chuckling.

"But at the mine, you were different."

Wynn sat there for a moment, thinking. Then he said, "Ever since I was old enough to hold a fishing pole, I had this dream of finding that old boxcar. Maybe it was for me, maybe it was for Josiah, I don't know. But the older I got, the more I wanted to solve the mystery. It was an obsession with me. I spent countless hours searching everywhere, scouring the woods, wading through rivers, combing the fields and trails. Year in and year out I searched. I wouldn't quit. That exercise kept me in pretty good shape, wouldn't you agree?" He patted his stomach and smiled.

"But at the mine you were like a different person."

"Sometimes in your life, Nathan, you find yourself in a situation where you have to push things out of your mind. You will them away with every ounce of strength you have—things like fear or pain, uncertainty... or being old."

Nathan knew exactly what he was referring to. He had done the very same thing in the darkened basement of the old courthouse. "Well, you didn't look old when you took down Ernie Bell."

"Yeah," Wynn said, relieved. "I guess not."

"Another thing I was wondering. Why did Josiah cover up for Little Bill?"

"My grandfather told me once, when I was very young, that Little Bill was the best brakeman in the country. He was hardworking, trustworthy, and a good friend. But that day, when they pulled into Stone Point, something was wrong. Little Bill wasn't drunk. It was something else, something worse. Josiah, being a decent man and a good friend, did what any of us would have done. He tried to help his friend. Unfortunately, it cost him his job, his railroad pension, and his honor."

"But it was Carson. He drugged him."

"That's right. But we didn't find that out until yesterday. The only proof that could explain what Carson had done was tucked in his coat pocket and buried behind a century of broken stone."

Nathan thought about that for a moment. Josiah Barrett *was* on to something with the magazine article.

"So what's the other one?" Wynn asked.

"Other one?" "Question."

"Oh, right. At the mine, you told us how they stole the boxcar."

"The flying switch."

"Yeah, that. If you knew about it, I mean, that it was possible, how come you didn't find the boxcar?"

"There was no evidence," Wynn said. "At least not until yesterday. In order to prove that a flying switch had actually happened, you needed physical evidence. Finding the boxcar would've explained everything, or maybe finding the tools they used to fix the old track. But without any of those things, there was no evidence of what the Carson Gang had done. The Whitney Spur was there one day and gone the next, like a phantom in the mist. A phantom vale."

"Huh?"

"The valley—or vale—that cradled the spur was scrubbed clean. After the storm hit, it was like it never existed."

Nathan nodded, remembering the massive landslides, uprooted trees, and giant boulders that littered the old track bed. If he hadn't seen the map in the library, he never would've imagined that railcars once passed through the break in those hills.

"Now I have a question for you," Wynn said.

"Sure," Nathan replied.

"How did you and Gina find out about Little Bill?"

Nathan froze. "Huh?" he mumbled.

"Little Bill. I heard the two of you discussing him in the library. He's not exactly a household name."

"Oh, that," Nathan said, stalling. "Well, um, let me think." Wynn's question had caught him off guard, and he looked down at the floor, his mind reeling. *What to say, what to say… THINK!* He couldn't reveal how he found Brooten's obituary, tucked in the back of the book. Nor did he want to answer the questions that would surely follow.

You found it in a book? What book? From a bookcase? What bookcase?

He looked up and saw Wynn watching him, waiting for an answer. "Uh, we were in the library, looking through some old newspapers…" he began.

Before he could finish, they heard a loud pounding on the side door. Wynn got up at once to see what it was, and when he reached the hallway, he saw a familiar face. He opened the door just as she raised her fist to pound again. "Good morning, Gina," he said.

Nathan came rushing out to the hallway.

"Nathan," she said, slightly out of breath. There was alarm in her voice. "You have to come back, right now."

"What's wrong?"

"They're freaking out."

"Who is?"

Her eyebrows flared. *Who do you think?*

"All right, all right," he said, doing his best to hide the relief in his voice. *Saved by Gina.*

He said goodbye to Wynn and followed Gina back to the cottage. It was slow going because Gina had only one good hand. The other was covered with the plaster cast that she kept cradled in her lap. As they rode across the lawn, he saw the minivan backed up to the porch, and his father was coming down the steps with a suitcase in each hand.

"Oh good, you found him," he said to Gina.

"What's going on?" Nathan asked.

"Change of plans, we're packing up."

"We're *leaving?*"

"Yup," his father said, as he loaded the suitcases in the back of the minivan.

"Why?" Nathan asked.

"Why do you think?" Gina mumbled.

His shoulders drooped.

"After you put those bikes back in the shed," his father said, "you need to go in the house and gather your things. We're leaving in 20 minutes."

"Twenty minutes?" Nathan protested. "You're kidding, right?"

Just then, his mother appeared on the porch. "Come on, Nathan, time to get a move on."

As they wheeled the bikes over to the shed, Nathan said, "They're doing it again. They're making us leave, just like before."

"Well, what did you expect?" Gina snapped.

"What are you talking about?"

"You don't think news of the boxcar discovery has already gotten out? How many reporters do you suppose will show up *this* time?"

"We don't need to worry about that," he told her. "I took care of it."

She stared at him suspiciously. "What did you do?"

He ignored her and wrestled the shed door open.

"Nathan?," she said, louder. "What. Did. You. Do?"

Twenty minutes later they were sitting in the van, waiting for Nathan's father to lock up the house. Nathan was in the third seat, staring out at the lake. Gina was next to him, puzzle book on her lap and pencil in hand. So far, there hadn't been much conversation. Nathan's father came down the porch steps and climbed into the van just as Wynn Barrett came around the corner of the house.

He walked up to the passenger-side window and leaned down, eyeing everyone inside. "Looks like you folks are headed out."

"Yes," Elizabeth replied. She didn't have to explain why. They both knew.

"Well then, I'm glad I caught you," Wynn said. "I snuck through the woods so they wouldn't see me."

"So who wouldn't see you?" Elizabeth asked.

"At least two dozen reporters, probably more. And that doesn't count the fellas walking around with those fancy cameras."

Gina looked away and smiled. *Fellas.*

"I knew we should've left at sunrise," her father fumed.

"Wait a minute," Elizabeth asked. "What are they doing at *your* house?"

"They want to know all about the boxcar I found. In case you haven't heard, it's a pretty big deal. Stolen boxcar. Hidden in the side of a mountain. Boxes of counterfeit money."

"Wait," Nathan's father said. "The boxcar *you* found?"

Nathan grinned and sat back in the seat with his arms crossed.

"Yeah," Wynn said, scratching his head. "It's the craziest thing. Seems someone told them it was me that found it after all these years. And given my family's involvement, you can just imagine all the questions they have. Lots and lots of questions."

"I wonder who...?" Elizabeth started to say. Her words fell off and she turned around and looked at Nathan. "That was the favor?" she asked.

"I told you not to worry, didn't I?" he said.

"So then, I guess this is goodbye," Wynn said. "I really want to thank you folks again, for everything."

"No, it's you we should thank," Elizabeth said. "If not for your quick thinking, I'm not sure what would have happened to Nathan and Gina." She turned around and looked at the two of them, then nodded toward the door. *Get out and say goodbye.*

Gina climbed out first.

"Bye, Wynn," she said with a shy smile. "Would you sign my cast?"

"I'd be honored to," he replied.

She handed him a black felt-tip marker, the one the nurse at the hospital had given her, and he signed his full name in a broad looping script. When he was done, he handed her the pen and said, "Goodbye, Gina. And thank you. I appreciate everything you did. My whole family does."

She blushed and said, "I have a confession to make."

"Oh?"

"I thought you were a crazy old man."

"Yeah, I kind of figured that," he said with a smile. He gave her a hug and whispered in her ear, "We all get a little crazy sometimes."

Nathan stepped up next and extended his hand. "Goodbye, Wynn. Thanks again for watching out for us."

"Goodbye, Nathan. And thank *you*, for making a crazy old man's dream come true." He gave Gina a wink and said, "I know Josiah would've enjoyed meeting both of you—the two most famous detectives in the world." He looked at Nathan's mother and grinned. "After me, of course."

A few minutes later, they pulled out of the driveway and headed toward town. News vans and satellite trucks were lined up on both sides of Jewel Lake Road, and a steady stream of locals drove by in both directions, trying to see what the commotion was all about. A throng of reporters were packed elbow-to-elbow in Wynn's driveway waiting for the local hero to emerge from his house. Catharine Chase was at the head of the pack, touching up her lipstick while the cameraman waited nearby.

Nathan's father drove past it all, slowly and without concern, blending in with the rest of the traffic.

Just another family.

Out for a drive.

Nothing to look at here.

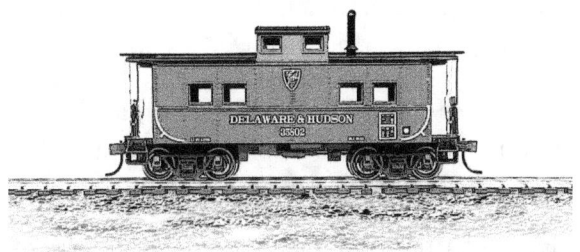

25

Slocum's

The following Saturday, Nathan was sitting alone in his bedroom. The past few days had been anything but boring.

Since their return from New Hampshire, his parents were glued to the television as every news station reported the amazing story of a long-lost boxcar, missing for nearly 150 years, deep in the woods, filled with thousands of dollars of counterfeit bank notes. At the center of it all was the lone descendant of the train's conductor and a resurrected hero, Josiah Barrett.

A sidebar to the story was the resolution of another unsolved case, the mysterious fire that destroyed *The Lakes Region Gazette* during that same year. At no time during the entire account were the names Nathan Cole or Gina McDermott ever mentioned. Better yet, it kept their parents distracted while he and Gina caught up on their homework, the same homework they'd told their parents they'd already finished at the cottage.

Nathan persuaded Gina to help him, but only after he convinced her that he, and not Wynn Barrett, had saved her life in the mine. He showed her the bruise on his elbow and explained how he got it while rushing outside to get his flashlight, proof that he was already working to save her when Wynn Barrett showed up.

On Wednesday afternoon, when he got home from school, two men in dark suits and ties were waiting in the living room. At first they looked like bankers, but they quickly identified themselves as special agents from the FBI. They asked the same questions Sgt. Reynolds had asked at the mine, but said very little about the counterfeit money or where it was from. He thought it was pretty cool, talking to the FBI. Too bad he couldn't tell anyone about it.

Now, with the mystery solved, and his truckload of homework behind him, one nagging question remained: the Bill Brooten obituary. Why was it stuck in the back of the book? It was a key clue to the entire mystery, so why wasn't it saved in Chapter 11, where he would've found it at the very start?

He flipped to the back of the book, to the chapter where he found the obituary. When he originally discovered it, the tiny scrap of paper was a mystery all to itself. But had he taken the time to read the pages that held it, he would've unearthed another important piece of the puzzle.

The chapter told of Major Eli Janney, a veteran of the Civil War on the Confederate side. It described a device he invented in the year 1868, called the knuckle coupler. It was a semi-automatic device that allowed rail cars to lock together without the help of a railroad worker. According to the story, workers risked serious injury, or worse, with the old "link and pin" coupler that required them to climb between the cars.

When he finished reading, he thought back to what Wynn told them outside the mine. How the back half of the train caught up to the front half and reconnected all by itself. It was a key part of the story, and helped explain how the Carson Gang was able to snatch the boxcar without anyone knowing. *Next time, he thought, pay attention.*

He took Brooten's obit from inside the front flap and placed it carefully at the start of Chapter 11. Then he closed the book and took it over to his bookcase, the one with his baseball trophies lined up on the top shelf. He knew that returning the book to the attic would be a waste of time, a lesson he learned with the first book. The bookcase on the third floor was for mysteries yet to be solved. Maybe someday he'd find a cool old bookcase of his own, but for now, this book would live in his bedroom, along with the first one.

Just as he was putting it on the shelf, he heard a knock on the door. Seconds later, it opened and his mother stuck her head in the room. "I've got an errand to run," she said. "It shouldn't take long."

He froze, using his body to shield the two books. "Okay Mom," he said.

As the seconds passed, she didn't move. That's when he looked over his shoulder and said, "Is something wrong?"

"No," she replied.

"I thought you were going."

"I am," she said, "and you're coming with me."

He exhaled loudly. "Do I *have* to?"

"You most certainly do," she said. She checked her watch and said, "Come on, let's go. I don't want to be late."

"Where are we going?"

"You'll see."

They drove for 20 minutes, out toward Lexington. Nathan sat slumped in the seat with his arms folded, thinking about the events of the past week. It was only when his mother slowed and pulled off the road that he glanced out the window. "What is this place?" he asked.

"Slocum's," she said, as she pulled into an empty parking space. "It's an auction house. My dad used to bring us here when I was young."

When Nathan heard that, he bolted upright in the seat. He saw a long, single-story building set back from the road. It was painted muddy brown and there wasn't a single window on the front. A huge parking lot ran the length of it and wrapped around both ends. Perched above the front doors was an old weather-beaten sign. Despite the flaked paint, the name was still visible.

"This is the errand?" he asked, raising both eyebrows.

She shut off the car and turned to face him. When she spoke, she took her time, choosing her words carefully, for a conversation that only she could have with him. One that was long overdue.

"What?" he asked, when he saw her staring at him.

"We need to talk about the bookcase."

"Huh?"

"The bookcase? In the attic? You've been taking books out of it, haven't you?"

"I don't know what you're talking about," he muttered, looking away.

"Actually, that's what I wanted you to say, but we both know it's not true."

He stared out the window, wishing he was back in his bedroom.

"Nathan?"

He slowly turned from the window and looked at her.

"The courthouse? The Whitney Mine? Those things didn't happen by accident, did they?" she asked.

His thoughts were spinning as he tried to think of something to say, but nothing was coming to mind. He was afraid of what would happen if he told her the truth.

"Did they?" she repeated.

"No," he said softly, looking away. It was all over now. After what happened at the Whitney Mine, the attic would be off limits for sure.

No more bookcase. No more books.

Just a big padlock on the door.

His mother took a deep breath and let it out. "After your grandfather died we hid the bookcase in the attic hoping no one would find it."

"No one? You mean, me?"

She nodded her head. "Yes, especially you."

"Why?"

"Because you're not ready for it."

"Not ready? What's that supposed to mean?"

"It's a long story," she said. "One day, when you're ready to hear it, I'll tell you."

Nathan said nothing.

She turned and looked out the window, her eyes fixed on the far side of the parking lot. "That bookcase has been around for as long as I can remember," she said softly, thinking back to the first time she saw it in the back room of Hammond Books. "The books in it are very special."

"You can say that again," he mumbled under his breath. He looked down at the floor, waiting for his punishment to come. *I can't believe she knows. All this time, and she never said a word.*

"Well," she said, turning to look at him. There was a look of resignation on her face. "What's done is done. There's no turning back now."

No turning back, he thought, *what does that mean?*

"There are some things about the bookcase that you need to know," she said. "For starters, no one, and I mean no one, can know about it. Are we clear on that? You can't share it with anyone."

He did a double take. *That's it? Don't tell anyone? Too late.*

"And don't worry," she said. "I know you told Gina."

He did another double take. "But... how?"

"She's a smart girl, Nathan. There's no way she would've gone in that mine if you hadn't told her *something*. The courthouse too, for that matter."

"Tell me about it," he said. Then he asked, "Does Dad know?"

302

"No, and you're not to tell him. Ever."

"Why not?"

"We'll talk about that another time," she said, checking her watch. "The other thing you need to know is that you can't just take books from the bookcase and not replace them."

"I tried to, but—"

"No," she cut in. "I didn't say put them back, I said *replace* them."

"I don't understand."

"When you first discovered the bookcase, were the shelves full?"

"Yes," he said. He didn't mention the one empty slot, or the book that belonged there. The one he found lying on the floor. *How this whole thing started.*

"The shelves were full because my father replaced the ones he took with new ones."

"Oh, right," he said slowly. It wasn't something he'd really thought about, but now that she mentioned it, it made perfect sense.

"Just like my father, you need to find new books to replace the ones you take."

"I do?"

"Yes," she said. The tone in her voice and the look on her face indicated there was more she wasn't telling him.

"Did you ever take a book from it?" he asked. "You know, read it and try to solve the mystery?"

"No," she said.

"Why not?"

"Because my father didn't choose me. He chose someone else. But that's a discussion for another time."

She picked up her purse and reached for the door handle.

"Hold on," he said. "Grampa *chose* someone?"

"Yes," she said softly, avoiding his eyes. She stared at the purse in her lap without speaking, her eyes betraying the pain she had buried deep inside for many years—one she would carry with her for the rest of her life.

In that moment, a series of vivid images, like exploding fireworks, flashed through Nathan's mind. His visit to the attic, where he found the first book on the floor; how he tried to put it back on the shelf but it refused to stay; the pages that turned by themselves; the glowing images. Then the second book, sitting still on his bureau for weeks, until he was packing to leave; how it stuck to the window, and how it refused to let him out of the room.

Ever since he found the first book, he couldn't help but feel that he was *supposed* to find it. Read it. Follow the clues. Find the secret buried within. But now, he realized the truth. Those things didn't happen by accident. He had been chosen. It was a realization that struck him like a thunderbolt, and he found it impossible to speak.

His mother checked her watch and said, "We need to go inside."

He sat motionless, too stunned to move.

"Are you all right?" his mother asked.

Her words were a muted jumble, like she had spoken them from somewhere beyond the car window. He managed to utter a series of words that she didn't understand, then he pushed the door open and slowly climbed out. They were halfway across the parking lot when he snapped out of his daze. "An auction house?" he asked.

"It's where people come to buy old things," his mother explained.

"Old things?"

"Yes, like books. Very old books."

They walked through the front door and stopped. It was a huge room, with long tables that lined the perimeter. Every table held stacks of books, each tagged with a lot number. Some lots had one book, other lots had up to 20 books. A throng of people were spread throughout the room, browsing the stacks and studying the list of lots to be auctioned off that day.

As Nathan took it all in, he could see why his grandfather came here. Many of the books were old and worn, their bindings cracked. There were bibles, several inches thick, small thin paperbacks bagged in plastic, almanacs, journals, illustrated histories, bird guides, and works of fiction. Included among them were newer books with embossed covers in dark green, royal red, and navy blue.

At the front of the room sat a podium with a single microphone. Rows of chairs were lined up before it, where a number of people sat waiting for the auction to start.

"Fifteen minutes," the auctioneer called out.

When Elizabeth heard that, she pulled Nathan aside, well out of earshot of the others. "My father once told me that there are many books, books with secrets. You're old enough now, and it's time you learned how to find them. Just like my father did, and his father before that."

Nathan scanned the room, eyeing the piles of books on each table with a look of fascination. *Just like my grandfather did, and his father before that.* In the back of his mind, a single word echoed like the tolling of a bell, and try as he might, he couldn't make it stop.

Chosen.

"The bidding is going to start soon," his mother said. She nudged him toward the tables. "Come on, let's go see what we can find."

Side Tracks

THE CARSON GANG is based on the real-life Reno Brothers, a family of bandits from Rockford, Indiana. They were among the very first of the Western outlaws and train robbers. The four Reno brothers were John, William, Frank, and Simon.

THE WHITNEY MINE was inspired by the Ruggles Mine in Grafton, New Hampshire, which began commercial production of mica in 1803. As of this writing, an estimated thirty million dollars worth of minerals have been recovered there.

SOFT BELLY is railroad slang for a wooden-framed rail car.

HARPER'S MAGAZINE first appeared in June of 1850 as *Harper's New Monthly Magazine*. It is the second-oldest continuously published monthly magazine in America.

THE TRAILING ARBUTUS (are-BYOO-tuss) would likely be extinct if not for a group of women in Boston, Massachusetts, who lobbied to have it named the state flower, which made it illegal to collect. That group would eventually become the New England Wildflower Society, which still exists today.

BOOMER, in railroad terminology, is a drifter who moves from one job to another, staying only a short time on each. During the heyday of the railroads, they were in high demand because of their vast experience.

MOOSE can be unpredictable, and they have been known to

respond aggressively if they feel threatened. It is common practice for drivers to "wait a moose out" if they encounter one in the road. This is smart strategy on two fronts, because anyone who provokes a moose risks serious damage, both to themselves and to their vehicle.

THE CLICK BEETLE belongs to the order Coleoptera. It clicks to warn off predators and sometimes to help right itself if it has been turned over onto its back.

THE ROSS & SHERIDAN OVERLAND EXPRESS and the stage mishap described in this book are fictional, but the incident is based on an actual stagecoach tragedy, The Cold River Disaster, which occurred on March 14, 1837, in Langdon, New Hampshire.

THE THREE SISTERS are a cluster of three separate islands in Squam Lake, located in the Lakes Region of central New Hampshire. They were purchased by Milton Richardson in the year 1886 for his daughters, Harriet, Louise, and Mildred.

THE GREAT TORNADO OF 1821 hit New Hampshire on September 9th of that year, with winds over 170 miles-per-hour. The funnel was half-a-mile wide and travelled 45 miles on the ground, killing six people and injuring hundreds more. It is still considered one of the most destructive storms in the state's history.

GOLD was first discovered in Lyman, New Hampshire in 1864, and several small mines soon opened in the nearby town of Bath. None of those mines are currently operating.

THE FLYING SWITCH is an outdated procedure for isolating

rail cars. It is highly frowned upon by railroad officials.

A BRIGANTINE SHIP was a two-masted sailing vessel, swifter and more maneuverable than a sloop or schooner, and used for a number of purposes including piracy and espionage.

VALE refers to an area of lowland between hills or mountains.

Acknowledgements

I was destined to write a railroad story. It was unavoidable. Ever since my childhood visit to Steamtown, U.S.A., in Bellows Falls, Vermont, trains have held a special place in my heart. That lifelong fascination, along with the help from the following amazing people, brought *The Phantom Vale* out of the attic. My heartfelt thanks go out to each of them.

Dale Russell, for his expert guidance and extraordinary knowledge of trains.

Brian Hackert, research librarian, for his fine detective work in the stacks.

Alan Rumrill, Executive Director of the Historical Society of Cheshire County, for sharing the Cold River Bridge Disaster, as well as his superb knowledge of 1800's life in New Hampshire.

Brett Bissonnette, for his help with police protocol.

Joe Bills, brother in arms and award-winning writer, for his support, guidance, and shared vision.

Marcia Lusted, relentless writer of books and editor supreme.

Steve Levy, for solving the riddle that made the train illustrations on the chapter pages possible.

Gyakyi Bonsu-Anane, Master of the Graphics Universe, for his help with the cover and chapter page illustrations. The force is strong with this one.

Jim Grant, teacher, educator, mentor and friend, who taught us all the meaning of grit.

Pam Wilder and the crew at Silver Direct.

The staff at the Toadstool Bookshops, for their continued support of readers and writers alike.

Teachers and librarians worldwide, the real superheroes who make a difference in the lives of readers young and old.

And to the fans of the Third Floor Mystery Series, who keep me up late at night, crafting, scheming, and searching for just the right words.

Illustrations

About the Author

Alfred M. Struthers lives in Peterborough, New Hampshire. In addition to crafting books that inspire, entertain and make a difference in the lives of readers young and old, he is a singer/songwriter, woodworker, photographer, and avid collector of fossils that line the streambeds around Cooperstown, New York.

To find out what he's been up to lately, visit: thirdfloorbooksllc.com.

Afterword

Catharine Chase was leaving the Channel 5 newsroom for the day when her news director stopped her in the hallway.

"All done with the train story?" he asked.

She checked the hallway in both directions. "Not exactly."

He studied the anxious look on her face, sensing she was holding something back. "What happened up there?" he asked. "What aren't you telling me?"

She did another quick check of the hallway, then grabbed his arm and dragged him into an empty office. When she spoke, there was urgency in her voice. "John, they were there."

"Who was there?"

"Those two kids... from the courthouse story."

"In New Hampshire? Are you sure?"

"I'm positive," she said. As she spoke, she tapped her foot nervously on the floor.

John gave her a curious look. "What were *they* doing in New Hampshire?"

"Nothing I can prove," she said. Then in a quieter voice, "Yet."

"I see," he said slowly. "And you're sure it was them?"

"Oh. Trust me. It was them, alright," she insisted. There was fire in her eyes.

"Are you suggesting they were involved?"

"*Those* two kids?" she said, eyebrows raised. "Another bizarre mystery solved? Yeah, they were involved. I'm sure of it."

"But you say you have no proof," John confirmed. He let out a heavy breath. "Wait," he said, "I thought the police had identified the local guy. What's his name... Barrett?"

"That fish story?" she huffed as she began to pace. "I'm not buying it for a minute."

"You don't think it's just a coincidence?"

"There are no coincidences," she fired back. "Not in our line of work."

"Well," he said cautiously, rubbing the stubble on his chin. "I'm not sure what to tell you."

"Don't worry," she said. "There's something going on there. I don't know what, but I'm going to find out."

She started for the door, then paused and looked back.

"This isn't over."

Book Three - Available now!

The Curse of Halim

Stuck to the bottom of the drawer was a piece of paper, and only by picking at it with his fingernail was he able to pry it free. It was a sheet of note paper folded in half. When he peeled it open, he found a triangular slip of paper inside, with lines of faded print on both sides. Two of the edges were perfectly straight, but the third edge, the longest of the three, was ragged and uneven. It was part of a page, taken from a book. Someone had done the unthinkable and torn it out.

He scanned both sides of it briefly and then examined the note paper. The outside was blank, but on the inside he saw a handwritten message.

This is all there was
SJ

He eyed both papers suspiciously. "This is it?" he said. "This is what you wanted me to see?"

Each of his previous visits to the attic had led him to a book— with page after page of details, descriptions, illustrations, and maps, each of them a clue to whatever unsolved mystery lay within. But this was just a single sentence, and someone's initials.

19 letters.

"Why save a scrap of paper?" he muttered, shaking his head. "A whole page, maybe, but just a corner?"

He slipped the torn page back into the folded note and stood there for a moment, thinking. When it came to solving riddles, there was one person he could always count on. "I need Gina," he said. "She'll make sense of this."

He returned to the bookcase and slid the drawer into the empty slot. This time it stayed shut. Then he tucked the note in his back pocket and fought his way toward the door, pulling spiders out of his hair and dropping them on the floor along the way. When he walked into the kitchen, his parents were nowhere in sight, so he quickly called Gina on the wall phone. She picked up on the second ring.

"Hello?" she said in a dreary tone.

"Hey, what are you doing?" he asked, keeping his voice low. "I need to show you something. It's the strangest thing—"

"Nathan!" she cut in, her voice dropping to a whisper.

"Yeah?" he replied. "Is something wrong?"

"Hold on." She lowered the receiver and shouted, "YES, I KNOW!"

"What's going on?" he asked, when she came back on the line.

She let out an angry breath and lowered the receiver again. "ALL RIGHT!" There was a brief pause. "Are you still there?" she asked, sniffling as she spoke.

"Of course," he said, "why wouldn't I be?"

"Never mind," she replied. "Listen, you have to—"

Click!

The line went dead.

"Gina? Hello? I have to *what*?"

For several seconds he stood there staring at the receiver. *Why was she crying?*